Serenity's Desire

Serenity's Desire

Kay Rizzo

**BROADMAN
&HOLMAN
PUBLISHERS**

Nashville, Tennessee

0-8054-6373-9

Published by Broadman & Holman Publishers, Nashville, Tennessee
Acquisitions Editor: Vicki Crumpton
Page Design: Sam Gantt Graphic Design Group
Page Composition: PerfecType, Nashville, Tennessee

Dewey Decimal Classification: 813.54
Subject Heading: FICTION
Library of Congress Card Catalog Number: 98-15560

Library of Congress Cataloging-in-Publication Data
Rizzo, Kay D., 1943–
    Serenity's desire / Kay D. Rizzo.
        p. cm.
    ISBN 0-8054-6373-9 (pbk.)
    I. Title. II. Series
  PS3568.I836S47   1998
  813'.54—dc21

                                        98-15560
                                           CIP

1 2 3 4 5 02 01 00 99 98

— ❧ *Dedication* ❧ —

To Janice Lindfors,
my good friend and my "Sis" in Christ
Proverbs 17:17

Contents

CONTENTS

WINDS GUSTING ACROSS THE FROZEN lake whipped the man's coat tails, staggering him with each icy blast. Caleb Cunard stared nervously at the imposing manse on the hill, waiting for the signal from the upstairs window. Behind him, three shivering forms huddled in the shadow of the boathouse.

Onyx, the estate's oversized, short-haired mutt, gave a low growl, pressing tighter against the man's pant leg. "Good boy, Onyx, good boy," Caleb whispered, patting the dog's head. "It's all right."

But all wasn't right. Yellow light streamed from the first-floor windows silhouetting the two horses tied to the hitching post while the upstairs windows remained dark. Even at such a distance Caleb recognized the mounts of Sheriff Broderick and his deputy, Will Johnsby.

Caleb blew on his hands and tucked them inside his brown suede jacket. Another gust jerked impatiently at the man's pant legs and fluttered the brim of his battered felt hat. A whimper came out of the shadows. The dog snorted softly and shifted his back to the wind whipping off the lake.

"Sh-sh, easy boy," Caleb coaxed. The dog vented a sigh

as if in reply. Exhausted after a harrowing game of hide and seek with the law, Caleb hunched into his jacket, grateful for the warmth it afforded him. He shivered when he remembered the loose, ragged garments worn by his charges hiding in the boat. *Was this trip number twelve or thirteen?* he wondered as he drew his hands out of his coat and blew hot air into the hollow of his palms. He'd lost count. It could just as well have been trip number twenty-five.

In the biting cold of the night, waiting for the all-clear signal, he felt the same surge of excitement he'd experienced on his first trek north from the Pennsylvania line to Assemblyman Pownell's lavish estate along the eastern shore of Lake Cayuga. From here, his charges would be transported north to Canada and freedom. The satisfaction of his work made the struggles and discomfort worthwhile.

Suddenly the mansion's double doors swung open and light bathed the broad porch and front steps. Sheriff Broderick stepped out onto the porch. Caleb watched Deputy Johnsby round the far end of the house. Abe, the estate's overseer, appeared in the doorway, his hands stuffed into his pants pockets. Abe Potter owed his life to New York State Assemblyman Samuel Pownell. Bought by the politician and set free, the former slave now ran the assemblyman's estate with the aplomb of a well-trained English butler.

"It's easy," he once told Caleb, "compared to operating an African head chief's household. That takes the wisdom of Solomon and the wit of Saint Paul." Abe had been the number one man to a regional chief until an ambitious coworker framed him for theft and Abe was sold to English slavers heading for America. Auctioned off to the owner of a New Orleans gambling establishment, Abe quickly learned to do figures. Evangeline, a saloon girl and fellow slave kidnapped from a mission compound in West Africa, taught him to read and write. She also taught him about a God who loved him, a God-man who died on a cross so all people could be free. When the owner learned of their clandestine meetings, he sold Evangeline to a local bordello and returned Abe to the auction block.

It was the matter-of-fact look of pride in Abe's soft brown eyes that caught the attention of Assemblyman and Mrs. Pownell. An hour later, the papers were signed and sealed. Abe was a free man. His heart spilled over with gratitude to the stranger and his comely wife. When they bade him good-bye, Abe begged to go with them. "I'll do anything for you, sir. Please take me with you." Since then his loyalty to the assemblyman had been unswerving. Even now, facing down the local lawmen, Abe would not waver in that loyalty, Caleb knew. In a few minutes the lawmen mounted their horses and headed toward the lake. Caleb crouched behind a gnarled oak tree stump and held his breath as the horsemen rode past. Onyx pressed his cold nose against the man's cheek. Even the wind seemed to hold its breath until the clopping of the horses faded into the night.

Caleb rose to his full height of six feet. He glanced toward the sky. A corner of the moon peeked from behind the bank of heavy clouds moving eastward, then disappeared. A light appeared in the second-story window. It went out, then on again. Caleb sighed with relief and waved to the people huddled in the shadows. "Quickly now! Run around to the back of the house and you'll be let in. Stay low. Go, before the moon reappears!"

Caleb watched as the three figures dashed across the lawn and disappeared into the shadows of the house. Onyx leaped to his feet, his tail wagging. "All right, boy. Let's go."

They jogged across the lawn and up the steps of the front porch. Caleb banged the door knocker three times. The door opened to Dory's smiling face. "Why Master Caleb, what a surprise to see you tonight. I suppose you're here to see Abe. He's out, but be back soon." Her dark eyes gleamed as the moonlight shone in the open doorway. "I just made a batch of shortbread cookies and a fresh pot of tea. Go on into the library."

When Onyx tried to follow Caleb, the butternut brown-skinned woman barred his way. "Onyx, get your bones out of here before I chase you with my broom!" The dog circled, his head bowed in submission but his tail wagging.

"Oh, all right. You go 'round to the back door, and I'll give you some supper scraps."

The animal bounded off the porch and disappeared into the shadows.

~ 1 ~
God Grants Serenity

"'GOD GRANTS SERENITY TO THE ONE who possesses a pure heart.' Can you believe that's what Matron Crookshank instructed me to repeat for an entire hour?" The seventeen-year-old daughter of New York State's Assemblyman Samuel Pownell hopped onto the center of her bed, her skirts spread around her. She brushed a stray ebony ringlet from her cheek. "I'll wager she wouldn't make Evangeline Buchanan repeat such a silly sentence."

"I should hope not, since her name isn't Serenity." Eulilia Northrop, Serenity's best friend and roommate, chuckled. "Be thankful your parents named you Serenity and not Chastity or Charity."

Serenity's crystal blue eyes deepened to thunderstorm gray. "My mother's name is Charity."

"O-o-h, sorry." The girl covered her mouth with one delicate hand.

"It's all my Grandma Mendoit's fault. She was a Quaker before she married my Huguenot grandfather. Mama says the only time she paid any mind to her childhood religion was when she birthed a child. She had six sons, all named after the disciples of Jesus, and seven daughters, including my mother, all named for Christian virtues."

Eulilia's eyes widened in genuine surprise. "I didn't know there were that many virtues."

"Tsk! Well, there are! But that's not the point. The point is my mother named me after her favorite sister, Aunt Serenity. . . ." Serenity rolled her eyes. "'A saint of a woman who never raises her voice or rushes about in an unladylike frenzy,'" Serenity chanted in a sing-song manner that mocked her mother. "How many times have I heard that?"

Eulilia giggled. Eulilia always giggled. Serenity averted her gaze toward the window to hide her tears of frustration. *She doesn't understand. How can she with a delicate name like Eulilia?*

The dormitory window faced the rugged Berkshire Mountains of Massachusetts and the gatekeeper's stone cottage. Beyond the massive iron gates Serenity could see the dusty roadway that led toward Boston, then home to western New York State. A twinge of loneliness stabbed at her stomach. Eight months at Martha Van Horne's Finishing Academy for Young Ladies and she longed for home on the shores of New York's Lake Cayuga. *Only a month to go . . .* she sighed. *Then Papa will come for me.*

"I don't know why they sent me here. A modern woman of 1850 doesn't need 'finishing'," Serenity said, rolling her eyes toward the ceiling. "I can only imagine what Lucritia Mott would say about Matron Crookshank and her little protégés. Besides, I can act as feminine as any other student here at the academy, when I want to, that is."

"Oh, ta-ta!" Eulilia hopped from her bed and sashayed across the faded blue Persian rug. "Ah, yes, as charming and witty as Evangeline Buchanan of the Baltimore Buchanans and her dearest friend, Annabelle Longworthy of Savannah.

You have heard of the Savannah Longworthys, of course." The girl straightened an imaginary wrinkle from the gathered skirt of her navy lindsey-woolsey uniform, with its regulation-starched, white blouse and pinafore.

Serenity lifted one eyebrow and smirked. "And you are the epitome of refinement, I presume?"

Eulilia waved one hand in the air, aping Matron Crookshank's mannerisms. "But of course, my deah."

"Indubitably!" Serenity responded in kind. "Especially the night we sneaked down to the pond so you could spark with the stable hand, while I twiddled my thumbs standing guard! Remember how you got stuck between the gate spikes on the way home and old Herman had to come to your rescue?"

"Seri! What a venomous tongue!"

"Oh, Eulia, stop complaining! I'd die to have a waistline like yours. You're the one the boys swarm around when we go to town." A movement outside the window caught both girls' attention.

"Speaking of Herman," Eulilia interrupted, signaling toward the window, "it's wash day." Her eyes sparkled with deviltry as she pointed at the caretaker's cottage. "Are you thinking what I'm thinking?"

"No, we can't." Serenity shook her head, but her grin belied her. "I'm already in trouble with Matron Crookshank because of you."

Eulilia's pink bow mouth bloomed into a pout. "Not fair! You enjoyed the ginger cookies just as much as I. It's not my fault you got caught and I didn't."

A growl rumbled in Serenity's throat. "I wouldn't have gotten caught if Herman hadn't seen me running from the milkhouse. Everyone knows you can't have fresh-baked ginger cookies without a glass of cold milk."

Eulilia's golden ringlets danced about her shoulders. "Which, I might add, is all the more reason we should. . . ." She rolled her eyes toward the window. "Sweet revenge."

"And if he catches us?"

"How can he? I'll wager he's wearing that silly robe of his by now!"

Every Monday evening, at the end of Mademoiselle DuChey's French class, the girls of the academy would watch as Herman Gustaffan, the gatekeeper, dragged a large tin wash tub from his shed and into the stone cottage. An hour later, from the dormitory's second-story window, they would see the old man, wrapped in a yellow satin robe printed with garish red poppies, drape two pairs of britches and two shirts to dry on the hedge growing between his cottage and the campus.

Suddenly the girls jumped up and ran to one of the west-facing rooms to catch a glimpse of the patched and baggy britches and the gatekeeper in his yellow satin robe. Looking down they saw him, right on schedule. As Serenity and Eulilia watched, the man carefully arranged the britches on the boxwood with the precision of a skilled quilter. The heavy canvas trousers looked defenseless and forlorn spread out on the hedge to dry.

"So?" Serenity shot a glance at Eulilia. "I dare you."

Eulilia's eyes widened with excitement. "I double dare you."

A slow smile spread across Serenity's freckled face. "We'll have to wait until after dinner and vespers."

"My, my!" Eulilia rubbed her stomach and giggled. "I do believe it is almost time for our evening repast." As if on cue, the dinner bell gonged. Instantly the sound of doors slamming and the clatter of black, button-topped, leather shoes clicking on the marble hallway filled the dormitory. "Shall we, Miss Pownell?"

"In a moment." Serenity tugged at a stray ringlet coursing the side of her left cheek as she straddled up to a mirror standing in the corner of the room, then spit-curled a shorter ringlet above her right eyebrow. "This hair of mine! Another curse!"

"Oh yes, naturally curly hair can be such a burden!" Eulilia said, nudging her way to the mirror. "You should have to roll your hair in rags every single night of your life!"

Serenity's stomach growled. She straightened her skirt over the many layers of embroidered petticoats and swished toward the door. "Are you coming, or are you going to primp all evening?"

Throughout dinner, the two girls eyed one another across the long, white linen-clad dinner table, barely suppressing their laughter. Constance Bidwell sighed impatiently. "Miss Northrup, would you please share with us the reason for yours and Miss Pownell's high spirits this evening?" As senior hostess at the table, it was her job to stimulate conversation.

"Sorry, Miss Bidwell." Eulilia blushed and averted her eyes to the plum cobbler in the berry dish before her. "It's a lovely evening, isn't it?"

"It's been threatening to rain all day long!" The older girl glared. "Perhaps you, Miss Pownell, would care to explain to the ladies present the reason for your breach of proper etiquette?"

"I'm afraid, there isn't much to tell. I . . . I . . . I—"

"Save your explanations for the cook. She and the kitchen staff will appreciate your humor much more than we, as you assist in cleaning up."

Serenity groaned. Beneath the table, her toe started tapping out her irritation. The noise grew louder. Suddenly someone kicked her. She yelped in pain and glared at Eulilia smiling sweetly at her.

"Did I detect a murmur of complaint, Miss Pownell?" Constance's gaze hovered over Serenity like a hawk over a field mouse.

"Oh no, ma'am."

A satisfied smile coursed the older girl's face. With deliberation, she poured a stream of heavy cream from the small silver pitcher onto her plum cobbler. "Perhaps tomorrow morning you both will regale us with humorous tidbits of kitchen trivia."

The vesper bell had rung by the time Eulilia and Serenity finished their assigned kitchen tasks. The two girls ducked out the kitchen delivery door without being seen and darted around the corner of the building where they stopped to catch their breath.

"So far, so good," Eulilia gasped. "For once Constance's ill humor worked in our favor. No one will look for us until after vespers."

"You didn't have to kick me so hard, you know." Serenity rubbed her shin through her heavy skirts. "I am sure to be bruised by morning."

Eulilia cast a quick glance around the corner. "No one's in sight. Come on!" She scooped up her skirts and darted across the moonlit lawn and into the shadow of a large elm tree. Serenity followed, certain someone would shout for her to stop at any moment. Not noticing Eulilia had stooped, Serenity charged into her, toppling them both to the ground. Eulilia scrambled to her feet. "Can't you watch where you're going?"

Serenity sat up, her button-topped shoes protruding from beneath the petticoats. "Why'd you stop?"

"Sh!"

"You sh!" Serenity stood up and straightened her dress.

"You don't need to get ugly!" Eulilia snapped, struggling to her feet.

"One more unpleasant word from you and I'm heading straight for the dormitory, Eulilia Northrup." Serenity laced her arms across her chest. Her toe started tapping.

"All right, let's not quarrel." Eulilia sighed and pointed toward the five-foot hedge surrounding the caretaker's house. "You wait here until I'm out of sight, then follow, all right?"

"That's better," Serenity snarled as Eulilia sprang from the shadows and broke into a run. Serenity watched, nervously glancing back at the dormitory, then toward her friend. The girl disappeared around the northwest corner of the hedge. *Oh, dear Father in heaven, what have I gotten myself into this time?*

—2—
The Purloined Britches

GATHERING HER SKIRTS INTO HER ARMS, Serenity raced across the second half of the moonlit lawn and into the shadows of the hedge. This time she stopped short of colliding with her roommate. A sudden light shone from the diamond-paned window above their heads. They crouched into the shadows until the light went out.

Taut as a carriage spring, Eulilia pressed one finger to her lips and gestured with her other hand in the direction of a trouser leg draped over the hedge. Serenity nodded. The two girls crept Indian fashion until they were directly beneath the dripping garment. One leg of a second pair of britches could be seen a yard farther down the hedge.

"You grab one pair and I'll grab the other," Eulilia whispered. Serenity nodded. Without warning, Eulilia stood up, seized the leg of the closest pair of trousers, and yanked it to her chest. "Go on! It's your turn."

"I . . . I . . . I c-c-can't." Serenity's breath stuck in her chest as she crept closer to her prey.

"Do it!"

Before she could carry out Eulilia's command, the back door to the cottage swung open. The girls froze. Silhouetted in the doorway, wrapped in a large towel, the caretaker shouted, his voice high and raspy, "Who's out there?" Without warning, Eulilia sprinted across the lawn toward the dormitory, leaving Serenity staring after her in surprise.

Herman's approaching steps spurred Serenity to action. She snatched the second pair of britches by the pant leg and began to run, only to have one of the pockets catch on a twig. The frightened girl tugged harder. The pants held fast. Determined not to be outdone by her friend, Serenity stood up to get a better hold. All color drained from her face when she found herself nose to nose with the equally startled gatekeeper, who quickly grasped the free leg of the same garment.

"Let go!" She ordered in her best Matron Crookshank voice.

"Whoa there, missy!" His mouth narrowed into a stubborn line. "Them's mine. You let go."

"No! I won't!" She tugged at the garment. They heard a loud rip.

Dismayed, the poor man eased his grip long enough to give her the advantage needed to yank the soggy garment free of the bush. Serenity whipped about and fled across the lawn, disappearing into the shadows of the dormitory with the garment clutched in her arms. Pressed against the cold, gray stone wall, the girls waited until the man stormed back inside his cottage before speaking.

"Now what?" Serenity inspected the dripping trousers.

"Up the flagpole?" Eulilia's eyes danced. A twenty-foot wooden pole stood in the middle of the grassy circle at the school's front entry. Each morning the "honor ladies," usually Evangeline and her buddies, raised the American flag, then lowered it again in the evening.

"No! We couldn't."

"Yes, we could." Eulilia's curls bobbed eagerly as her head nodded up and down. "Think how surprised Matron Crookshank will be to see two pairs of men's britches waving in the morning light!" Minutes later, the two giggling girls watched from the safety of their dormitory room as the garments waved in the chilly night breeze.

"We really did the man a favor, you know. Herman's britches will dry much better up there than they would on the hedge." Eulilia grinned and sighed from a job well done.

"Hmmph!" Serenity snuffed out the wick of the table lantern and began unbuttoning her bodice. "I am doomed," she wailed, "utterly doomed. He saw me! First thing in the morning, he'll report me to Matron Crookshank."

Eulilia chuckled. "Not before he rescues his britches from the flagpole."

Serenity untied the drawstrings on her petticoats and let them slip to the floor. "You don't think we were too mean, do you?"

"The way Herman reports on the girls' every little misdemeanor?" Eulilia sniffed indignantly. "I think we were too kind, personally."

"I don't know. . . ." Serenity's mother's words echoed in her head. "'Vengeance is mine,' saith the Lord. 'He who lives by the sword will die by the sword.'" She shuddered and lowered her flannel nightgown over her head. "I wish I'd never let you talk me into doing it." Feelings of guilt and regret lingered in the corners of her mind.

"Me? Talk you into it?"

"Yes. I never would have done it if you hadn't dared me. Do you think God will ever forgive us?"

Eulilia grabbed her hairbrush and hopped onto her bed. She unpinned her halo of blond curls and shook them free.

"Who knows? I'll leave that kind of stuff to you. You're the one whose mother is a Quaker preacher!"

"My mother isn't a Quaker preacher and you know it. She does believe as a Quaker, but that doesn't make her a preacher like Pastor Cunard." Serenity shook loose her own tangle of curls.

"Pastor Cunard? Who's he?"

"A circuit-riding Baptist preacher back home. His first name is Eli, but Mama calls him the Reverend. He and his family live next door to us on Daddy's tenant farm. Daddy doesn't think much of him, but his wife, Fay, and my mama are best of friends. They've only lived there for three years."

Serenity grew silent as she counted the brush strokes through her waist-length hair. Talking about the Cunard family brought back her homesickness, yet it was good to be away from her mother for awhile. It wasn't easy living up to the demands of her mother's God. *But if Mama's God is at all like her* . . . Serenity smiled knowing she could always tease a smile out of her mother . . . *He'll break down and forgive me sooner or later.*

In the moonlight filtering through the window, Serenity admired Eulilia's delicately featured face as the girl rolled her hair in rags. *She's so pretty. Not a freckle to mar her smooth, creamy complexion. Well at least I don't have to do that every night,* Serenity thought, tipping her head forward and dragging the pearl-handled hairbrush through her own luxurious curls.

Serenity held up a hand mirror and gazed at her own features. The oval jawline and petulant chin. A scowl deepened between her wide, naturally arched brows and crystal blue eyes. *Mama says beauty is fleeting and vanity is vexation of spirit. She says that true beauty lies within the woman.*

That's easy for her to say, a woman who brings all conversation to a halt the instant she enters a room.

Charity Pownell, the witty and statuesque wife of New York Assemblyman Samuel Pownell, had charm that could melt the hardest politician's heart to molasses. Admirers and opponents alike attributed her husband's long term in the state assembly as much to his wife's beauty as his success. *Next to her,* Serenity sighed, *I am a gawky gosling!*

Serenity hugged her knees to her chest. The lump in her throat grew with her deepening thoughts. She hated leaving the sprawling estate on the banks of Central New York's Lake Cayuga. She hated the New England finishing school that was supposed to turn her into a lady. She missed Abe and Dory, the family servants and her dearest friends. Most of all she missed Onyx, the gangly puppy her parents brought home to her after their first tour in Albany six years ago.

Eulilia chatted on, unaware that Serenity's mind was three hundred miles away. ". . . did frightfully on my Latin test. I can understand why I need to set a fine table, arrange flowers, and maintain polite conversation, but Latin? Why do I need to study Latin? Even Italians don't speak Latin! Or was it the Greeks?"

"Latin?" Serenity shook her head. "By the way, how did you do on the test today?"

Eulilia dropped her brush beside her on the crumpled quilt. "Have you heard a word I've said? Sometimes I worry about you, Serenity Pownell. How will you ever charm a marriage proposal out of a good-looking young politician if you can't follow the simplest of conversations?"

"I'm sorry. Wool gathering, I guess."

"Hmmph! Wool is all you'll ever gather if you don't pay attention when people speak to you."

Serenity yawned and stretched her arms into the air. She'd heard it all before. "I am sleepy tonight."

Eulilia chuckled. "A good adventure will do that to you."

"Oh, bosh! Be silent for a minute while I say my evening prayers." Serenity sprang from her bed and fell to her knees. A myriad of curls tumbled about her face as she bowed her head.

While Serenity might have questioned the importance of learning how to stitch French knots and serve bouillabaisse properly, she had no doubt about her need for her parents' God. Her parents attended services regularly when in residence in their Albany town house, but seldom rode the twenty miles from their country estate to the town of Auburn for services. Instead, her father would stay home while she and her mother attended one of Preacher Cunard's cottage meetings.

Serenity viewed God through her parents' eyes. So many times since she left home she'd wished for the security of her father's God and longed for the gentling nature of her mother's. *Not that the two are separated entities,* she reminded herself, *more like different faces of the same Being.*

Dear Heavenly Father, she began, *forgive the sins of Thy wayward daughter.* As she breathed the familiar phrase, she tensed. *Cleanse my heart from today's transgressions.* She grimaced. *Bless Mama and Papa, Abe and Dory. Bless my aunts and my uncles and my cousins.* She pursed her lips for a moment. *Bless Mrs. Mott and Elizabeth Cady Stanton, and of course, President Taylor. Amen.* Serenity smiled to herself, knowing that including the two suffragettes in her prayer would please her mother, and praying for the president would please her father. *And Sir, if it is possible, don't let old Herman remember who I am. Amen.*

She scrambled onto the bed and hauled the covers over her body. *What are you thinking, Serenity Louise? Of course Mr. Gustaffson will remember. How can he forget, you silly twig?* Thoughts of reprimand and the resulting punishment pummeled her brain as she tried to fall asleep. *What if I'm expelled? Poor Papa. What an embarrassment!* She analyzed the idea of being asked to leave school. *No, the only crimes serious enough for expulsion from the academy are immoral conduct or having one's parents unable to pay.* With that cynical thought to comfort her, she tucked the pillow around her shoulders and snuggled down to sleep.

The morning light of the overcast New England spring morning filtered through the lace curtains before either girl stirred awake. Serenity had barely untangled her long legs from the covers when the rising bell rang. She leaped from the bed with a bounce, threw off her nightgown, and hauled on the petticoats she'd left in the middle of the floor. "Wake up, Eulia, wake up!"

"Huh? What?" The girl sat up in bed and scratched her scalp between the masses of carefully tied rag curls.

Serenity's fingers fumbled with the buttons on her shoes. She mumbled to herself, "I mustn't be tardy. I mustn't be tardy. Another demerit and I'll be assigned to breakfast duty for the rest of my life!" She paused long enough to shape her high crown of hair into a cascade of curls. On each side of her head she inserted her favorite set of ivory combs, a gift to her from the governor's wife. "Are you coming?" Serenity snapped at her yawning friend. She ran behind the French screen, slipped into her uniform, and buttoned it down the back. She paused to straighten the prim little collar. "See you at worship," she called as she bounded from the room to join the thunder of feet filling the hallway.

At the foot of the stairs, Serenity paused and took a deep breath. *Like a lady,* she scolded herself. *Walk like a lady.* She had a special lilt to her walk as she descended the stairs, like a colt prancing in a field of spring grass. Her father compared her gait to that of the Russian ballerinas who sprang across the stages of Europe. Her proper Quaker mother preferred the simile of the colt to that of stage dancers. The instructors at Martha Van Horne's Finishing School for Young Ladies appreciated neither.

Worry knotted her forehead. *You don't need to attract any undue attention today!* She straightened her shoulders, lifted her chin, and walked into the chapel.

~3~

More Than a
Reprimand

 SERENITY APPRECIATED THE QUIET atmosphere of the chapel, especially in the morning. As she stepped into the darkened room, she felt a tap on her shoulder. She turned and smiled weakly. It was Constance. "Matron Crookshank wishes to see you in her office, Miss Pownell."

"Me?" Serenity pointed to herself. "What for?"

The older girl rolled her eyes. "Any number of things, I imagine."

Serenity sighed and caught sight of Eulilia coming down the stairs. A look of question passed between the two girls. Eulilia shrugged.

Constance paused outside the matron's office door. "I'm sure you know the way from here."

"Thank you," Serenity mumbled. She stepped onto the faded gold-and-blue flowered Persian carpet. Against one wall, the stone-faced Matron Crookshank sat muzzle-rod stiff in the middle of her yellow damask sofa. A blue delft tea set rested on a silver Revere tray on the Louis XIV occasional table beside the matron. Serenity swung her gaze to the right and gasped. Reflected in the gilt-framed, oversized diamond-backed mirror on the back wall of Matron Crookshank's parlor was the image of Caleb Cunard, Reverend Cunard's eldest son. *What is he doing here?*

A tingling of uncertainty shot up her spine. Taking a deep breath, she stepped across the entry into the parlor. "Mr. Cunard . . . " she breathed.

The young man took two steps toward her. "Mistress Serenity, I—"

"Oh, Seri, baby!" The ample form of Dory whirled from behind the doorjamb and into Serenity's startled arms. "My poor baby! My poor, poor baby."

Confused, Serenity hugged the ebony-skinned giant of a woman for a moment. *Whatever is going on?* A knot of terror formed in her stomach. She turned her gaze toward the silent young man. She sensed a deep sadness in his copper-brown eyes. "Something's wrong. What has happened?"

Gently, Caleb disentangled Serenity from the servant's arms. "Come here. Sit down."

Serenity allowed him to lead her to the winged-back chair beside the fireplace. Caleb knelt on one knee before her, taking her trembling hands in his.

"Your mother . . . " his voice wavered.

"My mother?" Serenity lunged forward, taking Caleb by surprise. He fell backward as she sprang to her feet. "What has happened to my mother? Is she sick?"

"It's terrible! Simply terrible!" Dory sniffed into her linen handkerchief.

Caleb grasped Serenity's shoulders. "Listen, Mistress Serenity. Listen to me!"

Fear coursed through her body. In a wave of hysteria the girl pushed against Caleb's chest, but he held fast.

"Something's happened to my mother? What is it? What has happened?" Serenity barked, choking back tears.

"Calm down, Seri. I'll tell you as soon as you calm down."

Serenity lifted her frightened eyes to meet his. He had never used her childhood nickname. She narrowed her eyes with sudden knowledge. "She's dead, isn't she? That's what you're trying to tell me. My mother's dead." As she asked the question, she prayed she was wrong.

The young man flexed the muscles in his jaw, but his eyes answered her question. The silent truth lingered between them. The room began to spin. Serenity's breath came in short hysterical gasps. She swayed and clutched at Caleb's coat. *I will not swoon. I will not swoon!*

"There was an accident on the way to the opera house in Albany. As the footman helped your mother from the carriage, one of the horses spooked. The animal reared—"

Serenity buried her face in Caleb's suede overcoat. The image of her beautiful mother clothed in a swirl of blush pink gossamer satin flashed before her eyes.

"She died instantly."

"When? When did it happen?"

"A week ago."

"And no one told me until now?" Her voice scaled up an octave. "Boston does have telegraph service, you know!" Her eyes flashed with fury.

Caleb tightened his grasp on her arms. "Your father didn't want you to hear the news from strangers."

"Strangers? Why didn't he come for me himself?"

Caleb glanced toward Dory, then up at the hand-carved, honeyed-oak ceiling. "He had to take care of the funeral arrangements."

"No! No, it can't be!" Serenity swung her head back and forth. "Not my mama. No! No, dear God, no! You can't take my mama from me!" Her wailing descended into a whimper.

He wrapped his arms around her and let her cry. At first she struggled to break free, but when she sensed that Dory had joined the tight little circle of grief, the girl gave in. Caleb eased her into Dory's arms.

"How long will it take for Dory to pack your belongings?" he asked.

Serenity tried to answer but no words came. Dory handed her a clean handkerchief. Serenity swallowed the massive lump in her throat.

"Can you be ready to leave before noon today?"

Serenity nodded. "Yes, sir." She walked across the room and stared at a Dutch painting on the wall. She could hear Dory talking with the matron. "If you'll show me to Serenity's room, I'll begin packing immediately."

When the massive oak door closed behind the two women, Serenity turned toward Caleb. "I-I-I'm sorry." She dabbed her handkerchief on the tear stains evident on his lapels.

He gathered her long slender fingers into his broad callused hands. "What is there to be sorry for? We all loved your mother. Aunt Charity was the kindest, gentlest woman I've ever known."

Serenity smiled at him in surprise. She'd never heard him refer to her mother as Aunt Charity. Serenity's mother and the Reverend's wife, opposites in every detail, had been friends since the Reverend and his family moved to the Cayuga Lake region from Massachusetts. Where Serenity's mother was tall and svelte, the embodiment of elegance and grace, Aunt Fay was short and pudgy, a fireball of energy and laughter. During the summers away from the capitol's stifling heat, the women spent afternoons popping green beans on the Cunard's back porch, discussing literature, theology, and politics. The daughter of a Harvard professor, Aunt Fay's interests far surpassed her role as a homespun, minister's wife.

After one such afternoon, Serenity said as much. In private, her mother shook her finger in her daughter's face. "Don't you ever imagine that wisdom wears Belgian lace and French brocade, young lady. Cotton and chambray cannot hide intellect and goodness, nor can the finest satin and softest linen conceal a dolt or rapscallion."

Serenity's father didn't share her mother's enthusiasm for the talkative little neighbor and her circuit-riding preacher husband. As a politician he greeted the Cunards with friendliness and good humor, but in the privacy of the family circle, he voiced his displeasure. "The man should get a legitimate job and support his brood," he said.

The Cunard brood included twenty-year-old Caleb, eighteen-year-old Aaron, ten-year-old Rebecca. Whether it was due to Serenity's mother's influence or to her father's tender heart, the assemblyman was always finding work on the estate for the two older boys. From her room above the library, Serenity sometimes heard Caleb and her father debate politics at night. While there was no doubt her father enjoyed Caleb's company, she herself fancied the company of Aaron, his younger brother.

One humid August evening, Serenity, accompanied by faithful Onyx, slipped out the kitchen door and skipped down to the lake for a late-night swim. On returning home, she plowed straight into the older Cunard son. Flustered, her hair dripping and clutching her dimity night gown and robe about her, Serenity mumbled her apologies and hurried inside the house.

Curious as to why Caleb was skulking around the estate at such an hour, she tiptoed onto the balcony outside her bedroom. Light and the sound of voices—Caleb and her father's—spilled out onto the lawn from the open windows below.

That tattler! That Benedict Arnold! she thought. But when her parents didn't mention her little adventure the next morning, the girl reconsidered her accusations.

Still standing before the Dutch painting in the matron's room, Serenity massaged her temples with her fingertips to ease the throbbing in her head. Why she'd recall such a memory on this day, the day she learned of her mother's death, she didn't know. "I'm sorry, but I need to change into proper traveling clothes."

"Are you sure you'll be all right?" the young man asked.

Serenity nodded. "I'm fine."

Caleb took a deep sigh of relief. "Good. I'll alert the driver."

"Please excuse me," Serenity said in a manner that belied her feelings. As soon as the door closed behind her, she fled toward the dormitory.

— 4 —

Good-bye and
Farewell

 THE CURIOUS GAZES OF CLASSMATES AND instructors followed Serenity's dash up the marble staircase. Tongues clicked and eyes rolled. No student of Martha Van Horne's Finishing School of Young Ladies should behave so unseemly.

"Seri?" Eulilia ran to catch up with her. "What happened, Seri? Matron Crookshank went into our room. She's having your trunks brought down from the luggage room. Did you get expelled? If old Herman tattled on you, I'll go to the matron and confess I was involved too. I won't let you take the blame alone."

"No, no, that's not it." Serenity willed herself to keep from crying.

"What is it then? What is wrong?" The girl circled around Serenity, her arms flailing with curiosity.

Serenity's steps faltered at the landing. "My mother—she—she died," she sobbed.

"Died? Oh, Seri, I'm so sorry." Eulilia drew back from her friend for a moment as if the news might be contagious. "Is there anything I can do?"

Serenity shook her head.

"I can help you pack," Eulilia volunteered. "Your clothing is mixed with mine anyway." The girl followed Serenity into the room. Dory looked up from the bureau's top drawer. A partially packed Saratoga trunk yawned at the foot of Serenity's bed.

"I'm glad you're here, missy. I laid out your gray pin-striped traveling dress for you." Dory dabbed at her nose. "I hope I chose wisely."

"Thank you, Dory. The gray will be fine." Serenity blinked through a new wave of tears. *Why should I care which traveling dress I wear? My mother's dead.* Remembering her manners, Serenity glanced over her shoulder at Eulilia. "Dory, this is my best friend, Eulilia Northrop. Eulilia, this is Dory." Dory smiled and bobbed her head in servile fashion.

Unaccustomed to being formally introduced to a servant, Eulilia gave an awkward nod in return. "Seri told me all about you. She says you make the best ginger snaps."

A sad little smile broke across Dory's face. "I wouldn't know if they're the best, but Miss Serenity and my husband, Abe, certainly like 'em."

"Well . . ." Eulilia surveyed the messy room. "I thought I'd check through my drawers for some of Seri's things. We, um, share back and forth a lot."

The older woman nodded.

Matron Crookshank strode through the open door. "Here's the trunk from the luggage room."

As the girls turned, they saw the hulking form of old Herman filling the doorway. On his shoulder he carried Serenity's second trunk. "Where would you like me to set this, Miss?" The man's gaze fell on Serenity. "You!" he exclaimed.

Embarrassment flooded Serenity's face. She averted her eyes toward Eulilia for help. Eulilia tilted her head. With an air of authority that comes from growing up on a tobacco plantation in the Carolinas, she pointed. "Over there by the window would be fine, sir."

The man continued to stare at Serenity.

"You may set it down anywhere, Herman." Matron Crookshank's strident tone didn't alter the man's demeanor.

"You . . ." He gasped a second time. The trunk hit the floor with a thud.

"That will be all, Herman." An impatient edge seeped into Matron Crookshank's voice. "You may go now."

Serenity glanced over her shoulder to see Herman bob his head and back out of the door. Matron Crookshank turned toward Dory. "If there is nothing else, I will be in my office."

As the door closed behind her, the girls heaved unanimous sighs of relief.

"Missy?" Dory lifted one suspicious eyebrow at Serenity.

The girls reddened. Eulilia recovered first. "I'd better get busy or I'll be late for deportment class."

"Deportment class?" Serenity mouthed, her eyebrows lost in the spray of curls on her forehead.

Eulilia shrugged and strode to the dresser. While Serenity searched through her desk for the key to unlock the second trunk, Dory returned to packing the first.

"Whatever is deportment class?" Serenity hissed.

Eulilia shrugged and grinned.

As Dory placed the last of Serenity's crinolines into the second trunk, she closed the lid and straightened. "That about does it, missy."

Serenity and Eulilia, standing by the window facing one another, nodded, their eyes brimming with tears. Clasping hands, they glanced out the window.

"Look!" Eulilia pointed at the flagpole and laughed. "The flag!"

Serenity drew back the curtain and gazed up at the red, white, and blue rectangle floating in the crisp New England breeze. She giggled and glanced toward Dory.

Serenity drew on her pearl-gray kidskin gloves and picked up her favorite blue-flowered damask hat box, the one her mother gave her when she left for school. She slipped the ribboned strap on her wrist and took a deep breath. "I'm afraid it's time for me to go."

As the two girls followed Dory down the stairs, they vowed to faithfully correspond with one another.

Serenity dabbed her nose with her handkerchief. "What am I going to do without you?"

"What are you going to do? What about me? Crook-shank will probably make Constance or Annabelle my new roommate!"

Serenity giggled at the prospect. "That would be justice, wouldn't it?"

"Justice? That would be eternal—"

"Eulilia Northrop," Serenity scolded, "don't you dare curse in front of me. You know I don't like it."

A look of mock innocence swept across the girl's face. "What do you mean, curse? I was going to say bliss—eternal bliss."

"Um-hmm, of course you were." Serenity tightened her lips. She paused when they reached the foyer. "Please come and visit me next summer like you promised?"

"I will."

"Promise?" The girls linked hands.

"Promise."

"Friends forever?"

"Forever."

The clatter of horses' hooves on the cobblestones out front brought Matron Crookshank from the office. The matron placed her porcelain hand on Serenity's and smiled. "God go with you, my dear. You will be missed."

"Thank you, Matron Crookshank. I shall remember everything I learned." Out of the corner of her eye, she caught sight of Eulilia grinning and gesturing with her eyes toward the flagpole. Serenity struggled to maintain proper decorum. The clapper on the door sounded.

Matron Crookshank opened the door. The girls turned to see Caleb enter the building.

"Who is that?" Eulilia whispered into Serenity's ear.

Serenity turned to look at her friend with surprise. "Just my neighbor, Caleb."

"Neighbor? Hmmm, a summertime visit sounds nice."

"Eulilia, I recognize that look in your eye. You should have been named after Diana, the huntress."

"Who me?" The girl fluttered her eyelashes innocently, then peered over Serenity's shoulder at the subject in question. "Have you taken a good look at him lately?"

Serenity appraised Caleb as one would a painting at the Boston Museum of Art. "Tsk! I really must question your taste, dear Eulilia; first the stable boy, Anthony, now Caleb?" she whispered as the entourage swept through the doorway onto the portico. The girls exchanged pointed looks with Herman as he loaded the second trunk into the boot of the rented carriage. Next he helped Serenity and Dory into the cabriolet.

Despite the nightmare surrounding her journey, a sense of anticipation caused Serenity's stomach to rumble. Caleb peered through the open carriage door. "Ladies, please make yourselves comfortable in there. I'll be riding with the driver." He exchanged a meaningful look with Dory, then closed the carriage door.

Everything's happening too fast—too fast. As the coach surged forward Serenity waved good-bye to her friend, maintaining her smile until they passed through the academy's iron gates and onto the Westboro-Boston roadway. She pushed her back against the carriage's leather seat and closed her eyes. "Dory? Why didn't my father come for me?"

"He had a number of details to clean up in Albany. He's waiting there for us," Dory explained. "He's arranging to borrow a friend's barge, to take us to Syracuse."

"Barge? But that's so slow compared to the train."

Dory patted Serenity's hand. "Maybe he's not too eager to return to the empty house any sooner than necessary," Dory said, squeezing Serenity's gloved hand. "Are you all right, child?"

Serenity opened her eyes and nodded absently. *Do you mean will I live through this nightmare? What choice do I have?* she thought.

Patterns of light and dark flashed by, sunlight shining through the young, tender leaves on the trees lining the roadway. She gazed idly at the green fields edged with rambling stone walls. A disturbing thought entered her mind. *It's my fault. God must be punishing me by taking my mother from me, punishing me for my bad behavior. Oh, God, I'm sorry. I didn't know!*

Tears blurred her vision as the carriage rolled past a stone gristmill. Water poured over the slowly turning wheel.

It's too late for regrets! She closed her eyes again. Her head throbbed with pain. *Maybe, it's a bad dream,* she thought. *I'll wake up to find myself in my bed at school. Please, God, make it only a terrible dream!*

The carriage jounced over the potholes in the road. At the outskirts of Boston, the clatter of horses' hooves increased, along with the clangor of cart wheels. The wide, cobblestoned streets allowed two wagons to pass easily as they approached the third largest city in America.

Face it, Serenity, she scolded the voices in her head, *you can't close your eyes to the truth! Your mother's gone and she won't be coming back.* The young woman swallowed her tears and took a ragged breath through gritted teeth.

The vitality of the metropolis stirred Serenity to open her eyes once again. Once Boston had been the hub of shipbuilding and commerce for the West Indies. Now New Orleans and Charleston vied for that title. Yet Boston remained the center of business for all of New England.

As the carriage passed the Boston Commons, she recalled the day in the fall when her parents first brought her to the finishing school. Before leaving her at the school, the three of them walked in the park and fed bread scraps to the ducks on the pond. Now that day seemed almost dreamlike in her memory.

The carriage turned right and headed down the hill on School Street toward King's Chapel, the first Episcopal church built in Boston. A cacophony of vendors peddling their wares, fishmongers hawking their catches, farmers selling milk out of their carts, town criers reporting the news and time, bells, horns, shouts, and neighs accosted Serenity's ears. Her nostrils pinched together from the pungent aromas of rancid grease, horse manure, dead fish, human body odor, and chimney smoke.

The carriage continued along Corn Hill Street, past Faneuil Hall. They rolled past the entrance to Damnation Alley, a street filled with shops and merchandise from around the world. Serenity grimaced at the memory of her mother's laughter when her father insisted on buying each of them a red Spanish mantilla and ivory combs from one of the stalls. *Mama loved red,* she thought, *but would never allow herself to wear the "Jezebel color" in public.*

~5~

The Interloper

 A FRENZY OF VEHICLES JAMMED THE main intersection en route to the depot. Carriages, wagons, and carts all rushing to the center created a helpless state of confusion. Dory tapped Serenity on the arm. "Look at that gold coach over there!" The servant pointed across the street toward a magnificent double-brougham, the sides of which were overlaid with gold. It was drawn by six matching sorrels. "Imagine! Four liveried servants!"

"Oh, that's a clarence, I think." Serenity had seen similar luxury carriages while visiting Albany with her parents. "It truly is impressive. The black scrollwork on the sides is quite pretty."

The driver of the admired vehicle cursed and waved a fist in the air at the driver of the business buggy in front of him.

"Hmmph!" Dory folded her arms across her ample stomach. "Pretty is as pretty does!"

Without warning, the left rear wheel of the two-passenger, open-air calash on their right jostled the side of their carriage, throwing their vehicle into the pathway of a loaded drummer's wagon. The two women bounced about the cab's interior like potatoes in a washtub. Serenity's elbows slammed against the walls of the carriage; the hat box on her lap flew to the floor. She grabbed for the armrest with one gloved hand, the back of the seat with the other. At the same time, Dory's hands flew into the air. "We shall be over, we shall all be over!" she screamed.

"Hey, you grog-swilling Jonathan! Watch your driving!" their driver shouted. Police whistles joined the shouts of other carriage drivers. A squad of burly policemen dashed into the tangle of vehicles and shouted orders.

"Why anyone would choose to live in this Babel of confusion is beyond me!" Dory snapped her jaw shut. Serenity grinned.

"Now, Dory, are you saying that if Abe took a notion to move to New York City or Boston, you wouldn't follow him?" she teased, her dimples deepening.

"My Abe has too much sense to do such a thing."

"But if he did, wouldn't you go? Doesn't the Good Book say, 'whither thou goest, I will go'?"

"Missy, don't you go quotin' the Good Book to me. Besides, that was what Ruth told her mother-in-law, not her husband!"

"True . . ." Regardless of her foul mood, Serenity couldn't resist teasing the woman. " . . . but doesn't the Bible also say something about 'leaving and cleaving'?"

"That's what God told the man, to leave his mother and father and cleave unto his wife, not the other way around."

Serenity giggled. "Sounds like hairsplitting to me."

"Hmmph!" Dory turned her face toward the window, her lips tightening. As the carriage rolled past The Blue Partridge Inn, church bells across the city gonged twelve and Serenity's stomach growled.

Dory withdrew a chunk of corn bread wrapped in a

linen napkin from the carpetbag by her feet. She offered it to Serenity. The girl shook her head. "No, thank you," she whispered.

"Child, you have to eat," Dory scolded. "You'll be no help to your papa if you take sick."

Serenity ignored her complaint. "Will my mama be . . .," Serenity paused and swallowed hard, ". . . coming home?"

Tears filled the older woman's eyes. "Your father had your mother's body interred in a small cemetery outside Albany. Mrs. Van der Mere helped him make the arrangements."

"Mrs. Van der Mere? The black widow spider?"

"Now, missy, that be mighty unchristian of you."

"Dory, everyone knows that since Captain Van der Mere died that woman's been casting her web around every eligible man on the East Coast, regardless of his age or rank. If a man breathes, he's ripe for her pickin'."

"Serenity Louise!" Dory clicked her tongue. "I'm sure your father is too destitute over the loss of your mother to be attracted to another woman's charms."

"I certainly hope so." Serenity's foot started tapping. "Mama was so nice to Mrs. Van der Mere, always inviting eligible men to her dinner parties."

Dory patted Serenity's arm three times. "Now don't go getting yourself upset, child. It's bad for your complexion, and—"

Tears sprang into Serenity's eyes. "It's not in the least unladylike!"

The carriage stopped in front of the railway station. Caleb assisted the ladies from the vehicle while the driver transferred Serenity's luggage. "This way, ladies," Caleb said, bowing graciously and extending his arms to both women. "If I may escort you to the railway car?"

Serenity noticed the look of surprise on Dory's face. To honor a servant of color in such a manner was rare in polite society. Yet Caleb behaved as if his gesture were most natural.

Travelers of every description and station in life surged past the threesome as they crossed the marble-tiled waiting area and onto the platform. The crowds dizzied Serenity. She and Dory settled into a railway car while Caleb retrieved the luggage receipts. Serenity patted the green velvet upholstered seats made of horsehair and strung rope. They were much more comfortable than the wooden seats in the lower class section.

Outside the curtained window, boarding passengers and uniformed workmen rushed about. Within minutes, the conductor signaled the engineer and the engineer clanged the bell. The great engine snorted; the iron wheels squealed. Steam hissed from the sides of the train, obliterating Serenity's view of the people waving farewell from the platform. The engine strained forward. The cars rumbled, gathering momentum. Serenity leaned back against the seat and closed her eyes. The six-hour ride from Boston to Albany would be a bone-wearying journey.

At each stop, while the train deposited and took on passengers and freight, a train butch strolled through the cars hawking newspapers, magazines, sandwiches, peanuts, and cigars. Bored, Serenity bought the newest issue of *Goedy's Lady's Book* from a twelve-year-old boy with railway smudge on his nose and hands. She tried to read, but couldn't concentrate. Somewhere in a secret pocket of her mind, she maintained the hope that somehow, someone had made a horrible mistake and her mother would be at the railway station to welcome her. She thought about her father's decision to travel across New York State by barge. *Maybe it's not such a bad idea after all. It will be nice to have time together before we get home.* She closed the magazine and hugged it to her chest. A fresh wave of loneliness engulfed her. She ached to have her father's comforting arms hold her and brush away her tears.

"Seri, dear," Dory interrupted her thoughts. "I miss your mama too. Would you like to talk?"

Serenity shook her head.

"That's why God gave us one another, for comfort."

"God?" Serenity clenched her teeth. "He let my mother die!"

Dory placed her hand on Serenity's arm. "Oh, child, God knows and . . ."

Serenity snatched away her arm. "Please, I don't wish to discuss this any longer."

Beyond the window, new growth budded forth along the tree-lined rail, but the young woman could see only the bleakness of a hard New England winter. *God, it isn't fair! If Thou needs to punish me for my misdeeds, then punish me! Don't take my mama away . . . I need her more than Thee does.*

As the train crossed into New York State, the smoke-stacks above the brawling industrial town of Troy came into view. The train chugged across the narrow trestle spanning the mighty Hudson River. Serenity's interest mounted as they approached the switching yards, eager to catch the first glimpse of her father.

The train screeched to a stop in a flurry of smoke and noise. Caleb, who'd been sitting across the aisle from the two women, stood and removed the ladies' valises from the overhead storage rack.

"Do you see him?" Serenity whispered to Dory. "Do you see my father?"

"No, not yet." The older woman craned her neck to get a better view, then pointed. "Wait! I think . . . yes, over there!"

Serenity gave a cry of anticipation. The tall, lean assemblyman with his charcoal-gray bowler stood a head above the crowd. As the crowd parted around him, Serenity saw a fashionably dressed, middle-aged woman clinging to his arm, Josephine Van der Mere.

Serenity's lower lip protruded. She folded her arms across her chest and bounded back against the railway seat. "I'm not going out there!"

"Come now, missy. Of course you are." Dory gently twisted a few of the girl's stray curls into place. "Besides, the train's heading toward Saratoga."

"Fine! I'll live the rest of my life in Saratoga! It may as well be California, for all I care!"

Caleb gazed down at the defiant young woman. "Miss Serenity, stop acting like a spoiled five-year-old. Your father needs you. Think of him and not yourself."

She blinked in surprise. Dory did the same. No one spoke to Miss Serenity Louise Pownell in that manner. Anger flashed across her face. A tear slipped down her cheek. "You don't understand—"

"I understand that your father's been through a terrible time and he desperately needs you. Can you understand that?"

With a sniff and a glare, Serenity gathered her skirts about her and joined the line of passengers at the rear of the car. The moment she appeared at the top of the stairs and reached for the conductor's hand, the tall man with the bowler and neatly groomed mustache and beard bounded toward her. "Seri, baby!"

"Papa!" All concern for proper decorum disappeared as he swept her into his arms and whirled her about the waiting area.

"My baby, my baby! I've missed you so much."

"Oh, Papa!" Their joy of seeing each other, mixed with the sorrow of the circumstances, made for a bittersweet reunion. The politician lowered his daughter until her feet touched the wooden platform. He tightened his arms about her and buried his face in her curls. They clung to one another for several seconds. For the first time that day, Serenity felt warm and safe. Neither father nor daughter noticed when Caleb left to reclaim Serenity's trunks.

"I need you, Papa," Serenity said, but her words were absorbed by her father's wool Chesterfield coat. With her ear pressed against his chest, she felt rather than heard his reply.

"I need you, too, Seri. I need you too."

Serenity would have stayed there, protected forever, except her father stepped back and held out his hand toward Mrs. Van der Mere. "Seri, you remember your mother's dear friend, Josephine?"

"Yes, of course, Mrs. Van der Mere." Serenity gave an abrupt curtsy.

Uninvited, the stylish, golden-tressed woman wrapped her arms around Serenity's suddenly arctic form. The feather on the woman's hat brushed against the girl's nose. "Oh, Serenity, dear, I am so sorry. Your mother, rest her soul . . . such a loss."

"Yes, Mrs. Van der Mere. Thank you." Serenity refused to thaw.

"Josephine. Call me Josephine, darling." The woman appeared not to notice the girl's icy response.

"Mrs. Van der Mere has graciously offered us the use of her barge for our journey home." Her father cast an appreciative glance at the woman, outfitted in an iridescent, midnight-blue taffeta afternoon dress and matching cape.

"Josephine's been such a friend through all of this. I don't know what I would have done without her," he continued. Josephine smiled coyly up into the man's face. A message passed between them that Serenity neither liked nor wanted to understand.

Her father offered his arms, one to Josephine and the other to his daughter. Instead of taking it, Serenity turned her coyest smile on Caleb. "Sir?" she said, slipping a gloved hand into the crook of the young man's right arm, taking him by surprise. Immediately, Caleb stiffened. Serenity tipped her head to one side and smiled again. A rigid smile lifted one corner of Caleb's mouth. Glancing first at the assemblyman, then back at Serenity, he touched the rim of his hat and nodded. Serenity batted her eyelids at him like she'd seen Eulilia do with the young men she'd meet. Then turning her face toward her father and Mrs. Van der Mere, she said in a snooty tone, "Are we ready?"

Serenity ignored the sadness that filled her father's eyes. Ever the proper gentleman, he suavely slipped his empty hand into his pocket. Arriving at the carriage, he turned to Mrs. Van de Mere. "Madam? May I assist you into the carriage?" he said. Serenity allowed Caleb to help her into the brougham her father kept in Albany. The fashionable carriage rolled over the cobblestoned streets, past the avenue leading to her parents' capitol city town house and turned instead up the broad, tree-lined boulevard where all the state senators, ambassadors, wealthy businessman, and diplomats resided. The carriage turned and paused outside a black wrought iron gate until the gateman allowed the carriage to enter the grounds of the Van der Mere estate. They would stay there for the night before continuing on by barge in the morning, the assemblyman said.

That evening, Serenity's mood deepened while Dory buttoned her into her favorite evening dress. At the dinner table, she watched the widow weave her spell over her father, and over Caleb as well.

Josephine's diamond necklace and multitude of rings glittered in the candlelight with every gesture, white diamond and ruby earrings dangled from her earlobes. Her deep-crimson silk dress emphasized her small stature, her carefully arranged corkscrew ringlets, creamy complexion, and tantalizing green eyes. By comparison, Serenity's sometimes awkward height, simple green dimity gown, and wild array of raven, black curls tumbling every which way down her back made her the perfect foil to the widow.

Josephine flashed a provocative smile toward the assemblyman. "Of course you have heard about New York City's latest addition to the medical profession? Dr. Blackwell— that is, Dr. Elizabeth Blackwell," she said waving a graceful hand in the air. "Can you imagine? A woman studying medicine. How indelicate."

"Personally," Serenity said, running her fingers along the embroidered neckline of her dinner dress, "I think she should be commended. My mother always believed a woman can do anything she desired if she put her mind to it."

"That's true." Her father beamed sadly.

Serenity glanced toward her father. "Remember how excited Mama was when she returned from the Women's Rights Convention in Senaca Falls?"

"Do I? She could talk of little else for weeks." He frowned. "That was almost two years ago; doesn't seem possible."

"Begging your pardon, Samuel, dear, but politics is hardly a world for ladies. Imagine believing women should have the right to vote in the elections! Dear Charity always seemed to be fighting one misguided cause or another." Josephine wiped at her eyes with her linen napkin and glanced around the room.

Serenity's father cleared his throat to pass the awkward moment. "For a woman who hated war of any kind, Charity found no end of hopeless battles to champion, I'll grant you."

"A dear, sweet woman." Josephine sniffled. "I cannot fault her for her causes since I, myself, was one of them."

Tears sprang into Serenity's eyes. All this talk of her mother was melting her stoic resolve. She dabbed at the cherries and heavy cream dessert in front of her with her spoon, willing the tears to disappear.

"I must confess, though, I never could understand her passion for that New England radical, Thoreau." Josephine fingered her necklace. "Why anyone would go to jail rather than pay his poll tax is beyond me. It would be much easier to pay the nuisance tax and be done with it."

"But to pay the tax would condone it," Caleb interjected. "Many great minds believe the man makes a lot of sense."

"Sense? Common sense or nonsense?" Josephine laughed at her play on words. "Breaking the law should not be tolerated in any form. How can a responsible American citizen justify such behavior?"

"I like Thoreau's spirit," Caleb countered. "Men who stand by their beliefs are rare in these modern times."

The politician sat silent. Josephine fluttered her eyelashes at him and coyly lifted one shoulder. "Well, I must admit. Every public speaker of merit quotes him."

"Then he must be good," the assemblyman finally said, arching an eyebrow and grinning. "All those senators, congressmen, and supreme court judges can't be wrong."

"Oh, Samuel, you are joshing me!" Josephine flung her hand in the air and giggled. "What can I say? I'm only a woman, you know."

An audible groan escaped from Serenity's lips. Realizing she'd been heard, her face reddened. "Sorry, Mrs. Van der Mere. I am afraid I am exhausted after my long journey."

"Of course you are, dear." Josephine rang the crystal bell to the left of her place setting. "How thoughtless of me. And tomorrow will be another long day. Gentlemen, please finish your dessert while I help Serenity settle in for the night."

Feeling relegated to the role of a twelve-year-old once more, Serenity cringed.

The butler entered the room. Josephine cast him a condescending smile. "Herschel, please tell Esther to turn down Serenity's bedding, and inform her that the child wishes to retire. She might need to prepare a bed warmer." The woman shuddered delicately. "It's been unseasonably cold this year, don't you think, Samuel?"

"Quite." He glanced toward his daughter. "Will you be all right?"

Since she couldn't think of a gracious way out of her predicament, Serenity nodded and placed her table napkin next to her dessert dish.

"Gentlemen, if you'll excuse us, I'll just see Serenity to her room." As Josephine began to rise, the two men leaped to their feet and rushed to the aid of the women—Caleb to Serenity's chair and the assemblyman to their hostess's. "Make yourselves comfortable in the drawing room. I'll return in a few moments," Josephine said, placing one glittering hand possessively on Samuel's shoulders. "Samuel, dear, you and I have so much to discuss before we depart tomorrow."

Serenity seethed. *This is disgusting! My mother's body is barely cold in the ground!*

Upstairs, Josephine couldn't have been nicer. Since Serenity bathed before dinner, there was little more for her to do than dress for bed. Josephine puttered around the room while Dory helped Serenity unbutton her dinner dress and slip into a chambray nightgown.

"Thank you, Dory. I can take care of the rest." Josephine waved Dory from the room, closing the door behind the servant. She paused, her back against the intricately carved bedroom door.

"Your mother spoke of you so often, I feel like I know you well." She nibbled on her lower lip. "I do hope you and I can be friends, Serenity."

"Mrs. Van der Mere, I—"

Josephine gestured toward Serenity. "No, please. Don't answer now. Just give me a chance, will you?"

Feeling hopelessly lost in a situation made unfamiliar by her own absence, Serenity nodded silently, then yawned.

"Oh dear, here I go again, keeping you awake. I am so sorry. We'll have plenty of time to talk on our trip to Union Springs."

Serenity's eyes widened. "You're coming with us? I thought—"

"Oh, yes. Your father needs me. It's the least I can do." Josephine blew her a kiss and left, closing the door silently behind her.

Serenity blew out the flame in the bedside lamp. Snuggling down under the covers, she squeezed her eyes shut. "Dear Father in heaven, where art Thou? My world is falling apart. I need Thee."

~6~

The Silver Garnish

WHEN SERENITY AWOKE THE NEXT morning, her head pounded. The muscles in her neck ached. Her eyes burned. She peered out from beneath a down-filled, scarlet satin quilt. Dory stood beside the massive oak canopy bed, her face breaking into a joyous grin. "Time to rise, Miss Serenity!"

Stop acting so cheery, Serenity wanted to scream. *But of course you're happy. You're going home to Abe!* Serenity burrowed her face beneath the covers once more.

"Now, child, I know you're awake. You can't fool me none." Dory dragged the covers off the struggling girl. Serenity rolled over onto her stomach.

"You don't want to keep your hostess waiting now, do you?"

Serenity groaned at the mention of Mrs. Van der Mere. "My head aches!"

"A cup of chamomile tea will do wonders for you." Faithful Dory leaned across the bed and began massaging the girl's shoulders and neck. "Your back muscles are so knotted, it's no wonder you're in pain. Relax, child, relax."

"Relax? While that lioness devours my father?"

Dory laughed. "I don't think devour is what Mrs. Van der Mere has in mind, child."

Reluctantly the girl climbed out of bed. "How can you laugh about a thing like this?" Serenity adjusted her corset over her hand-embroidered camisole. "Lace me in tighter today, Dory. I want to look my best."

"Child, if I lace you much tighter, you won't be able to breathe. Besides, I would think a twenty-one-inch waist is small enough for any lady of distinction."

"Twenty-one inches when I'm unlaced and eighteen when I'm laced. But today, I wish to be seventeen, if you please." Serenity cupped a hand on each hip and inhaled. "Hurry!" she hissed. "I can't hold my breath all day."

The older woman chuckled. "I declare, missy, I have the best of both worlds. I'm a free woman, simple as that may be, and I'm not so fancy so's I have to live in pain like you." She patted her ample stomach. "I'm free to be the way God made me."

"God didn't make you that way. Shortbread cookies and peppermint candies did," Serenity retorted.

Dory snorted and tied the corset strings into a bow. "Shortbread cookies! I never heard you complain about my shortbread cookies."

"And you never will." Serenity licked her lips as she stepped into her petticoats and tightened the drawstrings. Satisfied with the results, she raised her hands to allow the woman to slip a brown wool traveling dress over her head. While Dory fastened the long row of bone buttons on the dress's bodice, Serenity smoothed the swirls of black piping on the bodice and cuffs.

Dory tugged on the points of the French collar. "There!" Serenity swirled before the freestanding mahogany mirror. "How do I look? It feels wonderful to wear dresses other than that dingy school uniform."

"You look lovely, child. You'll have Mr. Cunard's eyes a bulgin'."

"Dory!"

The woman's eyes twinkled with delight. "Surely you've seen the way he watches you when you leave the room, or hangs on your every word when you speak."

"You are being ridiculous. Why he's an old prune." Serenity paused, studying her own face in the mirror. "Now, his brother Aaron . . ."

A slow smile spread across the girl's face.

"Hmmph! Aaron's a boy; Caleb is a man."

Serenity's curls danced in syncopation with her nodding head. "Exactly!"

"But then, you've plenty of time for such worries." Dory grabbed the hog-bristled brush and set about to tame Serenity's tousled curls. "The good Lord sure blessed you with an abundance of hair. So full, and black as ebony."

Serenity laughed. "When Papa's ancestors fled Paris for the Riviera during the Huguenot persecutions, one of my great-great-grandpas fell in love with a woman from Milan or Corsica . . . don't they have ebony hair in those parts of the world?"

"Serenity Louise! You mustn't speak of such things!" Dory smacked the girl on one shoulder.

Serenity sighed dramatically. "Dory, I took a class in biology, you know. I do understand a little about the life process."

"An excellent reason why young women should not be educated!" The woman tugged at a snarl.

"Ouch!" Serenity winced. "You don't mean that and

you know it. I've seen Mama teaching you how to read the Good Book."

"The Good Book, yes, but not a book that will increase your carnal knowledge."

"There are plenty of passages in the Good Book I wouldn't want to read before breakfast," the girl teased.

Dory clicked her tongue. "You are developing such an indelicate mouth, missy!"

"Sorry, Dory. I will endeavor to speak in a more ladylike manner." Serenity pinched her cheeks and moistened her lips. "Wasn't that the breakfast bell I heard?"

While the servants packed and transported the luggage to the waiting barge, the travelers rushed through breakfast. A liveried coachman transported Mrs. Van der Mere and her guests to the waterfront.

The waterfront breathed a life of its own. Gamblers, thieves, fortune-tellers, ruffians, and peddlers hawking their wares vied with one another for the attention of the wealthy travelers. Serenity stopped to watch a sad, molting, brown bear dancing to the tune of "Oh Suzanna," played on a flute by its owner. The girl loosened the drawstrings of her reticule and found two pence to drop into the coin bucket.

A young girl not much older than Serenity waved to her from on board one of the numerous shanty boats in the harbor. Two little children played at the girl's feet while a third child lay nursing at the young woman's breast. Serenity thought of the girls back at the academy. She couldn't imagine any one of them becoming a mother of one child at such an early age, let alone three.

Josephine followed Serenity's gaze. "She'll live her entire life on that barge. Her man is probably a peddler or a gambler."

Serenity glanced at the girl's soiled calico dress and tattered woolen shawl, then at her own tan suede cape with matching gloves and boots. "Life isn't fair." Her mother's words leaped unbidden to Serenity's lips.

"No, life isn't fair." Josephine patted Serenity's arm.

Serenity mulled over the woman's words.

"Gathering a skein of wool this morning?"

Serenity started at the voice breaking into her reverie. She glanced over her shoulder. "Mr. Cunard, I didn't hear you coming."

"I'm not surprised with all the commotion. I've been instructed to escort you aboard the *Silver Garnish*. She's readying to cast off. He gestured in the direction of the largest, most elegant packet docked in the canal.

Seventy feet long and fourteen feet wide, the *Silver Garnish* contained a roomy salon furnished with Brussels carpet, a Sheraton mahogany table veneered with a satin wood finish, and eight straight-back Windsor chairs. Mrs. Van der Mere's own French chef presided over the tidy little kitchen. And while the sleeping compartments, fore and aft, were definitely cramped compared to the commercial packets, the *Silver Garnish*'s sleeping accommodations were luxurious. The Van der Mere packet shone like an advertisement for canal travel in *Harper's Monthly*.

Mrs. Van der Mere directed Serenity to her stateroom. Once situated, the girl went in search of her father. She found him topside, watching as the packet captain shouted orders to the steersman. The hogee, a boy of no more than fourteen, sat astride the second of two matching gray mares, eager to embark on the journey west. When the captain shouted the command to be off, the hogee snapped a whip above the head of the front mare and the animals headed down the tow path beside the canal. The ropes grew taut and the barge inched forward.

Behind them a horn blew, warning the captain that a faster, lighter Clinton Line barge wanted to pass. The captain of the *Silver Garnish* gestured angrily at the commercial barge captain, who retorted in like manner. The steersmen of the two barges shouted commands to their respective hogees to tighten the lines. The two teams of horses strained, holding the ropes taut to allow the Clinton barge to pass. Serenity held her breath until the ropes cleared. She'd heard horror stories of tangled ropes and beached barges.

Once again under way, the *Garnish*'s hogee's high, off-key shanty song filled the calm morning air. His occasional glance toward Serenity brought a blush to her cheeks. She strolled aft and found her father leaning against the cabin wall. As she drew closer, Samuel Pownell turned and smiled. "Good morning, little one." He extended an arm to her. "It's been such a busy morning we've hardly had a chance to speak. Did you sleep well last night?"

She sidled easily into the protection of his grasp. "I guess."

"I didn't do very well either."

"I miss Mama."

He pulled her close to his side. "I do too."

They watched a canal walker inspecting the walls of the canal for any leaks that may have developed overnight. Whenever he spotted a leak, he lowered the gunny sack from his shoulders, scooped out a shovelful of manure and hay with his hand tool, and patched the hole. To have a hole develop in the dike walls or the walls of one of the locks would cause havoc to the canal traffic. Barges would run aground causing a traffic tie-up equal to farmer's day in Manhattan.

The singsong of the hogee and the occasional exchange between passing barge captains filled the morning air. At four miles per hour, it would be a three-day voyage from Troy to Syracuse. From there they would board a train for Auburn where Abe would meet them with the family coach and drive them the last twelve miles to their waterfront home.

Serenity ached for home, yet dreaded arriving there. Without her mother to greet her, the place would be mournful. The first few days would be especially difficult as the families in the surrounding community came to pay their respects. All Serenity longed for was to escape to her secret hideaway down by the lake and make the rest of the world go away.

The sun rose higher in the sky. A trickle of sweat slid down the girl's face. She brushed it aside. Her stomach growled. If only she could cool off by leaping into the canal. If she were at home she'd sneak down to the lake and take a dip.

Unseasonably warm temperatures had turned the barge's lower living quarters into a coffin, forcing most of the travelers to ride on wooden benches atop the main cabin. Caleb and Dory sat at the bow of the barge watching the busy world beyond the canal as the captain instructed his passengers on canal travel. As they floated up the Hudson River toward the mouth of the famous Erie Canal, Serenity thought she never imagined how robust one must be to survive canal travel. Whenever the helmsman cried, "Bridge!" those standing quickly scrapped their dignity and hit the deck. And when he cried, "Low bridge!" even those seated on the benches flattened themselves to avoid a conk on the head.

Despite the heat, Serenity wandered down the stairs into the central cabin where she found Mrs. Van der Mere's small library carefully stocked, not only with several of the classics, but with a number of the newest book titles from Europe as well. The natural light from the barge's side windows created a dusty warm atmosphere in the library. A mosquito lazily circled around Serenity's head as she browsed through the leather-bound volumes. Her fingertips caressed the leather bindings. Her eyes misted. *Mama would have loved this,* she thought. Her mother adored books, and she seldom missed the opportunity to instill that love into her only daughter.

"But Mama, why do I need all of this knowledge?" Serenity would argue. "I just want to be a wife and mother, like you."

"Just a wife and a mother? Serenity, you are a woman first and a child of God. That is enough reason to learn all you can about God's world." She would tug at one of her daughter's stray corkscrew curls. "Reading brings that world to your doorstep. A woman, a wife, and a mother needs to understand as much about that world as she can in order to make it a better place for herself and for those she loves."

Drawing Serenity into her arms, the woman would continue. "God has given you a keen mind, my dear. It is your responsibility to improve it so that when He calls upon you to wage war against the evils of the world, you will be prepared."

Serenity would then flash a wide-eyed, innocent grin at her mother. "War? But Mama, I thought Quakers didn't believe in war?"

"Friends, dear. And yes, friends do not believe in making war. Yet we do wage silent battles against injustices wherever and whenever we need to. Our weapons are our brains, not our brawn."

"Low bridge!" The captain's loud cry from the floor above was barely audible now. Without thinking Serenity brushed a stray curl from her cheek and discovered her face was wet with tears. *Oh, Mama, it wasn't time for you to go!* She leaned her head against a bookshelf and closed her eyes.

"You miss her, don't you?"

What a stupid question. Serenity straightened at the intrusive voice behind her. She blotted her tears on the sleeve of her traveling dress.

"Here . . ." Josephine handed her a linen handkerchief. "I do too, miss her, I mean." The woman removed a leather-bound volume from a shelf and handed it to the girl. "I know my loss is nothing compared to yours, but I'll never find another friend like your mother."

"And no one will ever replace her as my mother." Even as Serenity growled the words, she knew she sounded churlish and unladylike.

"Of course. I lost my mother when I was eleven. My Aunt Carolyn raised me. She was good to me, but she never could take Mama's place." Josephine shifted her gaze to the book now in Serenity's hand. "Your mother gave me that book for my birthday last year. She was always trying to get me to read more." The woman chuckled fondly. "An intellectual I'm not, but dear Charity never stopped trying."

Serenity ran her fingertips over the gold-leaf letters on the book's spine. *Autobiography: The Life and Times of Benjamin Franklin.*

"She said it's the first masterpiece of American litera-
A note of sadness seeped into Mrs. Van der Mere's
disappeared as quickly as it came. "Your mother

taught me to read, you know. Imagine an orphan, a Delancy Street orphan, being able to read."

Serenity bit her lip. The bulk of her tears remained dammed behind a wall of denial. "Excuse me, Mrs. Van der Mere, but I'm feeling a bit queasy. I'm not used to boating, I fear. I need fresh air." She covered her mouth with the handkerchief and rushed from the room.

Josephine called after her, "I'm not your enemy, Serenity!"

Serenity climbed the stairs to the deck and took in a deep breath of fresh air.

Her father called and waved to her. "So, how are you doing? You're just in time to enjoy the first set of locks."

The *Silver Garnish* inched toward a massive pair of iron gates where the Hudson and the Mohawk Rivers merged. The captain sounded the horn. Serenity gazed up at the three-story-high gates. Shouts to and from the workmen standing atop the gates split the peaceful afternoon air, sending a chill of expectancy through the passengers. Then a carefully choreographed drama unfolded before them. The gates swung open and the barge that had seemed so large back at the docks moved into the dark, ominous cavern. Water dripped from the mossy walls.

Another cry from high on the wall and several thick sisal ropes fell like paper streamers down the walls of the cavern. The barge crew scrambled to anchor the ropes to the *Silver Garnish*. High above their heads, bare-chested mule skinners, their black sweaty skin glistening in the remaining sunlight, shouted to the mules and the barge inched forward. Then, with the same slow deliberation, the gates closed behind the barge, trapping the barge and her passengers in the dark, frightening lock.

The passengers and crew of the *Silver Garnish* gathered at the railing to watch the lockskeeper turn the gigantic wheel that opened the floodgates at the western end of the lock. Gallons of water rushed in and the barge inched up the walls, higher and higher until Serenity could see the stocky little mules chomping on their grain on the other side of the iron gates. The barge pilot paid the toll and the lockskeeper gave the order to open the western gates. Again, the mules moved the barge steadily to the far end of the locks. There, the *Garnish*'s hogee and a team of fresh mares waited.

"It's unbelievable, man's inventions." Caleb whistled through his teeth. "The Bible tells us that man will increase in knowledge at the end of time."

Serenity cast a devilish grin toward her father. Unlike his wife, Samuel Pownell believed the Bible and God were subjects to be limited to Sunday morning. As Serenity expected, he ignored the biblical reference. "Three hundred miles from Troy to Buffalo and Lake Erie. The Canal makes travel much more pleasant than covering the miles by wagon or buggy."

"But sir," Caleb interjected, "isn't traveling by rail much faster?"

"Without a doubt, if you can tolerate the dirt and the cinders flying in your face, your food, and your personal belongings."

"But speed can make a difference."

"No doubt. In time, the continent will be crisscrossed with railroad tracks from New York to California, especially now they've struck gold out there."

"This Gold Rush, as the newspapers are calling it. Just how real do you think it is, sir?"

"It's real. I've seen the ore taken from the fields—everything from gold dust to gigantic chunks."

Caleb shook his head. "My dad's got a bee in his bonnet about preaching the gospel to the miners in California."

The older man chuckled. "If you ask me, the real money to be made in the gold fields of California will be made by the teamsters hauling food and mining supplies from San Francisco and the merchants selling the goods. Those are the men who will walk away wealthy, mark my word."

~7~
The Journey Home

 AFTER THE BARGE SLIPPED PAST THE LAST gate, Serenity watched as it glided through the countryside. Occasionally a child would wave or a field hand would lean on his hoe to watch until the *Silver Garnish* passed. Always the air was filled with the hogees' songs, keeping the team stepping to an easy rhythm.

Serenity glanced over her shoulder as Caleb hopped off the barge to walk along the tow path. Male passengers often did this to get some exercise. He would probably drop back on board at the next bridge. A quirky idea formed in her mind. *What if I*—she thought. *No, Papa would have a conniption. Besides, my feet would get tangled in my skirts.*

Serenity's stomach growled as the delicious aromas of native pheasant swimming in rich French sauces, vegetables au gratin, and decadent desserts wafted from the barge's open kitchen windows. Dinner would be welcome. The cuisine on the *Silver Garnish* didn't suffer from the cramped quarters.

After the sun disappeared, the lamp trimmers lit the lanterns on the barges, creating a wonderland of darkness and light. River towns sprang to life with floating gambling establishments, side shows, and houses of ill repute, but the *Silver Garnish* floated on into the night.

Serenity watched the lights dance on the canal water and listened to raucous banjo tunes filling the night air. A drunken canaler waved from the dock, beckoning her to join him. But the river traffic dwindled at the western edge of each small town. After that only the light from the hogee's lantern and the *Silver Garnish*'s lanterns broke through the darkness. The rich aroma of pine filled the air as the barge passed through the large pristine forests of Central New York. Occasionally Serenity could see the light from a farmhouse window and from open barn doors.

The third night of their journey, the aroma from the salt springs floated on the air outside the little town of Syracuse. Overcast skies shrouded the moon and the stars. Serenity stood at the bow of the barge and inhaled the salty air. On nights like this, Serenity could almost believe in her mother's God. Yet two nights of experience told her the silence wouldn't last long; in a few short moments the tranquillity of the night would be shattered by a fiddler's off-tune rendition of "Turkey in the Straw" or the "Blue Tail Fly." Then they'd float into view of the city lights, the ramshackled shanties strung together by webs spun of wasted lives and broken dreams.

A bat swooped from one side of the canal to the other. An owl hooted. A lone dog barked. She gazed into the somber forest and imagined what it must have been like for the pioneers pushing West for the first time. How frightening for them to leave the civilized cities of the East for the unknown regions of the West!

She wondered about the Onondaga Indians, reminiscing about the story told many times by her mother.

"The Indians of Central New York sided with the British during the Revolutionary War," she would say. "After the war, General Washington parceled the rich lands of this area to his soldiers, thus uprooting the tribes: hundreds of innocent people, people whose only crimes were to be of a certain race."

What would it be like to have the government drive one's family away from their homes?

"Low bridge!" The man at the helm called. Serenity ducked and inhaled the cool musty odor of moss—the covered underbelly of the bridge as it passed over her head.

"You always were a thoughtful child. . . . " A voice behind her said.

"Dory, you startled me."

The woman's dark skin made her invisible in the night. Serenity felt the warmth of a woolen shawl as it enveloped her shoulders. "Thank you. How did I ever manage at school without you?"

"I've been wondering how Abe has managed without me these last few days." Dory sat down on the wooden bench. "It will be good to sleep in my own bed again. I imagine you're eager to be home?"

"I guess so."

"Guess so? What's the matter, child?" Dory narrowed her eyes and arched a brow. "Are you sick?"

"Heartsick, if that counts, and a little afraid."

"Afraid? Afraid of what?"

"It sounds so silly to say. I guess I'm afraid of growing up." She gave a nervous little chuckle. "Some nights, when alone in my room, I'd hear thumpings on my bedroom walls and strange voices. I'd run to Mama and she'd hold me in her arms and make it all go away." Serenity choked back a new wash of tears. "Now, with Mama gone, where will I run?"

"Come here. Let old Dory hold you." Dory extended her arms. "God willing, I'll always be there for you."

The woman gathered the sobbing Serenity into her arms. As the tears subsided, Serenity dried her eyes on Dory's linen handkerchief. *God willing—that's the problem. What is God's will? Was it His will to take away my mother?*

~8~

Home Again

 THE EVENING MIST ROSE FROM THE LAKE, wrapping the Pownell mansion in a shroud of gossamer gray. The matching set of dapple grays hauling the family brougham stepped livelier as they caught the scent of home. A touch of sadness tugged at Serenity's heart.

A whitewashed rail fence edged the Pownell property. The horses paused at the wooden gate until Jonathan, Abe and Dory's eleven-year-old son, appeared out of the mist to open the gates.

"Jonathan!" Dory cried, attempting to unlatch the carriage door from inside.

"Whoa there. Caleb will get that for you!" Serenity's father laughed. Caleb opened the carriage door.

Dory ignored Caleb's outstretched hand and leaped from the carriage to the ground, engulfing her son in hugs.

Caleb extended his hand to Mr. Pownell. "I'll walk on home from here, sir."

The two men shook hands. "Thanks again for bringing my daughter home for me."

Caleb touched the rim of his hat. "A pleasure, sir. Ladies . . ."

Serenity's father watched the young man as he strode down the rutted road until the fog obscured his form. "A good man, a mighty good man. Onward, Abe!" he shouted.

Serenity held her breath as the shining carriage lights in front of the red brick manse came into view. Candlelight glowed from the tall narrow first-floor windows, adding a warmth of home to the large, imposing structure. *It's so beautiful,* she thought. A sigh escaped her lips.

Her father's voice broke through her thoughts. "Abe, take your wife and son and go home. We can manage."

"But sir, the horses and the carriage."

"Send one of the groomsmen to take care of them."

"The luggage?"

"Moses can take care of it from here."

"Yes, sir." The servant scrambled down from the driver's seat and rushed back down the driveway to meet his wife and son.

As Serenity's father helped her alight from the brougham, she glanced up toward her bedroom window and smiled. A lamp glowed faintly, lighting up the lace curtains. *Bless you, Annie,* she thought. Annie, the fifteen-year-old servant girl rescued from an abusive landowner, was Serenity's best friend. She had spent many long nights soothing Serenity's unreasonable fears of what Dory called "night noise." Until Serenity left for the finishing school in Massachusetts, the two girls had played dolls on the lawn, gone swimming in the lake, studied mathematics in the library, learned to read on the sunporch, and tormented Serenity's poor English governess, Miss Gorham, into a fluster.

Serenity's feet barely touched the ground when the front door swung open and Onyx bounded out of the house. He leaped upon her, his paws resting on her bodice. "Onyx! My dress will be ruined!"

The dog licked her cheek as she scratched him behind each ear. With Onyx dancing about her skirts, she followed her father and Mrs. Van der Mere up the steps into the house and into the arms of Annie. At the sight of her, Serenity burst into tears. The girl had also lost a mother in Charity, she knew.

Inside the marble-tiled foyer, the staff greeted the Pownell family. "Excuse me—" A strange voice broke through the cacophony of greetings. Everyone turned toward the open door. A stranger wearing a tattered waistcoat, britches tucked into weathered boots, and a battered felt hat held a folded note in his hand. "Excuse me . . . I'm looking for a Caleb Cunard."

Serenity's father snatched the note from the stranger's hand. "I'll get this to Master Cunard immediately. Thank you."

"But I . . ." The stranger glanced about uncertainly. Onyx stepped out of the milieu and growled. One glance at the massive pet convinced the stranger to leave immediately.

Everyone watched in silence as the stranger mounted his sorrel and rode off into the fog. Serenity's father stuffed the note into his pocket. "All right, everyone, let me introduce you to Mrs. Josephine Van der Mere, a dear friend of Charity's. Please make Mrs. Van der Mere at home during her stay."

Pansy, the housekeeper during Dory's absence, ordered about the younger staff members: "Moses, Harley, deliver the luggage to the proper rooms. Mrs. Van der Mere will stay in the green room."

The tall, angular housekeeper turned toward Josephine. "Mrs. Van der Mere, Benita will show you to your room and help you unpack. Perhaps you will want to freshen up before dinner?"

A look of awe and admiration filled the servant girl's eyes as she gazed at the elegantly dressed Mrs. Van der Mere. Serenity groaned and rolled her eyes toward Annie, who also stood dumb, goggling unashamedly at Josephine's jewels.

"That would be very nice." Josephine placed her gloved hand on the assemblyman's. "If you will excuse me, Samuel, Serenity?"

"Madam." Taking the woman's hand in his, Samuel touched her fingers lightly to his lips. The couple's eyes met. A smile tweaked the corners of Mrs. Van der Mere's mouth, sending a chill skittering down Serenity's spine. She watched the high society woman glide up the winding oak staircase after the simple, homespun Benita.

"Please take me to my room, Annie!" Serenity had spoken sharper than she'd intended, and touched her hand to her forehead. "I have a blistering headache. I wish to lie down before dinner."

Pansy placed a protective hand on Serenity's shoulder. "Come, Child, I'll help you to your room while Annie prepares you a cup of chamomile tea."

The two girls' eyes met for a moment. Serenity paused, her left foot resting on the first step. For the first time she saw her best friend through Eulilia's eyes. *Annie's a servant girl in my father's house!*

"Yes . . . that'll be fine," Serenity responded. Annie dipped her head and scurried from the room.

Serenity allowed Pansy to lead her up the staircase to her room. Onyx trailed behind.

"That dog doesn't belong in the house, let alone on the second floor!" Samuel bellowed. "Onyx!"

Head drooping and tail tucked between his legs, Onyx reluctantly obeyed his master's command.

Entering Serenity's room, Pansy gestured toward the balcony doors. "We opened these earlier to freshen the room. I'll close them now."

"No, leave them." Serenity gazed about the room—the lavender-and-white flowered tulip quilt the ladies of the community pieced for her birthday two summers ago; the hand-carved rosewood Louis XV four-poster bedstead with matching bureau and vanity; the delicate scroll carving on the secretary imported from France; the empty, hand-tooled, leather-bound journal her mother gave her last summer. Her mother wrote in hers every day. Somehow Serenity never found the time to do the same.

"There's water in the pitcher so you can freshen up. Or I can have the girls draw you a bath. . . ."

Serenity glanced toward the porcelain chamber set resting on the marble-topped table between the two sets of balcony doors. A sharp pain shot through her as she recalled the day she and her mother purchased the large-mouthed pitcher and matching basin, handpainted with tiny violets and wisps of baby's breath.

The pale lavender, lace-trimmed curtains ruffled with a gust of wind that set her Boston rocker in motion. Closing her eyes, she could hear waves lapping the shoreline. "Could we leave the unpacking until tomorrow?" Serenity untied the ribbons under her neck and tossed her bonnet onto the bureau. "I'm very tired tonight."

"Of course, Miss Serenity. Will you be wanting anything else then?"

"No, thank you. I'll be fine after I drink my tea."

"Oh, that girl. What could be keeping her?"

"You go ahead. Annie'll be here any moment."

Alone, Serenity sat next to her vanity and slowly removed the hair pins from her hair. Studying the face of the hollow-eyed girl in the mirror, worry etched her brow. Her usually springy black curls hung damp and limp around her pale face. *Who are you anyway? I neither know you nor like you.*

During Serenity's musing, Annie arrived with the tea. Serenity only partly heard the questions Annie asked about the finishing school and her trip home.

"I am so glad you're finally home," the servant girl said.

Serenity glanced at their reflections in the tall framed mirror before her—Annie's face, as fresh and shiny as Dory's favorite copper pots; and her own, drawn and porcelain white, touched with a blush from the cold, foggy night air. "I missed you too," she finally responded.

"Are you sure you don't want to dine with the others?"

"I want to be alone."

The eagerness in Annie's eyes faded. "Oh, of course. Shall I help you with your hair?"

"No, thank you. At school I've gotten quite used to preparing for bed on my own."

Annie tipped her head and left the room. Serenity braided her hair, then slipped out of her gray pique traveling dress, unlaced the whale-boned crinoline from her waist, and tossed everything into the corner behind the bed. As she ambled toward the bureau, she unfastened her corset and stretched.

Removing a white chambray nightgown from her luggage, she slipped it over her head and fastened the tiny pearl buttons at the neck and wrist, then poured herself a cup of tea.

The door to the hallway opened a crack. Annie peered around the edge of the door. Serenity glanced toward her.

"What is it now, Annie?" She didn't try to hide the impatience in her voice.

"Sorry, but Miss Pansy wanted me to give you an extra blanket, lest you be cold in the night." Annie glanced at the open balcony doors.

"Thank you. Just put it on the foot of the bed for now."

Annie placed the heavy woolen blanket on the bed and headed out the door.

"Annie, wait. I . . . I, uh, I'm sorry I was snappish with you. I'm very tired tonight. We'll talk tomorrow, all right?"

The corners of the girl's mouth lifted slightly. "I understand."

"Good night, Annie. And thank you for everything."

A sudden shyness overcame Annie. "It's so good to have you home again. You've grown up, like a real lady."

Serenity smiled sadly. "I don't know about being grown up, but it's good to be home."

As Annie left the room, Serenity closed her eyes and pinched the bridge of her nose. *Growing up isn't as much fun as I thought it would be.* She sighed and sat down to her lady's desk to write a letter to Eulilia.

"It's been quite an adventure. I thought of you every time one of the canallers flirted with me. The *Silver Garnish* is more than seventy feet long and fourteen feet wide. While the sleeping quarters were cramped, the salon and the dining room were both luxuriously appointed. In the salon, there was a purple velvet upholstered circular sofa with a column rising from the center as a backrest. What will the French think of next?

"I became pretty skilled at ducking for bridges. There were more than two hundred between Albany and Syracuse. I especially enjoyed the locks. There's something exciting and a little sinister about being trapped between the towering, slime-covered walls. Like the prophet Jonah must have felt inside the big fish."

Serenity paused. The sounds of laughter and piano music drifted up from the drawing room below. Serenity rolled her eyes toward the ceiling. "Josephine, in concert! Hardly appropriate in a house of mourning, even if she is playing a hymn."

Drawn by the melody of her mother's favorite hymn— hymns were the only concession her Quaker mother would make to having music in the house—Serenity laid aside her pen, donned her cotton plissé robe, and wandered onto the balcony.

As she stared out into the misty night, she mumbled the words to the hymn. ". . . Be of sin the double cure, Cleanse me from its guilt and power." *Guilt! Did my sins cause my mama's death? Is God punishing me for being bad, for pulling pranks on grouchy old Herman?*

A rustling in the lilac bushes beneath her balcony broke Serenity's mood. "Who's there?" she called. "I said, who's there?"

She was answered by a low, rumbling woof.

"Onyx!"

The dog bounded into view, barking excitedly.

"Sh! Be quiet and I'll let you in the house." He barked again and romped across the lawn toward the front of the house. "The back door, silly. The back door!"

She tiptoed from her room, her bare feet skimming along the Persian carpet runner to the end of the second floor hallway. She opened the door to the back stairs. At the foot of the stairs, she heard the servants working in the kitchen. Her stomach growled at the aroma of pan-dowdy, a deep-dish apple pie, the evening dessert.

She held her breath as she passed the dining room door, fearful that the servants clearing the dinner table might see her. With utmost caution, she unlatched the kitchen door and eased it open. "Onyx!" she whispered. "Onyx!"

The night wind tossed about the stray curls around her face. She opened the door further. "Onyx, where are you?"

Barefoot, she stepped across the threshold onto the wooden stoop. She heard a rustling near the forsythia bushes at the south corner of the house. "Onyx!" She hissed again.

Suddenly, a heavy masculine hand rested on her shoulder. "May I help you, Miss Serenity?"

Startled, she yelped and swung to face her attacker only to have her flailing wrists trapped in the cast-iron grip of Abe's hands. "Whoa there, missy."

"Abe! What are you doing out here at this hour?"

"I was going to ask you the same thing, Miss Serenity."

Before she could answer, Onyx whipped around the corner of the house, barking and charging the hedge of boxwood surrounding the rose garden. Caleb emerged from the bushes. "Hey there, Onyx, it's only me."

Serenity whirled in surprise. "And what are you doing there, Mr. Cunard?"

"Miss Serenity! I . . . uh . . . well."

Onyx bounded to Serenity's side and nuzzled her hands. "Onyx! Bad dog—I called and you didn't come."

Abe touched the rim of his hat respectfully. "If everything's all right, Miss Serenity, Caleb and I will be going."

Ignoring the two men, she knelt down beside Onyx. "If I take you inside the house, you must not bark, do you understand?"

The dog licked the side of her face. "Euugh! Do you

have to do that?" She wiped the moisture from her cheek and reached for the door latch. "Now, be quiet." Onyx panted eagerly.

Once safely in her bedroom with the dog by her side, Serenity removed her robe and slid into bed. "Go to sleep," she whispered, patting the dog's head. Onyx licked her hand, then stretched out on the braided rug beside the bed.

Serenity glanced toward the French doors and realized she'd left them open. She considered closing them, but the comfort of the feather mattress caressed her tired body, causing her to change her mind. She snuggled down under the quilt and allowed its warmth to lull her to sleep.

⁓ 9 ⁓

Unreasonable
Fear

 FEAR, BIRTHED IN THE SILENT, HIDDEN closets of the mind, slithers without warning into one's consciousness and onward until it permeates the entire person.

Serenity stared into the darkness. She'd heard them again—the "night sounds." Bumps, thuds, and soft murmurs like the voices of those who'd "crossed over," as Reverend Cunard described the departed. *Ghosts? Evil spirits?* She remembered the nights when her mother would hold her and assure her that no ghosts or evil spirits would have cause to visit their home.

"Mama, do you ever become afraid?"

"Of course."

"What do you do?"

"I recite Psalm 23. 'The Lord is my Shepherd, I shall not want. . . .'"

Serenity closed her eyes and imagined her mother's voice reciting the familiar scripture. "He maketh me lie down in green pastures."

She tried to feel her mother's arms around her but couldn't. She squeezed her eyes shut. "Oh, Mama . . ." Her eyes flew open at the sound of a soft moan. Had she groaned or had it come from beyond her bedroom wall?

"Serenity Louise! You are acting like a child. You're a seventeen-year-old woman now, it's time to start behaving as one." Her voice echoed off the twelve-foot walls in her room. She took a deep breath. *If Mama were here,* she thought, *she'd say, "Night sounds, child, just night sounds."*

"Night sounds," Serenity mumbled to herself. Scratch! There it was again, behind her massive headboard. "Is that you, Onyx?" Onyx growled. "If it is, stop it." The dog placed his snout on the bedding beside her. She patted his head when suddenly, she heard the sound again.

"There! That's not my imagination! And it certainly is not your fault either!" She leaped from the bed, stumbled over the dog, and ran out onto the balcony. Onyx followed, pressing close to her side.

A breeze off the lake ruffled the stray curls about her face. The fog had lifted and moonlight illuminated the lawn down to the grove of trees hugging the lake shore. She peered into the shadows searching for the source of her fears. A movement to her left caught her attention. She studied the area for several moments. Nothing. *Must have been a deer or something,* she decided.

A knock on her bedroom door distracted her. Onyx yipped in surprise. "Sh! Be quiet or Papa will make you go back outside."

"Who is it? Who's there?" Serenity called out.

"It's me, Annie. May I come in?"

"I suppose so." Serenity opened the door. "Why are you up in the middle of the night?"

The young girl held a tea tray in one hand and a lit candle in the other. "I thought you might be restless tonight, your first night at home, so I made you some hot chocolate."

Serenity scowled. "Did you hear the sounds? The night sounds?"

The servant girl set the tea tray on Serenity's desk. "Oh my, I forgot to take the other tray to the kitchen. I'll do that right away."

"Wait! Don't go. I don't want to be alone." Even to Serenity's own ears she sounded like a five-year-old afraid of spooks and goblins.

Annie walked toward the open French doors. "It's getting breezy. I'd better close the doors and latch them, don't you think?"

"Yes, I want them closed. I know it's silly of me, but I thought I saw someone running across the lawn a few minutes ago."

The servant girl smiled. "Probably a deer. Dory's had a terrible time keeping them out of her kitchen garden. As soon as a sprout breaks through the soil, it's devoured. I can only imagine how pesky they'll be once the plants produce vegetables. You climb back in bed while I pour you a cup of chocolate."

Serenity obeyed. She ran a finger over the gold filigree on the rim of the porcelain cup. "About earlier tonight, I didn't treat you very well, I'm sorry."

Annie's eyes misted. "That's all right. I was prepared for it."

"Prepared for it?"

"Yes. Dory told me that when you came back from your fancy school, you'd be different. And I would have to remember that I am servant girl and you, a lady."

"Oh . . ." Serenity sipped the hot liquid. *Have I really changed that much? What would Mama say?*

Annie frowned. "It's all right. I understand."

"No," Serenity shook her head. "It's not all right. I am sorry I took my ill humor out on you." Tears glistened in her eyes as she handed the empty cup back to the servant girl. "I feel so terribly alone with Mama gone. But you lost your mama too."

The girl nodded. "I was barely six when I was taken from her and put to work in the fields. That's where your mama found me. The next thing I knew I was going home with the pretty lady with the pink parasol."

Serenity remembered the day her mother brought the scruffy little copper-skinned child home. At first Serenity resented the attention lavished on the girl. But before long, Annie became the little sister she'd always wanted. Serenity blinked back a fresh wave of tears. "Annie, I need your friendship more than I need your service."

Annie eyes widened. "I'll always be your friend, Serenity."

The new day dawned with a procession of buggies, buckboards, and carriages. The people of the county came to pay their respects. While Assemblyman Pownell had always held himself aloof from the farmers and their wives, Charity Pownell had been loved and respected by all. She attended every quilting bee. When the Brown's farmhouse burned, she sent over a wagonload of bedding, clothing, furniture, and food. When the community church voted to sponsor a missionary to the Oregon Territory, Charity solicited donations from her friends at the state capitol and put the project over the top.

The neighbors brought food. Dory ordered the stable boys to bring the saw horses and planks from the carpentry shop to function as tables. Like a colonel in the local militia, she kept the household staff scurrying to cover the boards with white linen tablecloths and arranging the food gifts in two long rows. There were cherry, mince, apple, and black-berry pies; pastries, peppermint cakes, raisin cakes, brown betty, apple dumplings, and Boston brown bread. Casseroles of beans, macaroni, and potatoes prepared in a dozen different ways arrived.

Throughout the day, Serenity's father accepted the people's condolences graciously. Josephine assumed the role of hostess, flitting from cluster to cluster making certain all were well fed and happy. As Serenity mingled, she couldn't help overhearing the speculation regarding Josephine Van der Mere.

"You poor, poor dear child," Mrs. Creighton pulled Serenity to her ample bosom and patted the girl's head. "Growing up with no mama, and becoming a stepdaughter too. Tsk! Tsk! Oh, you poor child." The woman's breath smelled of spring leeks.

"Thank you, Mrs. Creighton, but I . . ." Before Sereni-ty could catch a breath of fresh air, she found her face crushed against the woman's stiff taffeta bodice again.

"I know. You don't have to say it, child. Life just isn't fair, is it?"

The woman's well-endowed chest muffled Serenity's attempt to answer. When Mrs. Creighton released her, Mrs. Borden repeated the process, followed by hugs from Mrs. Akers and Mrs. Roth, all reeking of compassion and onions. When she could bear the hugs, kisses, and tears of the well-meaning neighbors no longer, Serenity escaped to her room. That's where Aunt Fay found her, lying face down on her bed, sobbing.

"Serenity dear? May I come in?"

Serenity looked up from her pillow. "Aunt Fay." The girl swiped at her tears.

"I'm sorry to intrude on your privacy, but your bedroom door was partly open; I heard you crying. Is there
anything I can do?"

"No! There's nothing anyone can do."

Aunt Fay swept into the room and over to the bed. "Oh,
honey, I know how you must feel. . . ."

"No, you don't!" Serenity's words sounded sharp and
churlish. "No one understands." She dabbed at her eyes
with her pillow case.

"That's not true. I do understand. I lost my mother
when I was fifteen."

Serenity looked up at the woman standing beside her
bed. "Oh, I'm sorry. I-I-I didn't know."

Aunt Fay straightened the corner of the quilt covering
the bed. "It's all right. I understand your anger as well."

"My anger?"

"Yes, you're angry at your mother for leaving you. You
are also angry at Mrs. Van der Mere for usurping your
mother's place in your father's heart. And you are angry at
your father for encouraging her to do so. Am I right?"

"Uh . . . huh. . . ."

"And you are furious at God for allowing the tragedy to
happen in the first place. How am I doing?"

Serenity gave the woman a wry smile. "Pretty well."

"And you are angry at yourself for being angry!" Aunt
Fay brushed a sweaty curl from Serenity's left cheek. "It will
take a while before you forgive your mother for dying and
God for letting her die. But be patient. God will give you
the grace you need."

"What about forgiving my father and Josephine? That
spider is after his money."

"I doubt that. She looks financially well endowed to me."

"You're right. She seems to have more money than Satan himself."

"Serenity!"

"Sorry."

The woman pursed her lips. "Does caring for your father make her a bad woman? And what if she is lonely; does that make her evil for wanting to marry a friend's widowed husband?"

"But my mother is barely cold in the ground!"

Aunt Fay softened. "Your father is hurting and lonely, too, you know."

"Isn't my love enough?"

Aunt Fay smiled, her eyes filled with compassion. "I asked my father the same thing."

Serenity leaned forward.

"He said, 'Someday, you'll understand.'"

Serenity tightened her lips and glanced toward the ceiling.

"You're a beautiful young woman. Someday you will give a young man your love. Wouldn't you want the same joy for your father? Or would you want him to live without love?"

The girl examined her fingernails for several seconds. "But why must he choose Mrs. Van der Mere? She's so . . . so . . ."

"Affected?"

Serenity nodded. "About as real as one of my porcelain dolls from London. I hate being around the woman! She makes me feel like a dumb school girl."

The woman chuckled aloud. "Did you ever think that Mrs. Van der Mere might be uncomfortable around you too?"

"Around me?"

"I doubt you've hidden your animosity toward her." Aunt Fay caressed Serenity's cheek with the back of her hand. "You look so much like your mother, her hair, her eyes, her charm. I am sure you also possess a generous supply of your mother's compassion."

Serenity bit her lower lip.

Aunt Fay kissed the girl on the forehead. "Remember, you're not alone. Your Heavenly Father vowed never to leave you."

Minutes later, Serenity rejoined the crowd. The moment the girl appeared at the top of the portico steps, Aunt Fay moved to her side, rescuing her from the awkward situation. Reverend Cunard circulated through the crowd, comforting where needed. Serenity's father appeared to appreciate the assistance.

Serenity saw the Cunard's ten-year-old daughter, Becca, by the rose garden with her friends and eighteen-year-old Aaron in the carriage yard with his buddies. *Where is Caleb,* she wondered. The hairs on her neck bristled when she spied Sheriff Broderick and the ruffians he called a posse. While she'd never known a reason to dislike the man, there was something in his attitude that frightened her.

After the luncheon meal, a Victorian buggy with its top down and a team of four matching white horses rolled up the circular drive. All eyes turned to see Serenity's Uncle Joel Pownell and his wife, Eunice, disembark from the elegant slipper-shaped vehicle. Whispers scurried through the crowd. Serenity's father rushed to the carriage, embraced his brother, and kissed his sister-in-law on the cheek.

"It's so good of you to come." Samuel's eyes misted as he hugged his older brother a second time, patting him on the back as he spoke. "And you, too, Eunice."

"Where else would we be but here with you?" she asked.

"Auntie Eunice . . ." Serenity rushed into her aunt's outstretched arms.

Eunice held Serenity at arm's length. "I can't believe how you've grown! And such a young lady. I imagine you have all the young men in the county swooning!"

Serenity blushed.

Eunice put her arm around Serenity's shoulders and drew her aside. "Tell me, how are you managing?"

Tears came unbidden to Serenity's eyes. "It's difficult." Samuel urged Josephine into the circle with one arm and drew Eunice back into the circle with the other. "Charity's dear friend, Josephine Van der Mere, has been a great comfort," the politician said.

Eunice smiled at Josephine, then pursed her lips knowingly. "How nice to meet you, Miss Van der Mere."

"Josephine was recently widowed as well," Samuel corrected.

"Really?" Aunt Eunice's eyebrows disappeared into her hair line.

Serenity grinned at her aunt's accurate assessment of the situation. She glanced over her shoulder into the reassuring face of Aunt Fay. "Oh, Auntie Eunice and Uncle Joel, let me introduce you to my mama's dearest friend, Mrs. Fay Cunard." As she emphasized the word "dearest," she rolled her eyes toward Josephine. "Her husband is a Baptist circuit-riding preacher in the Finger Lake region. Aunt Fay, Auntie Eunice's father was a Methodist minister."

Eunice took Mrs. Cunard's hand in hers. "I've been eager to meet you. Charity wrote to me about you on many occasions. She said you were her spiritual mentor."

Aunt Fay bit her lip. "Thank you for sharing that. I never knew."

Eunice patted Fay's hand. "We seldom do. She also wrote about her weekly sewing bee and the delicate handiwork you ladies were doing for charity. I would be interested in seeing some of it, if I may."

"Of course. Let's find Dory. She'll be able to help us." Turning to Josephine, Aunt Fay asked, "Would you care to join us, Mrs. Van der Mere?"

"No, thank you." The woman smiled weakly. "I'll stay here and assist Samuel."

"I bet you will," Aunt Eunice muttered through her teeth.

Aunt Fay slipped an arm around the young widow's tiny waist. "You are welcome to join us, dear."

Even Serenity couldn't miss the look of gratitude in Josephine's eyes. "Thank you, but I think it would be better if—" She glanced toward Aunt Eunice, then toward Serenity.

"Then if you'll excuse us—" Aunt Eunice thrust her nose in the air. Her taffeta skirts rustled as the two women climbed the portico steps and entered the house. *Finally, someone's skirts out-rustled Josephine's,* Serenity thought.

"Aren't you going to join them?" Josephine asked.

"I . . . uh . . . well, yes." Serenity gathered her skirts and started toward the house. "If you'll excuse me—"

"Serenity, you and I are not enemies. Honest." Josephine's stare unnerved the girl. Serenity gave the woman a wry smile.

"That remains to be seen."

~10~

A Star Quilt

SERENITY RAN HER HAND OVER THE scrap quilt. Red, indigo, yellow, green, and multicolored ginghams and calicos danced in wild array. A second quilt of blues and browns stitched in the popular variable star design lay folded beneath the scrap quilt, as Fay displayed several more quilts of various designs.

Serenity tried to picture her mother and the other women stitching the scraps of cloth together. She didn't understand why her mother, the wife of the wealthiest man in the county, needed to spend her Wednesdays stitching quilts with the other townswomen.

Eunice squealed with delight. "Oh, I like that one! It reminds me of one I had as a child."

Serenity glanced toward the blue and white wedding ring quilt Fay held in her hands.

"Have you ever seen such neat little stitches? Incredible! The ladies circle certainly does exquisite work!"

Fay agreed.

"I'd love to have this one. . . ." Eunice caressed the quilt fondly.

"I think that can be arranged, Mrs. Pownell," Fay responded.

"Will the group continue meeting now that dear Charity is gone?"

"Of course, though her enthusiasm and good cheer will be missed." Fay dabbed at her eyes with a cotton handkerchief.

Serenity blinked back the tears in her own eyes and crossed to the sewing room window, gazing at the people milling about the lawn. *So many people cared about Mama.* She could see her father and Uncle Joel talking with Reverend Cunard. Her father looked worn and dejected. A lump formed in her throat. Aunt Fay was right. Her father was hurting badly. *Oh, Papa, I'm sorry I misjudged you. Only, let me help ease your loneliness.*

"Serenity?" Eunice placed her hand on Serenity's shoulder, the quilt folded over her other arm. "We should return to the other guests, don't you think?"

Serenity nodded and followed her aunt down the stairs.

"I'll see that Joel gives Samuel an adequate payment," Eunice said, caressing the quilt.

Fay straightened her bodice. "That will be fine. Mr. Pownell wholeheartedly supports our efforts."

As Serenity stepped out of the house into the sunlight, a bevy of neighbors accosted her to say their good-byes.

"Should you need anything, child . . ." Mrs. Carstairs patted Serenity's hand, ". . . let me know, especially if that hussy from Albany gives you any grief!"

Serenity swallowed her smile, catching the twinkle in Fay's eye. Fay moved closer. "Dear Mrs. Carstairs, you are always so thoughtful. I'm sure the entire Pownell family appreciates your concern. Serenity will not forget your kindness, will you, dear?"

Wide-eyed, Serenity shook her head. "Oh no, never."

Behind her, Eunice lifted a French lace handkerchief to her lips, coughed, and glided down the steps of the portico to join her husband.

Serenity turned to reenter the house when a gravelly voice called to her. "Miss Serenity, may I extend my wife's and my condolences for your loss?"

Serenity turned and bristled at Sheriff Broderick. His full mustache seemed to droop lower than usual, seen without his hat, which he held in one leather-gloved hand. The other hand was extended. His similarly dressed five-member posse stood behind him, with their hats in hand as well. Awkwardly, she took the man's hand.

"Your mother was a real lady, though I didn't much hold to her outrageous ideas about women and Negroes."

"Thank you, I think."

Suddenly an arm encircled her waist. Serenity's father drew her closer to his side. "Broderick, so good of you and your men to come and pay your respects."

"Well, to tell the truth—"

The assemblyman interrupted. "Be sure to tell the Missis hello. Serenity, honey, the Hogans are leaving. Would you please tell them good-bye for me while I bid farewell to the sheriff?"

"Of course, Papa." Serenity gathered her skirts and hurried toward the carriage yard. As she bade the Hogans good-bye, Onyx barked from inside the barn. Somehow he'd gotten locked in the tack room. Serenity ran to the barn. As she stepped into the shadows, a hand clapped over her mouth and she felt herself being dragged from view. She kicked at her assailant and grabbed for his hair.

"Sh! Stop fighting me, Miss Serenity," the man hissed. Serenity struggled harder. Finally, she slumped in defeat against the man's rough, sweaty wool shirt.

"If you promise not to scream, I'll let you go. Do you promise?"

She nodded. When he removed his hand from her mouth, Serenity lunged forward and let out a horrendous scream. The hand clamped over her mouth mid-scream causing little more than a yelp to be heard beyond the confines of the barn.

With the arm encircling her waist, he crushed her against his chest once more. "You said you wouldn't scream!"

She rolled her stormy gray eyes toward him but could see nothing more than his shirt sleeve. She struggled to escape. The more she fought, the tighter he held on to her. "Stop fighting and I'll let you go!"

She shook her head violently and stomped on the toe of his boot. "Ouch! You little spitfire!"

In his moment of weakness, Serenity broke free and dashed toward the open door. She would have escaped had it not been for her curiosity. The instant she turned to identify her captor, he grabbed her.

"Caleb Cunard!" she screeched. "What is the idea of you—"

Again he muffled her mouth. "Sh! You'll have Sheriff Broderick down here."

Anger shot from Serenity's stormy blue eyes. When Caleb finally released her, she placed her hands on her hips. "How dare you handle me in this manner, Mr. Cunard! Your ungentlemanly behavior will be reported to my father. You'll be lucky if he ever lets you on the Pownell premises again!"

Caleb backed away, his hands lifted in a gesture of peace. "I'm sorry, but I thought—oh, I don't know what I thought. Please forgive me. Just leave and don't tell anyone you saw me."

"I will go when I very well please. But first, I've come for Onyx. Most of the guests are gone." As she took a step toward the tack room, Caleb grabbed her arm.

"No! I can't let you do that!"

"You what?!"

Caleb peered around the corner toward the house. "Just leave the barn quietly. Go back to your guests and pretend you never saw me."

"I will do no such thing. Unhand me, sir!" She snatched her arm from his grasp. "My father shall hear about this!"

"Fine! You can tell your papa after your guests are gone, all right?"

"Hmmph! I will tell my father what I wish, when I wish!"

Caleb grabbed her arm, this time more gently. "Please, not for me, but for your father." His brown eyes pleaded for her understanding. "Don't say anything until the two of you are alone."

"What—?"

"I can't explain right now. Please go. I'll see to Onyx." She paused to rub her upper arm.

"Did I hurt you? I'm so sorry. The last thing I'd want to do is hurt you; you must know that."

Serenity sniffled. "I will probably be bruised by morning."

"I didn't intend . . ." He gently touched her upper arm as if he could heal the bruised flesh beneath her cotton frock. "Please forgive me."

"I will . . . as soon as you tell me what's going on."

His lips tightened. He bent to pick up his dusty felt hat resting on a nearby hay bale. "Can't do that. Sorry." He adjusted the hat on his head and touched the brim in respect. "If you'll excuse me? I must attend to my task and you must return to your guests." Caleb strode to the rear of the barn.

"Of all the—" Serenity huffed with indignation.

"Miss Serenity," Abe called from the carriage yard. "What are you doing out here? You's gonna soil that purty gingham dress of yours."

Serenity whipped about to stare at the closed door through which Caleb disappeared. "Abe, you'll never believe what just happened."

"Now, Miss Serenity, whatever happened can be taken care of later, don't you think? After your guests are gone?"

"That varmint dared to—"

"Pshaw! Whatever he did, I'm sure he meant nothing by it. Why don't you return to your guests? I'm sure your papa is wonderin' what happened to you."

"And I assure you, he will find out!"

Abe lifted a finger of warning. "Not until you are alone with him."

"But—"

"Not until the two of you are alone, understand?" Abe said with a gravity that disturbed her. She nodded slowly.

"Now, shoo, girl." The man waved her toward the open door.

After the last guest departed, Samuel Pownell retired to the parlor. "Well, this has been some day . . ." he said, putting an arm around his daughter's waist and one around Josephine's shoulders. ". . . hasn't it?"

Eunice cast him a cruel glance. "In more ways than you imagine."

Samuel ignored the woman's cryptic remark. "I do appreciate the support you gave us today. Family—you seldom realize how much you need 'em. Speaking of family, Joel, I have business to discuss with you before dinner."

Joel nodded solemnly.

Eunice fluttered her handkerchief. "Samuel, will we be staying in the green room, as usual?"

"I believe that's where Pansy put Josephine last night. Dory has readied the rose room for you."

"I'll be glad to show you the way," Josephine volunteered.

One of Eunice's eyebrows lifted into an insolent arch. "I believe I can find it. Family, you know." Like a prima donna exiting the opera stage to a thunderous applause, Eunice ascended the staircase.

"Father," Serenity interrupted, "I have to speak with you privately. It's very important."

"Can it wait until this evening, child? My business with your uncle is urgent."

"My business is rather urgent as well. Papa, I must tell you what happened out by the—"

"Later, child. We will talk later." His steely gaze stopped her mid-sentence.

"Yes, sir." Serenity's lips tightened into a fine line. "I just thought you might like to—"

"Serenity!"

The girl bowed her head to hide her indignation.

In a whisper, Josephine warned, "Beware of those petulant little lines forming around your mouth. They will rob you of your youthful bloom."

Speechless, Serenity looked at the woman in surprise.

"Besides, when men have important business to discuss, wise women willingly retire from their presence."

Serenity arched her brow. "Oh, really? What if my business is of equal importance?"

Josephine's wide, full mouth broadened into a motherly smile. "Serenity, darling, you are such a funny child."

Serenity's lips hardened into a pout.

"Let's go upstairs and freshen up, shall we? Perhaps you can show me what you intend to wear for dinner this evening?" Josephine put her arm around Serenity's waist as if they were two conspiring teenage girls. Serenity's back stiffened. Josephine ignored it. "I did so adore the little number you wore the first evening on the *Silver Garnish*. Cotton plissé wasn't it? Such a practical fabric for traveling."

Behind her, Serenity heard her father. "Well, Joel, let's get down to business. I've been concerned since the death of Charity. . . . My financial situation should be clarified for Serenity, should anything happen to me."

Serenity's head swiveled toward the foot of the stairs as the library door closed behind her father and Uncle Joel. The girl couldn't breathe for a moment. ". . . should anything happen to me . . ." The words became trapped on a demented carousel in her mind. *Should something happen? What could possibly happen to him?*

~11~
Lakeside
Strangers

"SERENITY . . ." HER FATHER LEANED one elbow on the fireplace mantle. "Uncle Joel has agreed to be my executor and guardian of my estate should anything happen to me before you marry or reach a responsible age."

Serenity stared, uncomprehending. "Papa, are you ill?"

"No, I am sound in both body and mind," he assured her. "I'm just carrying out your mother's wishes, a little late, I admit. She wanted me to make certain Uncle Joel and Aunt Eunice would be your guardians should anything happen . . ." He studied the unlit pipe in his hand for several seconds.

She inhaled the aromas of leather and expensive tobacco. She could almost smell her mother's favorite French perfume.

"Your mother and I thought you would enjoy living with members of my family rather than hers. The Quaker lifestyle can be a trifle confining."

Serenity remembered her mother's stories of growing up in the Society of Friends. It was quite different from her parents' whirlwind life of parties and balls in Albany.

Eunice smiled tenderly. "I hope you will never need to concern yourself with this precaution, but should you, we will be there for you."

"Thank you," Serenity stammered.

"Now, my dear, what was so important that could not wait?" her father asked.

"Papa, have you ever noticed how Caleb Cunard is always skulking around the premises at odd hours? Why, the other night—"

"My dear, we don't want to bore your aunt and uncle with neighborhood prattle," Samuel interrupted.

"But, Papa, this afternoon he—"

Again he cut her off mid-sentence. "Serenity, go see if Dory can whip up a chocolate drink for us. You know how Aunt Eunice loves our Spanish chocolate."

"My, yes," Aunt Eunice reminisced. "Your mother and I would sit out on the veranda, sipping hot chocolate and watching the first of the season's snow flurries. When your Uncle Joel and I first moved to Buffalo, I missed Charity terribly. She was the only sister I ever had."

Samuel took his daughter by the hand and led her toward the hallway. "We'll talk later, I promise."

Serenity seethed. "But, Papa, I . . ."

"Not now."

"Fine." Serenity gathered her skirts in her hands and fled out the front door.

"Serenity! Where are you going at this hour? Come back here!"

As she ran across the expanse of lawn toward the lake, she heard her father exclaim, "What has gotten into that child lately? She used to be so quiet and cooperative."

She glanced over her shoulder in time to see Onyx bounding across the lawn after her. The girl ran until she reached the shoreline. Exhausted, she doubled over to catch her breath. The dog, exuberant with her presence, licked her face.

"Don't do that," Serenity whined.

Onyx pranced about Serenity's skirts and barked excitedly. She tried unsuccessfully to brush away the dog. "Oh, you dumb animal. Be quiet!"

Picking up a stick, Serenity threw it down the beach. The dog bounded after it and returned it to her. She patted the dog and repeated the process several times as she walked toward her favorite retreat, a small cave dug into the side of a rocky overlook.

As a child, she would hide in the cave from her mother and Dory. Growing older, the cave became her quiet place to think "her deepest thoughts." The day before she left for the school in the East, Serenity had spent the afternoon in her hideaway.

While Onyx chased some night creature, Serenity hopped upon a large rock near the mouth of the cave. She scanned the quiet surface of the lake. Barely a ripple moved the ebony waters. A moonlit path across the waters held her attention. When she was five years old, she believed she could walk on the moon's silver path. Once she'd ruined a pair of black patent-leather slippers trying. She smiled to herself in remembrance.

Crossing her legs Indian style, she loosened the ivory combs in her hair. She tucked the combs in her dress pocket, then shook her head. Like wiry coils freed from a coach seat, the curls sprang into a wild disarray.

Serenity leaned forward and cupped her chin in her hands. The storm brewing on her face couldn't begin to match the one inside her stomach. Her father had silenced her a second time. The girl's heart ached with frustration. To whom could she turn when her own father refused to listen? "Why, even Abe and Caleb Cunard seem to have my father's ear more than I!"

At the sound of her voice, Onyx loped back to where she sat. "Woof!"

"Sh, Onyx."

The dog uttered a sequence of low barks.

"Oh, all right." Serenity slid off the rock and scratched the dog behind his ears. She straightened and glanced over her shoulder. Moonlight illuminated the entrance of the cave. Serenity had never explored the depths of the cave before, and this night was not the time to start, especially without the aid of a torch.

Remembering the small metal stationery box she'd hidden in a crevice in the wall, she entered the broad opening. She ran her left hand along the rock wall. "I know it's here somewhere." Her voice echoed throughout the cavern. Onyx growled. "It's all right, boy."

Suddenly, her hand touched a cold metal surface. "Ah, it's still here." She pulled the box from its cradle and minced her way back toward the entrance. She'd gone a few feet when she heard strange voices behind her—the voices of two men.

"Well, I woulda' thought the shipment'd be in here somewhere."

"Aw, Barney, you're always a day late and a penny shy! Talk about wild goose hunts!"

"Ain't geese we're huntin'."

"No, it sure ain't—no money in that."

Serenity trembled in fear. Suddenly the box slipped from her hands, hitting a small rock with a resounding clink. She bent to retrieve it.

"Did you hear that? Someone's in here with us."

Abandoning the box, Serenity scooped up her skirts and ran the last few feet to the mouth of the cave and scooted around the edge of its entrance.

The echo of heavy boots drew closer. Serenity shuddered, remembering tales of thieves haunting the seldom-traveled roads around Auburn. Travelers had been robbed and beaten for their purses. Occasionally a body was found. Fortunately, around these parts, violence to that extreme was rare. However a young girl, alone in the night, could not be certain of safety. Serenity could only imagine the horrors of what might happen if the men saw her. She considered running back to the house but not in the bright moonlight. She ducked behind a scraggly bush, pressing herself against the rocks. "Onyx," she hissed. "Come here." The branches of the bush rustled as she felt the dog press against her leg. His body quivered; his ears stood erect; his nose twitched. At the sound of scuffling feet, the dog growled.

"Sh," she scolded, then gasped as two men, each with a torch in hand, emerged from the cave. The light from the torches illuminated their faces.

"Look!" The shorter of the two pointed to the sand. "A footprint! Hey, here's a box too." He held it up for his partner to see.

"Hmm, let me have a gander at that print." The second man knelt in the sand. "This print was made by an expensive leather boot, a woman's, in fact. Hardly the print of a coon!"

As the first man opened the lid of the box, Onyx growled.

"What's that?" He shined his torch about the clearing. "Sounds like a dog. I hate dogs."

His buddy scoffed. "Aw, come on, you're hearing things."

Again Onyx growled. "Did you hear it this time?"

The first man aimed his torchlight toward the thick clump of weeds on the far side of the cave.

The second man stood up. "It came from over here." He approached Serenity's hiding place, his free hand rested easily on the butt of the rifle slung over his shoulder. As he swung the light toward Serenity's face, Onyx gave a fierce bark and leaped at the man's chest.

The man staggered back from the impact. His rifle fell to the ground. "Shoot! Hector! Shoot!" he howled.

Following the dog's lead, Serenity screamed and leaped from behind the bush, her nails aimed at the struggling man's face. She hadn't needed to worry about Hector. When Hector saw Onyx, he threw the box into the air and fled into the night.

The first man whirled about in time to see the charging, screaming girl, her hair flying and her eyes filled with fire. Tripping over his rifle he stumbled, fell to one knee, recovered, and bolted down the beach with Onyx in hot pursuit.

Serenity's knees went weak. *I need to get out of here!* she thought. Her hands shook as she picked up the box. Suddenly a giant blur leaped out of the shadows, as Onyx pushed her backward into the sand and covered her face with big sloppy kisses.

"Get off me, you big oaf!" She tried to escape his exuberant greeting. Serenity sat up and shook the sand from her hair. As she struggled to her knees, she looked in the dog's downcast eyes. "Oh, all right." She threw her arms around his massive shoulders. "You do deserve a big hug."

As Serenity tiptoed into the house through the back door she snickered, remembering the terror on the man's face. Her giggles turned to laughter by the time she climbed the stairs to her room.

Downstairs, the parlor door opened. "Serenity? Is that you?" her father asked.

"Yes, Papa."

"Are you all right? You sound out of breath."

She considered telling him about the two strangers until she heard Josephine's voice.

"Serenity, dear?"

Serenity ground her teeth and took a deep breath. "I'm fine, Papa, just a little tired. Good night. Good night, Mrs. Van der Mere."

"Josephine, please call me Josephine."

Serenity grimaced and closed her bedroom door behind her.

~ 12 ~
The Diary

 ONYX STRETCHED OUT HIS LANKY BODY on the braided rug beside Serenity's bed, his head resting on her crumpled dinner dress. A trail of sand and garments ran from the bedroom door to the bureau to the bed.

Snug in her flannel nightgown, Serenity perched in the middle of her bed, her ebony curls cascading around her shoulders. Light from the pewter lard-oil lamp on the Louis XV bedstand illuminated the rusty box in her hands. Slowly she lifted the lid hoping everything had not spilled out. She held up her dimity and Swiss lace pantalets and smiled. Mama had insisted she wear the false drawers whenever they went to town.

Since little girls' skirts swoosh more than ladies' and tend to expose one's lower extremities, the leggings gave the appearance that the wearer was wearing full-length pantaloons when in reality they covered only from the ankle to the knee. When the wearer didn't tie the ribbons tightly enough, they would slip down around the ankle without warning. Serenity didn't have the courage to destroy her hated hosiery just before leaving for Boston, so she hid them in the metal box.

Beneath the pantalets were the stubs of three circus tickets. She and her parents had traveled to Auburn to see the circus. She remembered Tom Thumb Jr., the littlest man; a bearded lady; a tiger from India; and the acrobats. The next day she tried to tightrope on a branch outside her balcony. Fortunate for her the rain-soaked lawn below provided a soft landing.

When Serenity lifted a picture postcard from the box, two coins fell into her lap, coins her father had given her after he returned from an official visit to Canada. She rolled them in the fingers of one hand while studying the sepia-toned card in the soft lamp light with the other. The daguerreotype of her family had been taken on her last visit to Albany.

Mama was beautiful. Serenity smiled sadly. *How can Papa compare Mrs. Van der Mere with Mama?* She smiled at the photo of a prissy nine-year-old, a little spoiled and a little impatient at having to stand frightfully still for such a long time, she remembered.

Serenity sighed, *Mama, I feel like I hardly knew you. Everyone had so many good things to say about you, even the sheriff, whom Papa cannot abide, declared you to be a good woman. I wish I knew you better. . . .* Her thoughts faded into a wishful sigh.

"Wait a minute!" She tossed the postcard into the metal box and bounced off the bed. Onyx yelped and scrambled out of her way. "I know how I can learn more about Mama! Why didn't I think of it sooner?" Serenity slipped her arms into her robe, grabbed the lamp from the bedstand, and padded into the hallway. The voices of her father, Mrs. Van der Mere, and her aunt and uncle talking in the library drifted up the stairwell. "Good!" she cried.

Onyx emitted a gentle "woof" and pressed against her legs.

"Sh!" Serenity tiptoed down the hall to her parents' bedroom. "Mama kept her journal in the drawer of the nightstand," she muttered to Onyx as she rounded the foot of her parents' massive Gothic Victorian four-poster bed. She opened the drawer. It was empty.

"Of course . . . Mama would have had it with her in Albany—Ouch!" Serenity stubbed her bare toes against her mother's steamer trunk. Her mother was never one to travel lightly. *Ten or more ball dresses plus all the accessories must easily fill that trunk,* Serenity thought, *plus all her personal items: French perfume, doe-skin dancing slippers, silk stockings and chemises, as well as her diary. If it's anywhere, it will be in there.*

Serenity's heart raced as she set the lamp on the bedstand and tried to unlatch the trunk. *Locked!* She glanced about the room. *Ah, of course, in the gentleman's bureau.* The gentleman's bureau had two drawers on top for smaller items, like a smoking pouch, handkerchiefs, and coins.

Serenity crept over to the bureau and tried the drawer on the left. Only coins and odd snippets of paper. Shining the lamplight into the drawer on the right, she spied his keys strung together with a leather thong. *Aha!* Snatching up the keys, Serenity began trying them in the trunk lock. She'd inserted the third key when she heard voices coming through the fireplace flue.

"She's still such a child," she could hear Mrs. Van der Mere say. "Surely you can't expect her to run your estate with any efficiency. It would be unfair to tie her down with such heavy responsibilities."

"Nonsense!" Samuel retorted. "Charity entered my home as a bride of eighteen."

"Josephine has a point. Charity was not an only child and had not been waited on her entire life," Aunt Eunice reminded her brother-in-law. "She needs feminine guidance in more ways than you men can ever imagine."

"Oh, spare me," Uncle Joel snorted. "Whenever a woman is losing an argument, she resorts to the female mystique."

"Of all the—!" Aunt Eunice huffed. "If you will excuse me, I am going to bed!"

"Retreating from the field of battle?" Samuel teased. "I've never known you to retreat."

"Hmmph! If my husband knows what's good for him, he'll retreat as well."

Serenity chuckled aloud.

Samuel laughed. "I don't disagree with you ladies, which is why I've asked Josephine to help train Serenity in the organization and operation of this place."

Serenity stiffened. Onyx growled.

"What was that?" Josephine asked.

"It sounded like a dog's growl to me," Eunice answered. "In the fireplace."

"A dog? In the house?" Samuel's words rose up the flue.

"Oh, no," Serenity whispered. "We'd better get out of here." She quickly fiddled with the keys until one released the lock. She opened the trunk and there, on top of her mother's rose satin negligee set, was her journal.

As Serenity grabbed the book and closed the trunk, she caught the leather thong between the trunk and the lid. She tugged. The thong broke, strewing keys across the floor. Suddenly the sound of a familiar tread hit the bottom step of the stairs. "Oh, no! Papa's coming!" she hissed.

At her warning, Onyx bounded to the bedroom door. Serenity scooped up the journal and the lamp, then raced from the room. Both she and Onyx skidded on the carpet runner as they rounded the corner of the staircase, catching themselves in time to disappear into her bedroom. She'd barely hidden Onyx under the bed, blown out the light, and climbed into bed herself when the hall door opened and her father appeared with lamp in hand.

"Are you all right, Puddin'-tuck?" he asked, glancing about the room for the dog.

She rubbed her eyes as if having just awakened from sleep. "Papa? Something wrong?"

"Nothing, child. I thought perhaps Onyx might have sneaked inside when you returned." He walked to the edge of her bed. "Are you feeling better?"

She nodded.

"What was it you wanted to tell me?"

"Nothing, Papa, nothing important."

"You didn't go down to the lake earlier, did you? Caleb Cunard told me he's seen some rather unsavory scoundrels lurking about down there."

Rather than answer, Serenity yawned, hugging her mother's diary to her side beneath the quilt. "I'm sleepy, Papa. Can we talk in the morning?"

He smiled and adjusted her quilts about her shoulders. "Good night, Puddin'. Sleep well."

Serenity waited several minutes after the door closed behind her father before she slipped out of bed and relit the lamp. Tenderly, she tugged on the red satin ribbon, opening the pages to her mother's last message. Serenity held it up before the flickering flame.

"In sixty-one days I will see my precious baby once again. I miss her so. I hope her year at a finishing school hasn't changed her into too much of a lady. I'd hate to have her spunk and vitality broken by too rigid a training. However, Sam is right, S does need to learn the finer points of social etiquette.

"I met with V and L for luncheon. We read together from Ps. 91. V's so fearful since W died. I hope the poet's words will give her courage, especially after Sam and I return home. Speaking of home, I can hardly wait to study with F once more. She is such a wise woman of God.

"Spoke with Sen. R regarding the suffragettes in Seneca Falls. I promised him that I would visit the colony and return with a full report when the assembly convenes in the fall. Surely the state and national officials have nothing to fear from these gentle women. Even my darling S recognizes the fairness of giving women a voice in their own destiny. Perhaps when she reaches her majority, she will benefit from the efforts of her forefa—no, fore-mothers."

Mama was thinking of me. Serenity smiled, and flipped back to the beginning of the book. By now she had discovered her mother's cryptic system—"Sam" for her papa and initials for everyone else, including "S" for herself. Of course, "Ps" was for the book of Psalms, which her mother frequently read aloud beside Serenity's bed when she was a child.

"January 1, 1845. A new year, a clean sheet. What a gift from God, to be able to start over again. But according to F, God gives us that privilege every day, every moment. How I miss her. Letters cannot substitute the blessing of speaking with her face to face. I try to read the book as she instructs, but much of the time I am lost. I daren't go to Sam for help. He can be such an agnostic at times. I don't need his intellectual analysis, I need F's simple, faith-filled explanations.

"I have decided to begin the new year by reading from St. L. I try to imagine what it would be like if my precious S were to be found with child at such a tender age. My stars, she probably doesn't even understand the biological processes of conception."

Serenity's face reddened. She could feel the heat growing on her neck and ears. Her knowledge of husband/wife intimacy was school-girl-sketchy but adequate enough.

"Who would believe such a tale—impregnated by God? How would I, as her mother, react? Hmm, perhaps it's time I have a little talk with S when she returns from school this summer."

St. L must be the book of Luke in the Bible, Serenity thought. As she turned to the second entry in her mother's diary, she vowed she'd finally read it for herself. Page after page, she read on. With each page, she learned more and more about the woman called Charity Elspeth Pownell, nee Sewell. Some pages were stained with tears, others had large blots of ink or tears where words had been smeared or scratched out. Serenity discovered that her mother's favorite color was lavender and her favorite scent, lilacs. She learned that her mother adored English truffles and had a penchant for hot chocolate, as well as Irish lace and silk from the Orient. But evidence of her mother's true spirit emerged whenever she wrote about the atrocities committed against the Negro slaves. In those passages, Serenity felt the whip of her mother's fury and the moisture of her tears.

"This morning I attended the Women's Reading Society and I met a woman named Arminta Smead, about my age. She told about her escape from a Mississippi plantation where she lived as a field slave. She was on her way to Canada.

"She told how one night, when everyone was asleep, she gathered together a small cache of food and some clothing and, stealing away from the slave quarters, left the plantation and plunged into the forest, a labyrinth of swamps and canebrakes. Night after night she traveled north, guided by the 'drinking gourd.' Always in the distance she could hear the baying of the hounds searching for fugitives like herself. She risked death by starvation, exposure, deadly moccasin snakes, and alligators to escape the keen cut of the overseer's leash.

"At one point, a pack of hounds caught up with her and had her surrounded. She prayed that God would protect her. In her hand she had a few crumbs of bread left from her food supply, which she offered to the dogs. They came up to her, but instead of seizing and tearing her body to shreds, they licked the crumbs from her hand, then ran off into the forest. What a woman! It was an honor to help her in even a small way to reach her goal. Dear Arminta may be poor in earthly goods, but rich in unwavering faith in Jesus."

At the end of the passage was another cryptic code: Ps. 34:7. The heavy mist of early morning hung over the lake before Serenity finally slipped the red ribbon back in its place, closed the book, and surrendered to sleep.

~13~

In Search of
the Book

 BEFORE SERENITY'S BOOTED FOOT touched the carpet at the base of the stairs the next morning, the explosion had already occurred. Serenity's father had assembled the household staff in his library. His bass voice boomed more threateningly than she'd ever before heard before. She peered into the crowded room to see the servants cowering before him, their terror permeating the air. Each one had come from a household where they'd felt their master's lash.

"Someone entered my bedchamber last night before I retired. Why I do not know. I found my key strap broken and my keys strewn across the floor." His razor sharp gaze studied each frightened face.

"Sir," Pansy raised a trembling hand, "when I turned down your bed, there were no keys on the floor—sir."

"Then the guilty party must have entered the room after that." Again the man's frigid gaze slowly circled the room. "I am a fair man. If there is a legitimate reason, tell me. I will deal fairly with you. Dory? Annie?"

A nauseating lump formed in Serenity's stomach. Slowly, she raised her hand. "Papa?"

His cold, hard stare threatened to dissolve her courage. "Not now, Serenity! I must resolve this before—"

"Papa, I did it. I went to your room last night to find Mama's diary. When I heard you coming up the stairs, I panicked and dropped the keys. It is my fault. I am sorry."

"You stole your dead mother's diary?"

His accusations accosted her like storm waves pounding against the New England shoreline.

"I . . . I . . . I will go up to my room and retrieve the diary for you."

"My own daughter violating my privacy?"

"I'm sorry!" Serenity fled up the stairs. Tears streamed down her cheeks as she pawed through the top drawer of her bureau. She drew the scored leather-covered book from beneath her folded bedclothes and lifted it to her lips. As she did, she caught a reflection of herself in the mirror over the dresser and the reflection of her father standing behind her, his face dripping with tears. Serenity whirled around.

"Papa, I didn't mean to hurt you. I just wanted to know my mama better. There is so much I didn't know about her and—" She threw herself in his arms.

"Seri, oh Seri . . ." Her father swept the girl into his arms. "I'm sorry too."

"I miss her so much." Serenity buried her face in his chest.

They held one another for some time as he caressed her head and shoulders. "What are we going to do without her?"

Serenity sniffed. "I don't know."

As he pulled away, he lifted her chin. "You may keep her journal, Seri."

"We can share it." Serenity answered. "She talks a lot about both of us, you know. She really loved us, didn't she?"

"Absolutely!" His eyes glistened in the morning light. "If you look in the library, on the top shelf left of the mantle, you'll find her earlier journals. There should be one for every year since we wed eighteen years ago." He laughed. "I think your mother would like knowing her journal writing helped us heal. Wait, I have something else for you."

He strode from the room and returned with a large book in his hands. "Your mother took a lot of comfort in this. I can't bring myself to read it, but maybe you'll appreciate it."

Serenity took the book from his hands. Running her fingers over the embossed words, she read aloud the title, "Holy Bible." "Aunt Fay and Mama read from this last summer."

Samuel scowled. "Frankly, I wasn't too pleased when your mother took up with the Cunard family. I don't have much tolerance for the religion of those circuit-riding preachers. I've run into my share of shams over the years . . . not that the Cunards aren't genuine. And, of course, Caleb is a fine upstanding lad."

Serenity frowned. "That reminds me. Yesterday, I was in the barn looking for Onyx when Caleb Cunard grabbed me and dragged me behind some bales of hay and—"

"Caleb told me about the misunderstanding you and he had. I am sure it won't occur again."

"But the other night, I heard and saw—"

"Now, don't worry your pretty little head about anything." He tousled her curls, kissed her cheek, and left the room.

Serenity clutched the diary and her mother's Bible to her chest and gritted her teeth. *He did it again. Why won't he listen to me?*

The day passed with Serenity lost in her mother's world. Once Josephine looked in on her. Another time her Aunt

Eunice checked on the girl to be sure she was all right. Mid-afternoon, Annie brought her a cup of hot soup and a watercress sandwich. With each interruption, Serenity shooed them all away.

The sun hung low over the lake before the girl closed the last diary. She figured out the rest of the coded references, most importantly, that "V" stood for Josephine Van der Mere. Serenity smiled to herself at her good detective work.

An hour before dinner, the library's double doors opened and Mrs. Van der Mere appeared carrying a lamp in her hand. Her forest-green dimity skirts swooshed past the spiral-turned leg of the tapestry sofa by the door. "It's getting dark in here. I thought you could use a light."

"Thank you," Serenity said in earnest.

"Dory asked me to remind you that dinner will be served in an hour."

Serenity frowned. "Mrs. Van der Mere?"

"Josephine," the woman reminded.

"Josephine, you really were one of Mama's best friends, weren't you? You and Aunt Fay."

The woman swallowed hard. "Yes, my dear, Charity was definitely my best friend, and I hope I was hers."

"Then you can probably help me."

The woman's face lit up. "Of course, if I can."

"I've a list of references my mother made to books of the Bible, but I don't know where they're found. Would you take a look at them?" Serenity handed the woman the sheet of linen paper on which she'd been working.

The instant Josephine saw Serenity's scribbles, she smiled. "Do you have a Bible?"

"Oh . . ." Serenity glanced about the room. *Where did*

I leave Mama's Bible? One corner of the leather cover protruded from beneath the stack of diaries. "Here, here it is." She handed the book to Josephine.

Josephine set the large book in front of her and angled the sheet of paper so that she could read it as well. "Ps. 91 is the ninety-first Psalm. This one's my favorite. Let me show you." The woman turned the gilt-edged pages.

"He that dwelleth in the secret place of the most High shall abide under the shadow of the Almighty. I will say to the Lord . . ."

Serenity listened as her mother's friend read the words aloud that her mother quoted whenever Serenity was afraid.

The night sounds.

"Thou shall not be afraid of the terror by night . . ."

Serenity shuddered.

". . . nor the arrow that flieth by day."

The young girl bit back her tears.

"He will call upon Me and I will answer him; I will be with him in trouble; I will deliver him and honor him."

Josephine scanned the other texts. "This one is in Hebrews, chapter 13 verse 5. 'I will never leave thee nor forsake—'"

"Why?" Serenity's question burst from her lips. "Why did Mama have to die? Why does God make such outlandish promises only to break them?"

If she'd expected to see censure in Josephine's eyes, Serenity was mistaken. Instead, a tear trickled down the woman's face. "I asked your mother the same questions after my husband passed on. When Mr. Van der Mere died, I thought I'd died too. Your mother helped me to want to live again, for his sake. He was the only man who ever treated me with respect and love." Josephine took a deep breath, then continued. "I wasn't born into wealth. When I married my husband, I had to learn all the little niceties that you learned from your mother's example. Your mother was the one who helped me. I owe her everything."

The woman drew a lace-edged handkerchief from her pocket and blew her nose.

"I was so frightened to be alone with no one to love. I wouldn't have survived if your mother hadn't taught me how to confront my fears." The woman's usual self-confidence had disappeared. "All I can tell you is what your mother shared with me." Josephine cast a timid smile toward Serenity. "But, if you would feel more comfortable talking with Mrs. Cunard, I wouldn't be offended."

"No, I'd like to know what Mama told you."

Josephine glanced at the watch fob pinned to her bodice. "Unfortunately, we need to dress for dinner right now. Perhaps we could chat a while this evening?"

A slow grin spread across Serenity's face. "I'd like that."

Aunt Eunice held court throughout the main course of chicken and dumplings. She told humorous tales of high society in the western regions of the state. As a former New York City debutante, moving to the hinterlands of western New York had been a trying experience. Yet it was obvious that she reigned over the new society at the edge of the Erie Canal civilization.

"Buffalo women have convinced themselves that they are the epitome of grace and style," Aunt Eunice said batting her eyelashes and fluttered her black lace fan in imitation. "Most of them come from backwoods cabins. Now, because oil was found beneath those cabins, they wear airs that don't fit and crinolines to match."

Joel dabbed a dollop of whipped cream atop a second

helping of blueberry cobbler. "Tell them about Mathilda, darling."

"Oh, yes, poor Mathilda traveled with her husband to New York City. When she returned home, she brought with her a few Eastern customs, including the finger bowl. At her next dinner party, she arranged for each guest to have one." Aunt Eunice arched one hand gracefully in the air. "Well, the guests, never having seen such a thing before, first used the finger bowls for dunking their toast. Then, to make matters worse . . ." Aunt Eunice leaned forward. ". . . the guest of honor, the city's mayor no less, drank from it. Imagine! I thought poor Mathilda would pass out from apoplexy."

Serenity giggled at both the story and the animation with which her aunt told it.

"If a hostess lays out more silverware than a spoon, knife, and fork, she's in for major confusion on the part of her guests. At the least, one of them will joke about 'eating out of both sides of one's mouth' or being 'two-faced.'"

Serenity could detect a certain fondness in Aunt Eunice's voice for the border ruffians she mocked.

"Why, my male guests are as likely to use one of my imported Italian dinner knives as an Arkansas toothpick as to spread butter on his muffin! In all my born days, I've never seen the likes of it."

"Codfish aristocracy, that's what we call them," Joel admitted.

"Now, Joel, you're not many generations removed from the source of your money, you must admit," Eunice teased.

Uncle Joel arched an eyebrow toward his wife. "Why, Eunice Pownell, how democratic of you."

Samuel chortled aloud. "Joel, must you and Eunice head home tomorrow morning? We'd love to have you stay longer. You've both been so encouraging, and you've brought laughter back into our lives."

Serenity started. "You're leaving? Oh, please stay longer, Auntie Eunice."

Eunice stretched her hand out toward the girl. "Darling, I wish we could, but your uncle has some important oil negotiations to settle. Talk about codfish aristocracy!" She huffed. "But, dear, why don't you come home with us for a few weeks?"

Serenity blinked in surprised. She glanced toward her father, who averted his eyes from hers. Josephine did the same. Sudden tremors of fear prickled at the base of her neck. She shook her head violently.

"Thank you for the offer Auntie Eunice, but I need to be with my father. Maybe at summer's end?"

"You'll be back at school by then, young lady." Her father lifted his crystal water goblet to his lips and took a sip.

"School? Papa, no! I don't want to go back—ever!"

"Nonsense, dear child. It's the best thing for you now, with . . ." His breath caught. "I can't raise you alone. You must become a proper lady for your mother's sake."

"But Papa!"

A forced smile spread across her father's face. "Serenity, let's not discuss this on your aunt and uncle's last night with us. So, Joel, what do you expect pork bellies to bring in this summer?"

Uncle Joel laughed. "Pork bellies? Ask me about lumber or coal and I could give you a fair estimate, but pork bellies? Might as well predict what those crackers in Washington might do!"

Everyone except Josephine left Samuel Pownell's announcement about finishing school behind and moved on to other topics. Serenity lifted her eyes toward Josephine, sitting across the table from her. The woman smiled an understanding smile. Serenity glanced away to hide the tears brimming in her eyes. The rap of the knocker at the front door disrupted the girl's thoughts.

~ 14 ~

Troubled
Dreams

 WHEN THE BRASS KNOCKER THUDDED against the front door, Joel shot a surprised look at Samuel. "Who'd come calling at this hour?"

Samuel picked up the plate of ginger cookies resting in front of him. "Serenity, dear, please pass the cookies to your aunt. You do want seconds, don't you, Eunice, dear?"

"You read my mind. You know I can't resist Dory's ginger cookies," Eunice responded.

Suddenly Dory appeared through the dining room door. Shall I get that, sir?" Mr. Pownell nodded, then turned to his brother. "And just what is your position on 'the Great Compromiser'?"

"Clay? Ah, the Southerners just can't wait until the man kicks the bucket. He won't be around to benefit from California, gold or no gold."

"That's a little harsh, don't you think?"

"Pshaw! Look at all the fools breaking their backs out there! The real gold is in merchandising, if you ask me. Supply shovels, tents, and pick axes—that's the line to riches. The city of Buffalo is certainly benefiting from the California Gold Rush, being at the western end of the Erie Canal."

Samuel's eyes narrowed. "What do you think about Clay's proposal to abolish slave trade in the District of Columbia and return runaways?"

"Makes sense. A man's property is his property; what's right is right."

"Hmm." Samuel placed his elbows on the table and slowly matched his hands, finger to finger. "And the popular sovereignty clause?"

"Well, I can't see slavery prospering in the newly acquired western territories anyway. Like Douglas says, the decision on whether or not to legalize slavery in an area shouldn't be made by government bureaucrats a thousand miles away."

Serenity tilted her head toward the voices coming from the vestibule.

"Please tell the assemblyman I am here," a deep bass voice ordered.

"Mr. Pownell and his guests are at dinner. I can't disturb—"

The male voice became insistent. "Then I shall find the assemblyman myself!"

Dory raised her voice as well. "Sheriff Broderick. You can't just barge in—"

Samuel continued his discourse. "If Senator Calhoun gets his way, we'll—"

The sheriff's massive form filled the dining room entrance. Serenity's father, sitting with his back to the intruder, paused. "Sheriff? What is the meaning of this interruption?"

The sheriff eyed the people around the table. "You'd best teach your girl, here, to keep her place."

Serenity stared in horror as her father lowered his eyelids to half-mast. Her mother called this his "ready for battle" look. Samuel rose to his feet. "Now, Sheriff, Mrs. Potter was just following instructions; the Pownell household and their guests expect to dine quietly, without interruption."

The sheriff stepped up to Samuel, nose-to-nose. "My business can't wait."

The assemblyman folded his arms. "Speak, by all means, then."

The sheriff looked around, reddened, and fumbled his hat from his head. "Sorry ladies. Not in front of the ladies, sir."

Aunt Eunice arched one eyebrow, then dabbed at her lips with her linen napkin. "And I thought the people of Buffalo were country bumpkins."

The sheriff's face hardened. "Pownell?"

Serenity's aunt waved him away with one bejeweled hand. "What a bore."

Serenity glanced from one face to another, around the room. *What is going on?* Her father yawned as if tired of the game the sheriff was playing. "If you ladies will excuse us, Joel and I will see to Mr. Broderick's concerns in the privacy of the library."

The sheriff answered through clenched teeth. "My business is with you and your boy, Abe, not with your brother."

Joel cast the sheriff a roguish grin. "What? Two lawyers in the same room make you nervous?"

"I know the law, Junior. It's you and your trouble-making brother's law that I can't abide."

"Interpretation," Joel drawled, "our interpretation of the law."

From the far end of the table, Aunt Eunice lifted one finger, her ruby and diamond rings glistening in the candlelight. "Oh, you mean God's law?"

The sheriff whirled in her direction. "Ma'am, you sure

can try a man's patience. Reckon I . . ." He paused, recon-
sidering his words. "Sorry, ma'am, but you know what happens when you tweak a polecat's tail."

Aunt Eunice stifled a grin. "From personal experience?
No, but out our way, men know how to deal with polecats."

"Eunice!" Joel growled.

The sheriff gritted his teeth. "Pownell, now! In the library!"

"Of course, Sheriff." Samuel gestured. "This way."

"By the way, where's your boy, Abe?" the sheriff asked.

"Boy? There are no boys named Abe on my estate.
However, if you're referring to my overseer, Abe Potter,
he's on his way to Auburn, I imagine. You must have passed
him on the highway."

The sheriff grunted. Serenity watched as the men left
the room. When the double doors to the library closed, she
gasped. "Auntie Eunice, that was a risky thing you did!"

Eunice smiled and sighed. "Not really. I've seen his type
before. The man is a bully and a coward. Besides, he tracked
mud onto your mother's Oriental carpet! What a buffoon!"

"Well, that buffoon looked angry enough to lambaste
you back to Buffalo," Josephine interjected.

"Mrs. Van der Mere!" Serenity gasped.

Defending herself, Josephine continued. "Well, he did!
If she'd been a man . . ."

Dimples formed on each side of Eunice's coy little smile.
"You're probably right. Perhaps we ladies should adjourn to
the parlor? I am sure I could play the piano and sing so
loudly that the men won't be able to hear themselves think
straight."

"Auntie Eunice!"

"Joshing, child. Just joshing," Eunice replied. The
women arose from the table and glided into the parlor. "May

I challenge either of you ladies to a game of checkers?"

Josephine glanced toward Serenity.

"Oh, Auntie, I'd love to, but you beat me every time!" Serenity moaned.

Her aunt giggled. "Being as this is my last night here with you, I'll play with one hand tied behind my back."

Serenity groaned. "Thank you so much. Mrs. Van der Mere, will you play the winner?"

Josephine shook her head. "I think I'll stick to my needlepoint."

"Stick to your needlepoint—that's a good one." The room filled with laughter. A comforting warmth spread through Serenity's body. *How good it feels to laugh again.*

As they passed through the hallway toward the front parlor, Serenity glanced out of an etched-glass window beside the door. Five rough-looking men lounged on the front portico. The glow from one man's pipe lit his leather-like face as he glanced her way and leered. She shuddered.

"Come away, child. He's a brute." Aunt Eunice placed her hand on Serenity's shoulder.

Serenity allowed herself to be led into her parents' luxurious pearl gray and ivory parlor. The flame from each of the oil lamps flickered and danced in the massive diamond-backed wall mirrors, multiplying the light scores of times. Eunice seated herself on the pink brocade settee. After adjusting her voluminous skirts about her, she set up the checkerboard on the table before her. "Are you ready to do battle, dear niece?"

Serenity seated herself on a silk damask footstool opposite her aunt. As they played and Josephine stitched, the evening wore on. The girl was losing her second game of checkers when she heard the front door open and close. She leaped to her feet and bounded into the hallway. "Papa, what did the sheriff want?"

Samuel placed his arm around his daughter's waist. "Man talk, nothing that you need to worry about, my dear."

"But Sheriff Broderick was so angry."

Her father laughed. "Yes, he was, wasn't he? And what have you ladies been doing in our absence? I'll wager that your aunt has been trouncing you at checkers, right?"

"Two games!" Serenity grimaced.

"Well, move over, let the master show her how it's done." Samuel chuckled aloud.

Uncle Joel appeared as Serenity and her father returned to the parlor.

"Are you ready to get beaten, Eunice, old girl?"

"Just who are you calling old?" Aunt Eunice retorted. "Draw up a chair and let me instruct you in the intricacies of winning, brother dear."

"Serenity, please tell Dory to have the stable boys release Onyx." Her father carried one of the tapestry-upholstered Louis XIV casual chairs to the coffee table. "I want him to have free reign of the grounds tonight."

Uncle Joel chortled. "Good idea. Great dog you have there. I'll bet he earns his keep, keeping unwanted varmints away."

"You can say that again. Now, Eunice, who leads, smoke or fire?"

"Ladies first, of course." She slid her first checker forward.

From the piano bench on the other side of the room, Joel warned, "Watch out, Samuel, don't fall for that simpering female routine. Take it from experience, she'll whip ya' for sure."

The raucous strains of "Buffalo Gals" followed Serenity into the hallway as she searched for Dory. She spied Annie on the second landing. "Can you take a message to the stables? Papa wants Onyx loose tonight."

"Oh, yes, ma'am." Annie placed a stack of fluffy white Turkish towels on the mahogany bench at the top of the stairs.

"On second thought," Serenity interjected, "I'd like some fresh air. I'll take care of it."

A look of fear crossed Annie's face. "Oh, no, I'd be glad to—"

"Nonsense. Why should you drop what you're doing to do something I can manage for myself? Besides, the fresh air will do me good." Before Annie could reply, Serenity gathered her skirts and rushed down the hallway to the rear door.

The cool evening breeze tossed about the loose curls surrounding Serenity's face as she skipped down the slate walkway toward the stables. Her silk skirts rustled as she ran. It felt good to be out of the stuffy house for a few minutes. She could hear the waves splashing on the sand down by the lake and the row boats thudding against the dock. High above her head, the wind whistled through the trees. In the distance, an owl hooted.

A light shone through the dusty tack room window. Serenity knocked on the door. "Hamish? Gus?" she called. The door opened. Gus held a lantern in his right hand; the light illuminated his ebony face. Beyond the door, the other groomers were seated around a table playing cards.

"Why, Miss Serenity, what are you doing out here at this hour? Does your papa know?"

"Of course. He wants you to set Onyx free tonight."

A look of pleasure swept across the horse trainer's face. "Yes, ma'am. Did you hear that Hamish? The boss man wants Onyx free tonight."

"Yes, sir!" The youngest man at the table, barely out of his teens, leaped from the table and disappeared into the stables.

Feeling awkward, Serenity mewed a thank you.

"Anytime, miss." The man peered beyond her into the darkness. "Don't know how safe it is for a young woman like yourself to be out at this hour. Would you like one of us to escort you back up to the house?"

At that instant, Onyx bounded around the corner, barking. He leaped at her, almost knocking her to the ground.

"Onyx!" Gus snapped. "Down!"

Serenity laughed, fending off Onyx's kisses. "That's all right, Gus. I think Onyx will be a sufficient escort."

The stable hand laughed. "Yes, missy. I'm sure he will."

~15~

The Scent of Trouble

 "SORRY, BOY, PAPA WANTS YOU OUTSIDE tonight." Serenity scratched behind the dog's ear. "Go on now, earn your keep."

Without encouragement, Onyx darted toward the rosebush hedge, barking. The dog stopped short of the bushes, growled, and snapped at the bush.

"Onyx? What did you find? A gray squirrel?" Serenity wandered over to where Onyx stood barking. Carefully, she pulled a branch away and peered into the bush; she found herself nose to nose with the face of Caleb Cunard.

"Ai-i-i-i!" she screamed, flailing her hands in the air. The branch popped back in the man's face. He yowled in pain as the branch stabbed him in the nose, and his hat flew to the top of the bush.

"What are you doing behind that rosebush?" she gasped.

"What are you doing out at this hour?" He nursed the end of his long aquiline nose where a thorn had left its impression.

"I live here, remember? This is my home!" Serenity placed her hands on her hips, school-marm style. "So what's your reason?"

He paused before he spoke. "I'm here to talk with your father."

"By way of the rosebush? And at this hour?"

"I was here earlier, but you had guests."

"You mean Sheriff Broderick and his posse? They left hours ago."

Caleb disengaged his hat from the thorny bush. "This is all very charming, Miss Serenity, but I have an appointment with your father." He tipped his head respectfully, adjusted his hat on his head, and started toward the front of the house.

"Wait, you didn't tell me why you're here," she called.

"No, I didn't, did I?"

"Of all the . . ." Suddenly the dog bounded up to her and laid a bleeding and terrified squirrel at her feet. "O-o-o-oh! Onyx! Take that thing away!"

The dog picked up his catch and trotted into the shadows to enjoy his evening repast. Serenity shook her head in disgust and returned to the house. As she passed Dory in the hallway, she asked, "Where is everybody?"

"They've gone to bed, except for your papa. He's in the library."

"With Caleb Cunard, I suppose?"

"Yes, ma'am."

Serenity gazed across the hall at the closed doors. "I guess I might as well go up to bed. Is Annie around to help me unfasten this dress?"

"I sent her to assist Mrs. Van der Mere. She must be finished by now and is probably waiting in your room."

Serenity paused to study the wedding cake scrollwork on the massive double doors. "Something's changed between Annie and me since I returned from school. I don't like it much, but I don't know what to do about it."

Dory nodded. "It has to be, child. It has to be."

"Why?"

"Because you are now the lady of the house and Annie, she will always be a servant."

"But can't we be friends as well, like you and my mama?"

Dory's eyes glistened at the mention of Charity. "Our friendship took years to forge. And as close as we grew, we both knew there was still a line that had to be maintained." The servant crossed the hallway and dimmed the silver wall sconces over the mahogany credenza. "When it came to running the house, I couldn't suppose on our friendship. Annie needs to find that line as well."

"I don't think of myself as the lady of the house. Serenity glanced toward the closed library doors. "I don't much like the changes around here."

"Life is a process of changes." Dory patted her shoulder. "Don't worry, you'll grow into your role as well."

Reluctantly, Serenity started up the staircase. "When do I start?"

"How about tomorrow morning?"

Serenity's eyes widened. "Truly?"

"Truly." Dory dimmed the light in the second sconce. "Good night."

"Good night."

The library doors swung open as Dory disappeared down the darkened hallway. Serenity heard her father speak. "I'm serious, Caleb, be careful. Broderick's no fool, you know."

"That could be debated in Congress!"

"Don't underestimate the man. The scent of money is in the air."

"Sir, I will be careful, I promise. I don't want to spend six months in jail and pay an enormous fine."

"You can be sure he'll impose the stiffest punishment possible, if given the opportunity."

The two men stepped into the hallway and froze at the sight of Serenity.

"What are you doing up at this hour?" her father asked.

Serenity tipped her head and cast a coy grin toward Caleb. "I could ask you two the same question. Actually, Papa, I came to kiss you good night." She glided to her father's side. He dipped his head to allow her to plant a gentle kiss on his whiskered cheek. She stepped back and cast another wry smile toward Caleb.

Caleb tipped his head respectfully toward Serenity, a bemused smile teasing the corners of his mouth. "Miss Serenity."

Whirling about, she swooshed up the stairs as hushed voices followed her.

"You don't suppose she heard . . ."

"I certainly hope not. It would increase the risks drastically."

Serenity paused at her bedroom door. *Risks? What risks? Fines? Imprisonment? Whatever can they be talking about?* She'd always believed her father to be an upstanding man as member of the state assembly, often mentioned in the press to run for a senate seat someday. That her father might consider breaking the law was unthinkable. Living along one of New York State's Finger Lakes, she'd heard rumors of smuggling illegal goods in from Canada, but her father? *Never!*

All the while Annie helped her dress for bed, Serenity mulled over the men's conversation. Annie was so eager to describe Mrs. Van der Mere's wardrobe of crinolines and chemises she barely noticed Serenity's silence. When the servant girl finished brushing the snarls out of Serenity's hair, Serenity put on her nightcap and hopped into bed.

Sometime in the night, an owl hooted and Onyx barked. Annie hurried in, scurrying to the French doors. "There's a brisk wind blowing out there tonight, Miss Serenity. Best I close these before you catch your death."

Serenity pulled the quilts up under her chin. "Yes, I suppose . . ."

"Would you like me to stay with you? I could sleep on a mat at the foot of—"

"No, no. I'll be fine."

"If you need anything in the night, just pull the bell rope and I'll be here for you." Annie smoothed the quilts at the foot of the bed. "Sleep well."

The little maid picked up the pewter lamp she carried with her and turned to leave. Serenity glanced toward the French doors. "You sleep well too. And don't worry, I'll be fine."

Without a word, Annie slipped from the room and pulled the door closed. Soft moon glow replaced the lamplight in the room. Serenity watched as a cloud drifted across the face of the moon, thrusting the room into darkness. The worrisome questions of the day faded as she surrendered to exhaustion.

She hadn't been sleeping long when she awoke again with a start. *There! There it was again. That scratching sound! The night sounds. They always began with scratching, like a squirrel scampering up the side of the house.*

Serenity cowered under the covers, leaving nothing but her frightened blue eyes peering into the darkness. "He that dwelleth in the secret place of the most High shall ab—" *Again! The sounds are real, not part of my dreams!* ". . . shall abide under the shadow of the Almighty. I will say to my Lord, He is my refuge and my fortress; my God, in Him will I t-t-t-trust."

A series of thumping sounds followed the scratches, then the voices, strange voices, thick and frightening. Serenity lay awake for a long time after the sounds ceased. *Face your fears, that's what Mama told Josephine to do.* But the very thought of abandoning the safety of her bedroom to confront the source of the noises sent a new wave of shivers up and down her spine.

Serenity climbed out of bed and lit her lamp; its comforting glow filled the room and the girl with reassurance. She reached for her mother's Bible. It fell open to Psalm 91. She read it aloud. After completing the chapter, she idly flipped through the pages of the book, stopping at verses her mother had underlined: Psalm 140:1 "Deliver me, O Lord, from the evil man . . ."; Proverbs 15:1 "A soft answer turneth away wrath . . ." Beside the 29th verse of Proverbs 31, Serenity found her name written in the margin with a note. "Many daughters have done virtuously, but thou excellest them all."

Warmth crept over her, the warmth of knowing she'd been in her mother's thoughts so often. She turned a few more pages and found the book of Ecclesiastes. She sounded out the strange name, E-clee-see-as-tees. "To every thing is a season . . . a time to be born and a time to die . . ."

Had this been Mama's time to die? The thought niggled at her mind. "A time of war, and a time for peace. . ." *But aren't Friends against war?*

Serenity flipped through several more pages. Her thoughts bounced about like an empty picnic basket in a runaway buckboard. Charity Pownell had always been Mama to the young woman, nothing less, nothing more. Now, like a prism breaking the sunlight into a rainbow of colors, her mother's comments in her diaries and the underlined texts in her Bible revealed so many new facets that Serenity had never seen before.

The girl yawned and stretched. The walls had been silent for quite some time. Perhaps now she could sleep. She placed the book on the nightstand. The room darkened as she turned down the wick in the silver oil lamp beside her bed. She snuggled down under her covers to await sleep once more.

~16~

More Than She Wanted to Know

 UNCLE JOEL AND AUNT EUNICE HEADED for Buffalo the next morning and Serenity set her mind to learning, first how to be the "lady of the house," and second, to discover more about her mother. Both Dory and Josephine were eager to teach her everything she wanted to learn. The three women gathered in the dining room—Dory removed the silver candlesticks and matching compote from the shining mahogany table as Josephine set stacks of ledgers in their place.

"See, dear . . ." Dory handed Serenity the current household ledger book. " . . . Gloria, the head cook, keeps a running account of supplies, like flour, sugar, and spices, so that when Abe or one of the other men go to town for our monthly supplies, she knows exactly what's needed. Pansy does the same for laundry supplies and linens. Your mother, being gone so much with your father, entrusted me to oversee the household operation."

"Good! I'll do the same." Serenity handed the book back to Dory.

"Whoa there. Your mother didn't hand over the operation without first understanding how it worked. You need to be able to do it yourself in order to maintain control, especially of the spending of dishonest employees."

"I detest mathematics. I thought being the lady of the house meant giving parties and teas and setting a gracious table, the things I learned at finishing school."

"That's part of it, my dear," Josephine interjected. "A very small part of it. You also must plan daily menus and work schedules. You will need to be Lady Wisdom, arbitrating disputes between staff members."

"It's a full-time job," Dory added.

Serenity glanced at the stack of ledger books and sighed. "Where do I start?"

The two women eyed each other, then Dory spoke. "How about in the kitchen learning how to bake a good loaf of bread?"

That evening, when Serenity served her first loaf of bread to her father, she better understood the workings of the kitchen and the responsibilities of the kitchen staff. She'd peeled potatoes, creamed corn, soaked black beans, and practiced her multiplication and long division. To give her a break, Josephine suggested she arrange the floral centerpiece for the dinner table. By the time the family finished their evening meal, the flowers in the crystal bowl had wilted, as had Serenity.

Her father leaned back and patted his well-filled stomach. "You did a fine job, Puddin'-tuck. A fine job. Your mother would have been proud." He turned to Josephine. "Thank you for taking the time with my girl."

Josephine's eyes twinkled. "Dory is the one responsible for today's instruction. My turn comes tomorrow."

A groan came from the other end of the table.

"Serenity? Are you all right?" Josephine asked.

"I'm not sure. There's so much to learn."

"Yes, there is," Josephine admitted. "But you'll do just fine."

"One thing is certain, I have more respect for what goes into the preparation of one evening meal now, and one loaf of bread. I'll never look at a slice of bread the same way again!"

Josephine and Samuel laughed. "If you keep making bread as good as this, I'll have to hire you full time!" he said.

"Oh no! Not me!" Serenity shuddered. "I don't know how Gloria does it day after day after day."

"Most women in the world do that and a whole lot more, day after day after day," Josephine reminded her.

Serenity shook her head. "I can't imagine living in such menial drudgery."

Her father smiled sadly. "According to the wealth of the man you marry, you may find yourself in similar surroundings."

"No! Never! I'd rather not marry in any case," Serenity declared. She couldn't miss the knowing look that passed between her father and Josephine.

"Love makes the difference," Josephine mumbled into her table napkin.

"So what's on the agenda for tomorrow? Cherry cobbler?" her father asked.

Serenity shook her head. "Tomorrow I learn how to freshen the beds."

Days passed. The vibrant yellow of the forsythias gave way to the soft, gentle blush of her mother's favorite old-fashioned yellow roses. With each day, Serenity became more competent at operating the large estate house. And with each night, she tumbled into bed, too exhausted to give much thought or attention to the night sounds that often skittered along her bedroom walls. Dory and Josephine shared stories about her mother as well. In the process, Serenity learned more about her mother's God. When lonely or sad, she began to seek out that God. Talking to her mother's God brought her mother closer somehow. She enjoyed talking with Him when at work on the washboard, when weeding the garden, canning berries, even repairing the family linen.

Serenity had hundreds of questions to ask. Whenever Dory or Josephine couldn't answer her sufficiently, she hiked the half mile to the Cunard place to see Aunt Fay. Once there, they'd sit on the porch and repair socks or pop string beans and talk. In a short time, Serenity realized she was studying the Bible not so much to learn more about her mother, but for her own interest in God.

"God is truly remarkable, isn't He?" Serenity remarked one day to her aunt.

The woman chuckled. "Yes, He certainly is. He goes far beyond anything we can even imagine."

"It's like the first time I saw the Atlantic Ocean. I'd read about it and tried to imagine it, but it was far more vast in reality. I remember standing on the Long Island shore trying to see France." A string bean popped between her fingers. She dropped the pieces in Aunt Fay's iron kettle. "In the last few weeks, God has become like that to me. No matter how much of Him I see in there," she pointed to the Bible, "I still can't see the other side."

"The wisdom of the ages spoken through your lips." Aunt Fay nodded her head sagely. "No matter how much you study and learn about the Creator of the universe and about His unbelievable sacrifice for you, there will always be one more lesson to learn, one more aspect to consider . . ." She laughed again. " . . . even on the other side."

Things went smoothly for weeks, until June 13, her

father's birthday. At breakfast, her father announced that he and Josephine were driving into Auburn for the day. Serenity felt piqued that she hadn't been invited along. But when Dory suggested that she bake a birthday cake for her father, Serenity forgot about her disappointment. This would be her very first cake. Since Dory would be busy all day catching up on the expense ledgers, Gloria agreed to supervise. She handed Serenity her mother's recipe for yellow cake and Serenity followed it faithfully. Except for Onyx being underfoot at every turn, all went well.

With the return of warm weather the baking was done in the summer house, a small stone building attached by a short breezeway to the main kitchen. Serenity always liked the little summer kitchen with its stone floors and brick walls, and its giant iron stoves and ovens. "Put the filled pans in the oven and leave them for forty-five minutes," the experienced cook instructed. "I need to begin lunch. The field hands will be in and hungry as bears."

Serenity ran her finger around the rim of the bowl and slurped the sweet batter into her mouth. She placed the batter bowl in the summer kitchen's deep metal dish tub, then cranked the pump handle to fill it with water. Picking up a cake of lye soap, she began washing the dishes she'd used. One of the lessons Gloria included in her education had been, "Clean up after yourself! Don't expect someone else to do it." With the dishes washed and draining on the oak drain board, Serenity dried her hands on her apron. Onyx sniffed the air appreciatively. "M-m-m, that sure smells good," she sighed. Serenity scratched the top of his head. She took a few steps toward the breezeway, then paused, turned, and eyed the oven. "One little peek won't hurt," she reasoned. "After all, how can I be sure it isn't burning?"

Carefully, Serenity opened the oven door just a crack. She smiled to herself at the smooth, even yellow-brown crust forming across the top of the cake. "Perfect," she said to herself.

Suddenly the screen door to the kitchen slammed. Startled, Serenity released the oven door. She straightened.

"You aren't worryin' that cake are you, missy?" Gloria demanded.

"Oh! No, ma'am. I-I-I . . . was just heading into the house."

"Good!" The woman passed on to the small herb garden at the side of the building.

Serenity followed her to the garden. "How do you know which herb to use with what food?"

"Experience partly and partly from what my mama taught me."

"Will you teach me?"

Gloria's belly shook with laughter. "Child, is there no end to the things you want to learn? It seems your brain would burst from everything you've packed in it these last few weeks." She knelt down at the edge of the series of neat little rows. Small tender plants had already begun to sprout up in the rich brown soil. "All right, I'll do what I can. This one here is basil. I use it to flavor baked beans and meats like beef, lamb, and rabbit. This one will produce dill seeds. I put a sprig of it in each jar of cucumber pickles. It adds great flavor to fish, green beans, cabbage—" Suddenly the woman sniffed the air. "What's that? You'd better check your cake!"

"Oh!" Serenity leaped to her feet and ran into the summer kitchen. She opened the oven. Gloria followed her.

"Hot!" Serenity grabbed an oven pad and hauled the

cake pans from the oven. She took a sprig of broom corn she'd washed earlier, pricked the center of the first cake, then removed it. Instead of coming out clean, the sprig was covered with cake batter. "No! It has to be done. Look how brown the crust is!"

There, before her eyes, the centers of the two nicely rounded layers of cake sank into a wrinkled mess. "No! You can't do that! No!"

She heard a chuckle from the doorway. She glanced up to see Caleb Cunard leaning against the door jamb. "Problems?"

"Laugh, will you?" She fought back tears. "Fine! If you want to fall, fall!" She picked up one cake pan and flung it across the room.

Onyx, who had entered the summer kitchen after Gloria, gave chase to the pan as it sailed through the air. The pan skidded to a stop at the back wall, as did the dog. Before Serenity could react, the animal plowed into the steaming hot cake batter, yelped, then dashed out of the summer kitchen, spinning out on the slippery stones as he ran.

Caleb doubled over with laughter, making Serenity angrier than ever. "It's all your fault, Mister Cunard. How dare you sneak up on me like that!"

"Sneak up on you? I didn't sneak up on you."

"What's going on here?" Dory peered into the summer kitchen. "Why is your father's birthday cake on the floor?"

"It fell! Caleb made me so angry I . . ." Her face flushed with embarrassment, Serenity rushed into the house. She ran past a startled Annie, knocking the clean towels the girl was carrying from her arms. She ran up the stairs and threw herself onto her bed.

"What is the meaning of that display?"

Looking up, Serenity saw Dory filling the doorway.

"Believe it or not, Annie has better things to do than refold the stack of towels you knocked from her arms."

"Everything's ruined!" Serenity's lower lip protruded; her eyes flashed with anger. "Papa's cake fell, and it's all Caleb Cunard's fault!"

"Tsk! Tsk! Tsk!" Dory wagged her head. "You want to be so grown up, yet you blame everyone else for your mistakes."

"It wasn't my mistake! The cake was doing well until he—"

"Tell me the truth. Did you open the oven at least once to check on the cake after Gloria told you not to?"

Serenity's face reddened.

Dory nodded. "That's what I thought." The woman ambled over to the bed and placed a tender hand on Serenity's shoulder. "A sign of maturity is learning to take the blame for your own mistakes. A child blames everyone else. An adult accepts responsibility for her actions." She brushed a stray curl from Serenity's cheek. "Now, you freshen up a bit and come back downstairs. I'm sure Gloria will give you another shot at cake-baking."

Dory left Serenity to her thoughts. The more Serenity thought about what happened, the funnier it became. When she stopped laughing, she hurried down to the summer kitchen to start over. As a new cake rose steadily in the oven, she thought her troubles were over.

At dinner that evening, her father praised her for the cake she'd baked. Even Josephine ate a second slice, something the slight woman never did. But midway through dessert, her father stood, came around behind Josephine's chair, and rested his hands on the woman's shoulders.

Serenity stared in surprise.

"Serenity, dear, Josephine and I have something to tell you. I . . . uh . . . we—Josephine has consented to become my wife."

Serenity opened her mouth to speak, but no words came.

"We're planning an August wedding, just before you return to school. The wedding will, of course, be held in Albany."

Her father's words washed over Serenity in thunderous waves. She gazed first at her father, then at Josephine. *You traitor*, she thought. Her eyes hardened. Josephine reached out to touch her hand. Serenity drew back. For a moment she closed her eyes, trying to quiet the deafening ringing in her ears.

"Now, darlin'" her father soothed, "you're a big girl now, almost a woman. I'm sure you can understand." Her father planted a kiss on Josephine's cheek. Josephine tipped her face toward him, her gaze never leaving Serenity's.

"Serenity, I—" Josephine started.

"If you will excuse me . . ." Serenity pushed her chair back and rose to her feet. "Annie is teaching me how to crochet. Tonight she promised to teach me the popcorn stitch. Besides, I am sure the two of you have wedding plans to discuss." With her back as stiff as a newly starched crinoline and her jaw clamped shut, Serenity glided from the room and up the stairs.

"Serenity—" Josephine repeated, her voice sounding pained.

"Let her go," Samuel advised. "She needs time to think."

Serenity paused at the top of the stairs to listen.

"Samuel, are we doing the right thing? The poor child barely has had time to mourn her mother. Perhaps we should have waited. We still could—"

"Nonsense. It's practical for us to marry before the new state assembly opens. If we wait, the first break wouldn't be until Christmas. I need you at my table before then."

"Not exactly the plea of a romantic, Mr. Pownell." An edge had come into Josephine's voice.

"My dear, I'm too old and too rusty at this courting stuff, I fear. Please be patient with me."

"I do so want Serenity's approval. I thought she'd finally grown to like me."

"She will come around. I know my daughter."

Serenity narrowed her eyes and mumbled. "Don't be so certain. . . ."

-17-
In the Face of Fear

 SERENITY'S HAND QUIVERED AS SHE tugged at the bell rope beside her bed. An hour had passed since her father made his grand announcement at the dinner table, an hour of shouting at and pleading with God. "If You are all powerful, You can stop them from marrying! My mother's been gone less than three months. Couldn't he have had the decency to wait six months or a year before taking a second wife? And why her?"

Serenity bounded off her bed, draped a woolen shawl about her shoulders, threw open the French doors, and stormed onto the balcony. "What a fake she turned out to be! Being nice to me to hornswaggle my father!" She paced back and forth between the balcony's two main support pillars until the setting sun cast a golden pathway on Lake Cayuga.

A woodpecker tattooed the side of a giant oak tree behind the house. Onyx chased a rabbit into the berry bushes at the edge of the lawn.

If only I had someone to talk to. Once I could talk with Annie. I suppose Dory would listen, but it wouldn't be fair since Josephine will soon be her employer. Serenity turned her face north in time to see a light come on at the Cunard home. "Aunt Fay . . ."

Serenity dashed back into her room, changed from her wrinkled dinner dress into her heather gray lindsey-woolsey, pinned her disheveled hair into a roll at the nape of her neck, and grabbed her woolen shawl. Lighting the portable lantern from her dresser, she ran down the back stairs and into the summer twilight.

She considered taking the road, but knew the path through the pines was faster. As a child, the woods had been the home of monsters and goblins. "I am old enough to know better now!" She said aloud with an authority she didn't feel.

As she stepped into the thick darkness of the pine woods separating the Pownell estate from the Cunard's, she paused and glanced back at the light shining from the parlor windows. "Maybe I should tell someone where I'm going," she thought, then shrugged. "No! Who would miss me?"

As she skipped along the path, her skirt caught on the briers of a raspberry bush. The fabric tore, but she didn't stop to check the damage. When a ground squirrel skittered across her pathway, she squealed and leaped backward. An owl hooted over her head. Looking up into the maze of tree limbs and pine needles, she shouted, "You can't scare me this time!"

However, she did run a little faster until she reached the wooden foot bridge at the edge of the Cunard property. The sight of their two-story log cabin caused her to breathe a deep sigh of relief.

On Serenity's first knock, Aunt Fay gave her a big hug and drew her into the house. "Are you all by yourself, girl? Here, let me take your wrap."

"I hope I'm not intruding—" Serenity's eyes filled with tears.

"No. In fact, it's a nice surprise. Just we women are home tonight. The Reverend and Aaron are down state attending to a funeral, and Caleb is late getting home from Auburn. Rebecca's asleep. Come over here and set yourself down."

Aunt Fay led her across the wide plank flooring of the Cunard's keeping room to a rough, hand-carved, oak settee. Plump, forest-green pillows filled with wood shavings padded the seats and back. Serenity sat down and gazed about the room. A fire roared in the massive stone fireplace. Beside the fireplace, a crocheted throw lay across the back of a Boston rocker. The lanterns on each end of the large stone mantle and two smaller lamps at the ends of the long narrow oak table behind the settee illuminated the great room. Over the fireplace, an oak-framed sampler read, "Give us this day, our daily bread." Serenity smiled to herself, remembering the alphabet sampler she'd stitched for her mother's birthday a few years back. It still hung in her mother's sewing room. *Josephine will probably take it down, that and every other reminder of Mama.*

"Would you like a cup of tea? With a sugar cookie?" Fay offered.

"Uh, no, thank you." Serenity smiled shyly. "I just came to talk with you."

Fay sat down on the far end of the sofa. "What can I do for you?"

Running through the woods, Serenity had rehearsed exactly what she'd tell Fay. But when the moment arrived, the words and the tears cascaded from her like the water from an early spring runoff. Fay listened attentively.

"And come to find out she's been pretending to be my friend in order to marry my father!"

Fay pursed her lips for a moment. "Are you sure that's what she was doing? Pretending?"

"What else? She knew I didn't like her and so she purposely set out to win my affections. It was all a ruse. And now, I'm suppose to accept her as my mother?"

"No, dear. Neither Mrs. Van der Mere, nor any other woman, will ever be your mother. Trust me, no one can ever take Charity's place in your heart."

Serenity's lower lip quivered. "I wish that were true for my father."

Aunt Fay laughed. "I promise, it is, honey. He will never love a second wife in the same way as he loved Charity." She placed her hand on Serenity's. "You see, we love each person in our lives in a uniquely different way. I love all of my children, but not in the same way. I love each of my thirteen brothers and sisters differently."

The woman squeezed Serenity's hand. "God gave us the capacity to love and love and love. And just as people are different, so our love is different with each person."

Serenity stared into the dancing flames, refusing to speak.

"What are you really afraid of, Serenity? Losing your father's affection? That won't happen. Believe me, I know. I'm a parent."

Serenity said nothing, but tears betrayed her feelings. Aunt Fay handed her a cotton handkerchief. Serenity buried her head in the woman's shoulder. Fay held her until the tears stopped flowing. "It's all right to cry. I've cried many tears in my life; some alone and even some with your mama. Did you know the day she and your father agreed that you needed to attend that finishing school, she came over here and we cried almost all afternoon?"

Serenity straightened, sniffled, and blew her nose. "This

might sound crazy, but . . ." Serenity paused. " . . . is it possible God would punish me by taking away my mother? Could my badness be the reason she died?"

"Heavens no!" Fay gasped. "Where did you get an idea like that?" She took Serenity by the shoulders. "Girl, look at me. If you forget everything else, remember this. God is the giver of good gifts, not bad. Bad things come from Satan, the father of lies! Your mother's death was a horrid accident, caused by a poorly trained horse or driver, who knows which?"

"But, but if God rules the universe, how come He can't stop Satan? If He can do anything, He could have kept that horse from killing my mother."

Fay shook her head. "You ask some pretty tough questions, Honey, questions that the world's greatest theologians have struggled with for centuries."

"But, it just seems that if God promises to keep us from danger, He should have kept His promise with Mama. Like in Psalm 91."

"Let me ask you a question. Is it possible that your view and my view of what happened to your mother is too small?"

Serenity wrinkled her brow. "I don't understand."

"Who am I to explain God's actions? His wisdom far surpasses either of ours." Fay thought for a moment, then took her Bible from the polished oak sofa table. She reached in the pocket of her apron and pulled out a pair of spectacles and adjusted the bows over her ears. She flipped through the pages. "Here it is, read this." She handed the book to Serenity. "Isaiah 57, verses 1 and 2."

Serenity positioned the book in the light from the sofa lamp. "The righteous perisheth, and no man layeth it to heart; and merciful men are taken away, none considering that the righteous is taken away from the evil to come. He shall enter into peace: they shall rest in their beds, each one walking in his uprightness." The girl looked at her mother's friend. "I don't understand. That doesn't make sense to me."

"I think the prophet is saying that humans can't understand why good people die, that sometimes the death of a good person is to give him rest and to protect him from evil that will come. Turn back a few chapters to Isaiah 55:8, where it says, 'My thoughts are not your thoughts and My ways your ways, saith the Lord.'"

"Doesn't that contradict the promises in Psalm 91? He promised to be with my mama. She was a good person and He failed her." Her angry words hung in the air. "How can I trust Him, if He can't keep His promises?"

"Child, the only way I know to build trust in Him is by getting to know Him better. Trust comes through understanding."

The girl's lips tightened and her eyes hardened. "And just how can I do that if I don't understand half the things I read in this book?"

"I suppose the same way I do. Before Jesus returned to heaven, He said, 'I will send you a Comforter.' He was talking about the Holy Spirit. Now, I don't pretend to understand the Holy Spirit, but I do know that when I ask God for the Holy Spirit to open my mind to His words, things I didn't understand begin to make sense."

Fay took a deep breath and exhaled slowly. "Sometimes I have questions about the way God leads me and the way He leads those I love. For that matter, after your mother's death, I spent several nights pouring over God's Word, searching for answers."

"You doubted God?"

"Doubted is the wrong word. Questioned might be more accurate. I didn't understand why things happened as they did."

"Did you ask Mr. Cunard?"

Fay smiled. "No, he's a busy man. I went to the Bible. I asked God for wisdom and peace with what had happened."

"You're talking in riddles. I don't understand."

"None of us have all the answers, honey. Sometimes I wonder if we ever will, at least, on this earth." The woman chuckled to herself. "But, one answer is constant. That is, God loves me. John 3:16. I believe doubt comes from not knowing Him well enough. That's when I go to the Gospels and read again the story of my loving, compassionate Savior."

"The Gospels?" Serenity scowled.

"Matthew, Mark, Luke, and John, the first four books of the New Testament," Fay explained. "They tell the story of Jesus' life when He was on this earth. He demonstrated love. He touched the lepers, blessed the children, fed the hungry, healed the blind. That's the Jesus I find in the Gospels. And Jesus Himself said, 'I came to reveal the Father.' He came to show His people what God is really like."

"But—"

Fay raised her hand to silence Serenity. "Since Jesus and God are one, I figure that by getting to know Jesus better, I can understand God better. Does that make any sense?"

Serenity nodded.

"When I have a clear picture of my Savior, I evaluate my understanding of God's behavior with the loving behavior of Jesus. And when something doesn't fit the loving picture the Gospels portray, I figure I must not have all the answers yet and I choose to trust the Jesus I've come to know as my friend."

Fay studied Serenity's face as she spoke. "Then I pray, 'Father, I don't understand all of this, but You do. Please take my questions and take my doubts. Keep them until You think I'm ready to understand the answers; then, and only then, make all things clear to me. Until that time, I choose to trust in Your love and not in my wisdom.'"

Serenity nibbled on her upper lip for a few minutes. Suddenly a flood of questions burst from her, like storm waters through an earthen dam. Fay struggled to keep up with the girl's probing mind.

"Does God ever punish one person for the sins of another?"

The woman smiled and shook her head. "Never."

"How can you know that?" Serenity's forehead wrinkled. "How can you be sure? Where does it say that in here?" She held up the Bible.

"There is a story in the New Testament about a man who had been blind from birth." Fay cleared her throat, then continued. "The disciples asked Jesus who sinned to bring about this man's curse, the man or his parents? And Jesus answered, 'Neither.' In a world of sin, bad things happen. The rain falls on the good and the bad."

Serenity closed her eyes. The face of old Herman surfaced before her. She took in a ragged sigh. *If only Aunt Fay is right? Please be right!*

When the grandfather clock in the corner of the room gonged, Serenity jumped. "Oh! I'd better hurry home before someone discovers I'm missing!"

"You didn't tell anyone where you were going?" Fay's voice rose an octave.

"I, uh, left the dinner table abruptly . . ." Serenity studied her fingernails for a moment. " . . . when my father announced his plans to marry Josephine before the end of the summer. If Annie comes to my room to check on me . . ."

"Well, then. It's time you dashed home." Fay rose from the sofa and held out her hand to the girl. She led her to the door, opened it, and gazed out at the moonlit terrain. She frowned. "I don't like sending you home alone after dark. I wish Caleb or the Reverend were home. They should be, in fact, any time. I can't imagine what's keeping them!"

"I'll be fine." Serenity answered with more confidence than she felt. She picked up the pewter lamp she'd left on the console table by the door. "I'll take the road home. It's a ways longer, but not as scary."

"I think that's a good idea. Wait, I want to pray with you before you leave."

Serenity bowed her head and listened as Fay prayed for her safety. In the same breath as her "Amen," the woman warned, "Don't dally. I'll stand here and watch until you're out of sight."

Serenity kissed the woman and hurried down the steps to the roadway. She paused to turn and wave, but Fay was already engulfed by the shadows of the night.

-18-
Mysteries of the Night

 SERENITY STRODE ALONG THE RUTTED dirt road, jumping at every sound or movement in the forest around her. "Oh, dear God," she whispered, "I'm a fraidy cat, I know, and my faith in You and Your promises to protect me is equally weak. But if You are the God Mama and Aunt Fay claim You to be, please help me to reach home safely. And, if You could throw in a little courage, I'd be most obliged." She opened her eyes in time to sidestep a large frost heave.

Maybe if I sing . . . She remembered a little ditty she'd heard Gloria singing while making bread.

"Da-da-da-da-da-da-da, follow the drinking gourd." Serenity couldn't remember the words. "Da-da-da-da-da-da-da, follow the drinking gourd."

Strutting confidently down the center of the road, she sang until the sound of rustling bushes interrupted her impromptu concert. A niggling fear skittered up her spine. *Run. Run!* Her mind ordered her legs, but they failed to respond.

"Run!" She shouted to herself. This time her legs obeyed. She darted down the road, the light from her lamp bobbing ahead of her as she ran. A glance over her shoulder and she knew something or someone was chasing her. "Oh, dear God," she panted, "if You're ever going to help me, make it now!"

Without warning, the toe of her boot smashed against a rock in the road, sending her sprawling onto the roadway. Before she could scramble to her feet her assailant was upon her, licking her face and slobbering her with kisses.

"Onyx, oh, Onyx, you scared me to death!" She threw her arms around the dog's neck and shoulders. She pushed him away and clambered to her feet. "Why ever did you— What's the matter, boy?"

Instead of staying by her side while she dusted off her clothing, the dog dashed into the woods, then returned. He repeated that several times. "Stop playing games, Onyx. Let's go home."

The dog tugged at her skirt, dashed into the woods again, then returned to her side. "Onyx! I'm tired and I'm dirty. I don't want to play games." But again, the dog turned and disappeared into the shadows.

As she took another step, she heard what sounded like a baby's cry. She paused, but all was silent. Suddenly Onyx burst from the woods once more and tugged at her skirts. "All right! All right! I'll follow you. But this had better be good, you spastic mutt!"

The dog pranced in the direction of the woods, stopping every few feet to be certain she was following. She climbed over brambles and straddled fallen logs. "I can't believe I'm doing this, in the middle of the night, no less! I must be out of my—a-i-e-e-e!" She felt herself flying through the air, her lamp swinging in the opposite direction. She landed on a berry bush.

"Ouch!" Angry tears sprang into her eyes. "That's it!

I've had enough. If you think I'm going to follow you any further on your wild goose chase, you're crazy!"

She looked around for her lamp, but the light had gone out. Intense darkness settled in about her. The moon, which earlier had been lighting the terrain, had slipped behind a bank of clouds. With trees on all sides, Serenity had no idea where she was. She heard waves lapping the shores of the lake. *At least I'm heading in the proper direction,* she thought.

Her left hip ached. When she stood, she rubbed it gently. "O-o-oh, I'll be sore tomorrow morning." While brushing twigs and briers from her clothes, she heard it again, a baby's cry. She stopped to listen. "There it is again," she said aloud, gathering her skirts about her legs and plunging into the brush.

Suddenly, a male voice commanded, "Stop!"

"A-a-a-ah!" Serenity screamed. Her hand flew to her chest as she panted to regain her breath.

"Be quiet, girl! It's me, Abe. Over here under the pine tree!"

Serenity peered into the brush. "Abe? Whatever are you—"

"Sh-sh, Miss Serenity, be quiet or they'll hear you! As it is, Onyx heard you and recognized your song."

"Who'll hear me? What song?"

"Be still, child. This isn't a game. You were singing 'The Drinking Gourd.' That's what Onyx heard. If they'd heard it we'd be in big trouble right now." Abe had never used such a harsh tone with her. "I want you to listen carefully. I think I broke my leg—"

"Oh! I'll run and get help."

"No! You can't do that yet. I need you to go down to the cave and . . ." he paused. Serenity couldn't see his face in the shadows, but heard fear in his voice.

"The cave? Why? What for?"

"Be quiet and listen. Go to the cave and hum the same tune you were humming before—'The Drinking Gourd.' Then take the six adults and two children to the main house." He groaned in pain. "Take them into the basement through the hatch beside the lilac bush. Are you following me?"

"I think so."

"There is a canning shelf on the wall to your left. It's filled with jars of peaches and applesauce, except for one jar of plums. Behind the jar of plums there is a leather strap. Pull the strap and the canning shelf will pivot, revealing a narrow staircase."

Serenity's eyes widened with surprise.

"Take the people up to the attic. There's food, water, and blankets there for them. Then return immediately down the staircase and push the shelf in place. You'll know it's secure when you hear a snap." Abe grunted. "Then find my son and tell him I've been injured. He'll take care of the rest."

"You're hiding runaway slaves in my father's house?" Her whispers climbed to a dangerously high pitch. "I can't believe you would betray my father's trust in this way!"

"Just do as I say, and as quickly as possible. Bounty hunters are in the area tonight."

"Bounty hunters?" Serenity's skin crawled with fear. She knew the punishment for harboring and abetting runaway slaves. Everyone did. To think that her father's most trusted servant could be breaking the law right under her father's nose appalled her. "You're using my father's home for an underground railroad station? You could go to jail for this and Papa could be fined thousands of dollars, and that's if you're both lucky."

"Look, we can sort this all out later. Right now, those

people need your help. We can't fail them now, not after they've come so far."

"Papa's going to be furious!"

"Just do as I say! Now! Onyx, go with her!" The dog gave a short woof and obediently headed toward the lake. Abe's harsh tone jogged Serenity to action as well. She turned and followed the dog through the thicket.

When her feet touched the gray sands of the beach, Serenity broke into a run toward the mouth of the cave. Onyx ran ahead and disappeared into the darkness. Serenity stopped at the mouth of the cave. Terrified, she braced herself against the granite wall. Cautiously she peered into the cave. She could see and hear nothing, not even Onyx.

"Onyx!" She hissed. "Onyx, where are you?"

She paused to listen. She heard voices, not from the cave, but from the lake behind her. She could hear the scraping of a rowboat being hauled across stones. She froze, her back pressed against the wall of the cave. After several seconds, the forms of two men emerged through the mist. "Stop being so picayune, Leroy! It don't matter if the boat is two feet or four out the water, as long as it's leashed to that tree back there!"

"Is that a fact? Well, I don't want to come back and find it bobbin' in the middle of the lake."

The light from one of the lanterns flashed across the mouth of the cave. Serenity pressed further into the shadows. As she did, her foot scraped against a stone.

"Hush!"

Serenity held her breath. She felt Onyx's moist nose touch her hand, his body quivering with excitement.

One of the men whispered. "I heard somethin'."

"Clyde, you're always hearin' things."

"You would, too, if you stopped yappin'."

"Sh! I heard it ag'in."

The light drew closer to the cave, piercing Serenity's protective cloak of darkness. The girl realized she'd have to stop the men from entering the cave. Remembering how well the element of surprise worked the last time she'd visited the lake, Serenity ripped the hair combs from her hair and shook it free.

When the lead man was within a foot of her face, Serenity let out an ear-piercing scream that ricocheted off the walls of the cave. At the same time, she lunged at the man, her fingernails clawing at his face.

"A-i-i-e-e-e!" The lead man howled from shock and pain, then whipped about and plowed into his startled companion. The two men wrestled to maintain their footing. As if on cue, Onyx set to barking. The walls of the cave echoed with the dog's barks, multiplying the sound to that of a pack of wild dogs.

The two men didn't wait to discover how many canines were in the pack before breaking into a hasty retreat to their boat. Serenity giggled with glee, but her merriment stopped when she heard a baby cry from deep inside the cave. She whirled about. *The people! I'd forgotten the people.*

She peered into the darkness. "Yoo-hoo! Anyone here? I'm suppose to take you to the hideout."

She listened and except for the sound of Onyx trotting to her side, heard nothing. "Please, come out. I must move you right away. I don't know how long those bounty hunters will stay away." Still, all was silent. Then she remembered the song. "La-la-la-la-la, follow the drinking gourd. La-la-la-la-la-la, follow the drinking gourd . . ."

She paused to hear a soft echo of her song being

hummed an octave lower coming from deep inside the cave, followed by the sound of scuffling feet. Onyx didn't growl or bark at the appearance of the seven strangers.

A woman, not much older than Serenity, held an infant in her arms. Another woman's shawl was moth-eaten. Her sleeve was ripped and threadbare. The knee of the men's trousers sported patches. Four of them wore shoes the soles of which were secured with rags laced around their toes.

"You guide us?" The patriarch of the group, a tall man as black as the midnight sky, stepped out of the shadows. "A mere slip of a girl?"

Serenity laughed nervously. "'Fraid so. Follow me."

"But we were told that a man . . ."

"I'm all you've got. Either follow me or return to your owners."

A gasp swept through the cluster of terrified runaways. Ashamed of herself for making such a threat, Serenity begged, "Please follow me." She tromped through the brush to the edge of the estate's grounds. Slipping between the split rails of the fence, she straightened and turned to help the woman carrying the baby. "Here, let me hold him."

"She a girl-child, Mabel be her name." The mother handed the infant to Serenity, then crawled through the railings. "She a good baby, but hungry. My milk dry up the last day."

Serenity placed the child in her mother's arms. "Then let's hurry to the house so she can eat." Serenity broke into a gentle trot across the lawn as Onyx loped along by her side. The seven runaways matched their pace.

Serenity skirted the light flooding from the library. She could see Josephine seated on the brocade settee and her father leaning one elbow against the mantle and smoking his pipe. A fire roared in the fireplace. Serenity shuddered. *Oh, Papa, if you only knew what your darling daughter is doing right now!*

"This way," she hissed. She led the stowaways to the trap door. When she tried to lift it, it wouldn't budge. The leader of the group lifted the door with ease. Onyx, satisfied everyone was safe, trotted back toward the lake.

Serenity and her charges filed into the basement. "Stay here while I sneak into the house for a lantern," she warned.

She tiptoed up the inside basement stairs and into the kitchen pantry where the spare lanterns were kept. Grabbing a lantern, she lit it from the fire in the fireplace.

"Just what do you think you're doing?" A voice behind her exclaimed.

Serenity jumped and turned to face Dory.

"I thought you were asleep in your room."

"Oh, you startled me! Abe's been hurt. He sent me for help." She paused and squinted up at Dory. "How much do you know about what he's been up to?"

Dory's eyes narrowed. "What do you mean?"

"Do you know he's been breaking the law, and using this house as a—"

Dory grinned. "I not only know, I help him."

"You do? Does my father know about this?"

Dory smiled. "You'd better ask him that. So where are the passengers?"

"Passengers? Oh, they're in the basement. I came up for a lantern and some milk for the baby."

Dory spun Serenity about, aiming her in the direction of the basement door. "Go! Get them to safety. I'll bring the milk and a sugarplum for the baby."

"Sugarplum?"

"To pacify the child. Now, go! The longer they're standing around the greater the possibility they'll be discovered."

—19—

Lawbreaker

 THE DOOR SLAMMED BEHIND SERENITY as she hurried down the stairs to the basement. She shined the light about the room, but could not find her charges. "Where are you?" she called softly. As she crossed the shale floor of the basement, she spotted the runaways huddled behind several large pickle barrels. "Come on, it's not safe for you here."

She shined the light around the room at the canning shelves lining the stone walls. "Peaches, peaches," she mumbled, "where are the peaches? Beets, string beans, squash." She examined the jars for their contents. The runaways dogged her every step.

"Corn, corn, peas, peas . . . Ah, that looks like it might be peaches." She shined the light toward the shelves near the back wall. The light shined on the shiny jars and their labels. "Peaches—1849. Last year's batch. Here's the applesauce and, ah-ah! The one jar of plums."

Behind the quart jar of plums, Serenity found the leather strap. She pulled the strap as Abe had directed. The shelf wouldn't budge. She tugged at it again.

"Let me," the older gentleman of the group whispered. He took the strap from her hand and pulled. As he pulled, the canning shelf pivoted, revealing a narrow wooden staircase. Serenity led the way up the stairs to a small partitioned room, separate of the attic Serenity had played in as a child. She glanced about the space in amazement. In one corner she saw a stack of mats with blankets for sleeping. In another corner were several barrels and boxes. Hay covered the floor, muffling the sound of their footsteps as the runaways moved about the confined space. Three large trunks stood open and empty in the corner behind the stairs.

"There's food and water up here somewhere. Make yourself at home." She flashed the lantern about the area. "Dory will be up in a few minutes with some milk for the baby. I would leave the lantern, but—"

"No . . ." The older gentleman shook his head and pointed to the air vent in the peak of the roof. "The light would give us away."

"Yes, of course. Will you be all right here?" she asked, looking at the woman holding the baby.

"Oh, yes. This is so much nicer than the musty barn where we slept last night. And that was better than the night we slept burrowed in the riverbank to avoid the dogs."

"When we first saw your dog, we thought he was one of the hunter's dogs," the older man explained. "We never expected to find a handsome young woman like yourself as a conductor."

Serenity grinned. "That's all right, I never expected to be a conductor either. I don't know what happens next, but I'm sure Dory will help you in any way she can."

The young mother yawned. "Next, we eat a few bites, then sleep until tomorrow night when we will move on—"

"Toward Canada," one of the men volunteered, "and freedom."

Serenity said good night, then holding her lamp before her, tiptoed back down the stairs. As she did, the sleeve of her dress scraped against the unfinished slat wall of the stairway. She stopped and stared at the lathe and plaster. She'd heard that sound before. Of course! It was one of the sounds that had awakened her in the night. Night sounds! They weren't caused by ghosts and goblins, but by runaways hiding in the attic! She laughed to herself and continued down the staircase to the basement.

Carefully, she pushed the canning shelf back and set the plum jar in its proper place. She glanced about the basement. Nothing seemed out of place. The trapdoor had been closed. There were no footprints on the shale floor and no fingerprints on the shelves. Taking a deep breath, she hurried up the kitchen stairs. She could hear Dory humming as she slipped up the back stairs to her bedroom. At the second floor landing, she paused to listen to the sounds of laughter coming from the library below.

The thought crossed her mind that she should tell her father what was happening. She walked slowly toward the front staircase leading to the main floor. *If I tell him and he gets angry enough at Abe to throw those poor people out into the night, what will become of the woman and her baby?* She paused, her hand resting on the polished oak finial at the top of the stairs. *It can wait until morning.*

Suddenly a loud commotion in front of the house sent her flying to the arched window overlooking the portico. "Who would be visiting at this time of night?" she mumbled. She set her lantern on a mahogany lady's desk beside the window, then cupped her hands about her eyes trying to see what was happening. The portico roof was in her way.

The door knocker hammered against the front door.

The laughter from the library stopped. Only the grandfather clock at the foot of the stairs continued ticking away the seconds. Serenity held her breath. Several seconds passed and the knocking began again. "Isn't anyone going to answer the door?" she muttered. The knocking stopped, then began again.

Serenity considered going down the stairs to answer ituntil she remembered her torn, mud-spattered dress. A gentle swoosh-swoosh interrupted her thoughts. She ran to the stairs and leaned over the railing to see Dory, lantern in hand, walking slowly to the door. *How'd she get back from the basement so fast?*

The rapping sounded again, this time more impatiently than before. Slowly, Dory unlocked the front door and opened it. Serenity could see the glint of Sheriff Broderick's badge as he and two of his deputies pushed their way past Dory and into the house. "All right, where is she?" the sheriff shouted.

Dory caught up with him. "Excuse me, Sir, but it is late. If you wish to speak with the master of the house, you should come back tomorrow. The family is about to retire for the night."

"Girl, where is she?"

The sheriff stood glaring at the housekeeper. Serenity saw Dory's back straighten the way it always did whenever her hackles got up. "She? Who might she be?"

"I don't know for sure, but I suspect it's Miss Serenity, by the description I got."

Serenity's eyes widened in surprise just as her father approached the sheriff.

"A young woman was sighted down by the lake a few minutes ago. She attacked two bounty hunters hot on the trail of a family of runaways from Arkansas."

Samuel Pownell laughed. "My daughter, attack two bounty hunters?" His laughter rang throughout the three-story entryway. "What kind of balderdash are you spouting, Sheriff? My delicate little girl is sound asleep in her bed. Sounds to me like those plug-ugly varmints of yours were too liquored up to know what's up."

"They aren't my men, Mr. Pownell. If I could talk with your daughter, please?"

One of the two deputies strolled toward the library. Mr. Pownell's eyes blazed.

"You got a warrant to search this place, Sheriff?"

"Hiram, get back here!" the sheriff ordered. "Your daughter, sir?"

"In the morning, Sheriff. I do not wish to disturb her sleep. Besides, where do you think she might go in the night? To Washington?"

"All right. Out of respect for your recently departed wife . . ." The sheriff eyed Josephine, who was standing in the doorway to the library. " . . . I will return tomorrow morning after breakfast. By the way, when I'm ready to search your house, I will have that warrant. Be sure of it!"

The sheriff tipped his hat toward Josephine, whirled about and stomped out of the house. The deputies followed. Dory closed the door behind them.

Serenity leaned against the railing and heaved a giant sigh of relief. "What in tarnation was that all about?" her father's voice boomed.

"I'm sure it was a terrible mistake, darling." Josephine glided to his side and took his arm.

"Well, Dory?"

"Sir, I'm but a humble, obedient servant. I know nothing. I see nothing. I hear nothing."

"Hmmph! You say that every time something's afoot. Where's Abe?" Samuel strode across the entryway and peered out the portico windows. "Well?"

"I understand he's been injured. I sent our boy to fetch him."

When her father looked up the stairs, Serenity ducked back. "Something's fishy here. I don't like it. Maybe I'd better have a word with my darling daughter."

Spurred to action, Serenity dashed down the hall, unbuttoning her soiled dress as she ran. Ripping the last three buttons from the waist of the dress, she yanked it and her crinolines over her head, tossed them under the bed, and blew out the lantern on the nightstand.

She hauled her nightdress down over her head and leaped into bed, shoes and all. She'd barely fastened the buttons at the neck of her nightdress when her bedroom door opened. Her father's shadow filled the doorway.

"Serenity? Serenity, are you awake?"

Pretending to be waking from a deep sleep, she sat up and rubbed her eyes. "Papa? What's the matter?"

He strode into the room carrying a lamp. "Were you sleeping?"

"What time is it? Is it morning yet? Is something wrong?"

Samuel shined the light about the room, then on the floor beside the bed. "No, nothing's wrong. Sorry I wakened you. We'll talk in the morning."

She snuggled beneath her down-filled quilt and yawned. "Good night, Papa."

"Good night, Punkin'." He bent over and kissed her forehead, straightened, then left the room.

As the door latched behind him, Serenity exhaled sharply. Leaping from her bed she dropped to the floor to unbuckle her boots. Once removed, she finished undressing and hopped back into bed. She closed her eyes and thought about the terrifying night sounds she'd heard so many times. *Abe's been harboring runaways for years! How many others are involved in his schemes?* She sat up in bed. "Annie must be, of course! Every time I was afraid, she was always here with her herb tea to comfort me. And Gloria! She's hummed that 'drinking gourd' song as long as I can remember!"

Laying back down against her pillow, Serenity stared into the night. "I can't believe they're up to so much mischief without my parents knowing!"

She thought of Eulilia, her roommate from school, and giggled. *The girl would be horrified to find out that her best friend's servants operate a "station" on the underground railroad. Or she'd be captivated by the danger of it all!*

So where does that leave me? The moonlight beyond the balcony doors cast gyrating shadows on the ceiling. She sighed, closed her eyes, and drifted off into an uneasy sleep.

"Run! Run!" someone shouted. "The bounty hunters are after you. Run!" Serenity grasped the tiny black baby to her breast and sped down the road. She glanced over her shoulder at her pursuers. Terror swept through her like an express train to Syracuse.

"They're gaining on me! And they have dogs. Dogs?" She charged forward with renewed energy. When she heard her mother shout, "Run, my darling, run," the girl looked ahead toward the end of the road. There stood her mother, arms outstretched, beckoning to her. "Run faster! Run!" But no matter how hard she tried, Serenity couldn't catch up to her mother.

It was as if she were running, but not running. Behind her, the barking dogs drew ever closer. She could see their yellow fangs in their slobbering mouths. She could see the wild frenzy in their eyes. Suddenly a baby cried.

Serenity's eyes flew open; she sat bolt upright. The hunters, the dogs, the road, and her mother's face disappeared. Her breath came in short gasps. "Where am I?" She pressed one hand against her heart as she glanced about the darkened room. "Oh, dear God, I'm safe."

Then she heard the baby cry again. She looked toward the ceiling. "Please," she begged, "please, quiet that baby. They'll find her if you don't."

As if in response to her plea, the child quieted. Outside the French doors, an owl hooted, a dove cooed, and the night breeze whistled through the branches of the elm tree beside her window.

~20~

A Higher Law

"Here, let me do that for you." Annie took the pearl-handled hairbrush from Serenity's hand. "You must have slept fitfully last night. Look at all these tangles."

"Ouch!" Serenity winced.

"Why didn't you wear your nightcap?" the little maid scolded as she tugged at the tangles. A breeze wafted through the open French doors, fanning the white dimity canopy ruffle above Serenity's bed. "By the way, just where were you 'til all hours? I came upstairs to help you dress for bed and no one was here. I was tempted to tell your papa."

"I'm very glad you didn't. Papa would have been furious if he knew that I walked over to Aunt Fay's place after dark."

"Ah . . ." Annie grinned broadly. "So, that's it. You went to see Mrs. Cunard. Not the young Mr. Cunard, of course."

Serenity whipped about to face the young servant. "Of course not! Why would I want to do such a thing as that?"

"Oh, come on, this is Annie you're talking to, remember? The household staff is wagering as to how long it will be before the two of you post your bands."

"Our bands? You mean become engaged? To one another? We can't stand the sight of each other!" Serenity's eyes snapped with fire. "That's ridiculous! I've never heard anything so ridiculous! In fact, last night at the Cunard's, the young Mr. Cunard wasn't even home—not that I minded!"

Annie giggled. "What was that phrase your mama used to quote from Mr. Shakespeare's play? 'Me thinks thou dost protest too much.'"

"I certainly don't remember any such quote!" Serenity yanked on the collar to her pink gingham bodice. "Why doesn't this thing lay flat like it's suppose to?" She looked up at the grinning face of her friend and personal maid. "Wipe that smile off your face. You look like a clown from one of those traveling circus acts."

Annie's smile broadened. Her eyes twinkled.

"Stop it! Honestly, I went to the Cunard home to see Aunt Fay. I was upset about my father's announcement last night and needed someone to talk to. Surely you can understand that?"

"'The excuse that thou dost make in this delay is longer than the tale thou dost excuse.' I believe that one's from—"

"Stop quoting Shakespeare and brush these snarls out of my hair!"

"Oh, you recognize that one?"

Serenity glared at Annie. "Yes! *Romeo and Juliet,* scene five."

The girl tugged at a snarl in the back of Serenity's hair.

"Ouch! Be gentle."

Annie waved the hairbrush in the air like a stick. "Which do you want? Me to remove the snarls or to be gentle? You can't have both."

Serenity exhaled sharply. "I can tell this is going to be a very long day!"

Annie brushed Serenity's hair back and tied it in a blush-pink grosgrain bow. "There! That should hold as long as you behave ladylike."

"Ladylike? Of all the—"

A knock sounded at the bedroom door.

"Who in the world can that be at this hour?" Serenity stood and straightened the wrinkles out of her skirt while Annie walked to the door and opened it.

"Pansy?"

The woman entered the room. "Miss Serenity, your papa is in the library. He wishes to speak with you right away."

Serenity glanced at Annie and grimaced. Annie shrugged her shoulders and rolled her eyes in reply.

Pasting on a bright smile, Serenity turned toward the family chambermaid. "Please tell my father I will be down as soon as I finish dressing."

Annie looked at her questioningly. Serenity glared. "I still need to put on my shoes, you know."

"Yes, ma'am." Pansy left the room. The instant the door closed, Serenity grabbed Annie's forearms.

"What am I going to do? I did something stupid last night. I broke the law."

"You what?" the little maid asked.

"I broke the law. It's a very long story and the sheriff will be here any minute. He could arrest me!"

Annie clicked her tongue. "You're becoming hysterical. Sheriff Broderick won't arrest you, I promise."

"How do you know? How can you be sure?"

"Trust me, I just know." Annie patted her mistress's hand, then glanced down at the house slippers on Serenity's feet. "Now you'd better scoot downstairs before your father sends out the militia."

Serenity inhaled and exhaled several times, trying to calm herself, then left the room. She paused at the open library door. "Oh, dear God, if You're really the God Aunt

Fay claims You to be, I need You!" Timidly, she peeked around the corner of the doorjamb. Her father sat at his cluttered mahogany desk, tapping his bone-handled letter opener on the forest green ink blotter. "Papa?" Her mouth broadened into a sick smile. "You wanted to see me?"

He looked up and scowled. "Serenity, please come in and close the door behind you."

She swallowed hard, but obeyed.

"Come, sit down." He motioned to the straight-back, Hepplewhite chair beside his desk. Slowly, she advanced toward the chair.

"Serenity, I've called you in here this morning to—"

"I know why, Papa, and I'm—"

"Wait, what I have to say is important. Please hear me out."

She swallowed the lump in her throat and sat down.

"I know about your little adventure last night. I went to see Abe this morning. He told me what you did."

"But, Papa, I can explain."

"It's all right. I'm not faulting you for what you did. I'm faulting me for causing you and too many of the household staff to break the law." He exhaled sharply. "Where do I start? As you know, your mother felt very strongly about the abolition of slavery. I do, too, but because of my position felt it better not to be so open about my feelings. When we built the last addition to the house, we—with the help of Abe and Caleb Cunard—decided to become a station on the underground railroad to Canada. Hence the secret stairwell and hidden attic."

"All those years, I thought the night sounds—"

"I know. We hated deceiving you, but you were a child. We never intended to involve you in any way. But after last night . . ." Her father studied his hands for a moment. "By the way, what were you doing on the road at such an ungodly hour?"

The girl reddened. "I, uh, went to see Aunt Fay. After your announcement, I—"

"Yes, I handled it poorly, didn't I?"

"Yes, sir." Her eyes filled with tears.

"Understand, while I'm sorry about my clumsy announcement, nothing has changed regarding the engagement. Josephine and I will be wed before you return to school. But that's not important right now."

"Not important? You're marrying another woman, almost before my mother's body is cold in the ground, and that's not important?"

Samuel placed his hand on Serenity's forearm. "I didn't mean it isn't important. I just mean that we have other issues to discuss at this time, not the least of which is Sheriff Broderick's visit this morning. You do know about his visit?"

She glanced across the room at the mantle clock.

"He'll ask you several questions. Think before you speak. People's lives are depending on your answers."

A sudden defiance welled up inside Serenity. She eyed her father. "You want me to lie?"

"I didn't say that."

"Yes, you did. First, you make me break the law, then you want me to lie? What's going on here? You're a state assemblyman. Your job is to uphold the law, not break it!"

"That's true. One should always obey the laws of this country. They are designed to protect us. And, for the most part, elected officials like Sheriff Broderick are honorable men."

"But—"

"But," he interrupted, "but, there are times when God's laws take precedence over man's. I believe that enslaving another human being or, in this case, returning a runaway slave to his master to be beaten and possibly killed, is one of those times."

Serenity remembered cradling the infant in her arms while her mother crawled through the fence. She could feel the warmth of the baby's tiny body as it nestled close to her breast, even for such a short time. Then she remembered her own mother's fury whenever someone was being mistreated.

"I-I understand, Papa."

The clatter of approaching hoofbeats sounded on the redbrick roadway in front of the house. Her father strode to the window.

"Sheriff Broderick?" Serenity asked.

"No, it's just the Garvey boy exercising my mare. But the sheriff will be here soon, mark my word."

"Don't worry, Papa," She walked to his side and touched her father's arm. "I'll do my best."

"I know you will, Puddin'-tuck."

She held up a warning finger. "But only if you promise to answer the millions of questions spinning around in my head."

He grinned, offering her his arm. "I'll do the best I can. But for now, may I escort you to breakfast, my dear?"

She curtsied with a flourish. "I would like that, kind sir."

Josephine met them in the hallway. Serenity, clinging possessively to her father's arm, mumbled a respectable greeting. She looked away when her father planted a kiss on Josephine's cheek.

Putting Josephine's hand in the crux of his spare arm, Serenity's father said, "Josephine rose extra early this morning to plan a special breakfast for us. She's chosen to have us dine in the sunroom this morning. Gloria prepared one of your new pancake recipes, didn't she, dear?"

Josephine smiled nervously. "They're not pancakes, exactly. The French call them crepes."

"Crepes? Like funeral draping?" he asked.

The woman chuckled. "They're thin, like the fabric, but quite edible, I assure you."

Samuel led the two women into the sunroom. Serenity gazed about the window-lined room in which her mother had invested so much time and love. Serenity remembered watching her mother cut the yellow flowered chintz for the Priscilla-style curtains and for the matching chair cushions. She slipped her hand from her father's arm and ran it along the polished split-reed back of her mother's rocker. She touched the glass tray on top of the tea cart. Her fingers caressed the cool surface of the ornate silver tea service. This was the first time since her mother's death that she'd entered the quiet little sanctuary.

A bouquet of pink rosebuds and daisies sat in the middle of the Hepplewhite table. Blue and white English porcelain breakfastware rested on a white linen tablecloth her mother had embroidered with daisy chains. Serenity's hand flew to her mouth. She backed away from the table. "I . . . I . . . I'm not hungry. May I please be excused?"

"Whatever is the matter?" Her father stopped in mid-action as he pulled out a chair for Josephine.

"I—" Her breath came in short gasps. "Do we have to eat in here, on those dishes and that tablecloth?"

"No, but, I don't understand."

"They're Mama's favorite dishes—English Abbey, they're called. And the tablecloth . . ." She pointed to the hand-stitched daisies.

Her father blanched as if remembering his wife stitching the daisies on the fabric. He shook his head and swallowed hard. "Nonsense! Everything in this house was your mother's. She would be irate if she thought we'd set up a shrine to her memory. Things are only things. They are meant to be used."

Serenity gulped. "But they're . . ." When the words to express her thoughts refused to come, she glared at the other woman.

Her father's lips tightened into a thin line. "Look, Serenity, I tolerated your outbursts last evening because I understood the shock you must have felt, but will every meal we have together include an emotional outburst?"

Serenity's lower lip quivered. "No, sir." She slipped unaided into her chair and lowered her eyes. They ate their blueberry crepes in silence. Even the dollop of fresh whipped cream did little to sweeten Serenity's mood. While Samuel and Josephine chatted about the weather and their favorite opera, Serenity glowered into her plate.

"All right!" Samuel's napkin hit the table. "I've had all the pouting and fussing I can stomach. Serenity, if you insist upon acting like a child, you will be treated like one. I will expect you to eat your meals in the kitchen until you can apologize to Josephine for your irreprehensible behavior!"

Josephine blanched. "Samuel, that's not nec—"

He lifted his hand to silence her. "Don't interfere. This is between my daughter and me."

Serenity dotted her lips with her table napkin. "May I please be excused?"

"Not only will I excuse you, but I insist upon it." He rose to help her from her chair.

"No, thank you, Father." She choked back her tears. "I

can manage. Excuse me, please, Mrs. Van der Mere." She ran from the room, plowing into Gloria carrying a fresh pitcher of apple juice. The women screeched as the juice spilled on both of them. Serenity stepped back, her hands and clothes dripping with the sticky liquid. "Ooh!" she wailed and ran for the stairs.

A knock sounded on the front door as she passed, but she didn't stop. Behind her, she heard Dory open the door to the visitor. When she reached the landing, she paused.

"Sheriff Broderick. Aren't you about a little early?"

"Ma'am, I'm here to see—"

"Mr. Pownell is at the breakfast table, I'm afraid. Would you like to—"

"I'm not here to see the assemblyman, but his daughter, Miss Serenity."

"Miss Serenity? Whatever reason could you have to harass that poor girl? Don't you know she's in mourning for her recently departed mother?"

"Look, just get the Pownell kid. I didn't ask for an argument!"

"Sheriff Broderick," Dory hissed, "it will be up to Mr. Pownell whether or not Miss Serenity will be allowed to speak with you." Serenity could hear the irritation in Dory's voice.

"Then get him for me, woman. Because, like it or not, I will talk with Miss Serenity this morning, either here or in my jail."

"It's fine, Dory," Serenity's father interrupted. "The sheriff can wait in the parlor until I finish my breakfast. And then we will speak with my daughter together."

Serenity glanced about quickly, gathered her skirts, and dashed into her room. "Annie," she mumbled as she unbuttoned the top buttons on her dress, "where are you when I need you?"

Suddenly, the girl appeared around the edge of the door. "Did you call me?"

"Oh, bless you! Here, help me with these stupid pearl buttons. I can't get them to—"

"Stand still. Let me do it."

"The juice sprayed all over my face and hair. My fingers are sticking together."

"Gloria isn't faring much better." Annie laughed. "Boy, is she mad! She's in the kitchen chewing out her staff."

Serenity looked at the girl in surprise. "I never knew Gloria had a temper."

"Temper? She'd make Shakespeare's Kate look like a pussycat!"

Serenity laughed, remembering how she and Annie eavesdropped on Serenity's parents as they read aloud Shakespeare's *Taming of the Shrew*.

With the last button unfastened, Serenity stepped out of the soiled dress and crossed the room to the washstand. "Pick out something for me to wear while I wash off this sticky mess."

Annie went to the wardrobe and withdrew a yellow and white gingham dress. "This one should make you look younger and, hopefully, innocent."

Serenity laughed, then patted her face dry with a Turkish towel. She checked her hair. "Guess I'd better lose this pink bow."

"Sit down at the dressing table and let me redo your hair." Annie slipped the dress over Serenity's head. "I'll take five years off of you."

"Wonderful! Just what I want to be, a twelve-year-old again."

"Today, being twelve years old might not be a bad idea. After all, what lawman would want to badger a child?" As she talked, Annie brushed Serenity's curls, then pinned a large yellow satin bow on the side of her head. "Especially a lovely little girl wearing a perky yellow ribbon in her hair."

~21~
Trouble Brewing

 "MISS SERENITY, I APPRECIATE YOUR being willing to speak with me this morning. I have a few questions I'd like to ask, with your father's permission, of course." Sheriff Broderick gestured toward Samuel sitting ramrod stiff on the sofa. Josephine sat beside him, holding his hand. "Is it appropriate for your guest, Mrs. Van der Mere, to be present on such an occasion?" the sheriff asked.

Samuel lifted his chin. "It is, considering Mrs. Van der Mere has agreed to become my wife and Serenity's stepmother."

Serenity straightened a wrinkle in her skirt and waited for the sheriff to continue.

"Miss Serenity, what were you doing down by the lake last night?"

The girl lifted her tear-filled eyes and batted her lashes prettily. "Do I have to tell him, Papa?"

Her father nodded.

"My father and I had a disagreement at the dinner table and I needed someone to talk to, so I went to see Aunt Fay."

"Aunt Fay?"

"Yes. Mrs. Cunard, next door."

The sheriff cleared his throat. "Go on."

"By the time I returned home, it was dark, so I went by way of the road instead of going through the woods." Serenity twisted the linen handkerchief in her hands.

"How did you get to the lake?"

"Sheriff, did I do something wrong? I was hardly trespassing. The lakefront is my Papa's property."

"That's right, Sheriff." Her father interjected. "My daughter can walk down to our private beach anytime she pleases."

"Sir, please," the sheriff growled, "let your daughter explain why she would detour to the beach instead of going straight home."

Serenity took a deep breath before speaking. "It's very simple. I was almost home when I heard something in the brush. I became frightened and started to run. It was Onyx, our dog, but I didn't know that until he chased me and I fell."

"Yes, go on."

"When I got to my feet, Onyx ran into the woods and I followed him. We ended up on the beach."

The sheriff narrowed his eyes. "Hmm. Did you see any strangers down there?"

Serenity breathed a sigh of relief. She wouldn't have to mention Abe. "Yes, I did."

Samuel leaned forward, his body tense, the muscles in his jaw flexing. The sheriff's eyebrows raised. "And?"

"And what?"

"Who did you see?" The sheriff looked like he might pop a blood vessel.

"I don't know. They were strangers."

The lawman closed his eyes and steadied his breath. In condescending tones, he asked, "Can you describe the strangers?"

"Oh, yes." Serenity's eyes brightened. "The two men were dressed in dark clothes. They each wore felt hats—kind of like yours, Sheriff—and vests. They both wore vests."

"I don't mean—"

"They came by rowboat. I was so frightened, I screamed for help and tried to run." A coy smile formed at the corners of her lips. "My scream must have frightened them because they left in a hurry."

"And that's all? That's the end of your story?"

"Well, I didn't want to hang around to see if they would return." Serenity acted indignant.

Without warning, Josephine rose to her feet. The two men automatically did the same. "If that's all you wanted, Sheriff, Serenity and I have a busy day ahead of us. She's learning how to knit."

Flustered by the abrupt end to the girl's statement, the sheriff mumbled, "Yes, that will do."

"Wonderful!" Josephine clapped her hands delicately. "Come, child, we'll retire to the sunroom while these two gentlemen discuss whatever business they must discuss."

Josephine took Serenity's hand and urged the girl from the chair. As the two women left the room, Serenity glanced over her shoulder at the sheriff and her father, both stunned and baffled at the abrupt change of events. Josephine stepped up the pace once they reached the hall. She didn't slow down until they closed the sunroom's door behind them. Once there, she leaned her back against the door and took a deep breath.

Serenity covered her mouth to suppress a giggle. "You were terrific."

Josephine's eyes twinkled. "A little trick I learned from your mother. She could use arrogance and humility better than I can use my knitting needles, and I'm a master at knitting!"

"Well, thank you. I was so afraid he'd ask me questions I couldn't answer without hurting someone."

"I know all about it. It was the underground movement that brought your mother and me together in the first place. My townhouse in Albany and my summer place in Saratoga have been used as stations for years." She paused. "I know you don't like me. And maybe I shouldn't tell you this, but my mother's grandfather was the son of a slave woman and a plantation master in Alabama."

Serenity stared in disbelief. The woman standing before her was blonde with blue eyes; her features aquiline. Her skin was porcelain white. "I never would have guessed." She thought of her own ebony curls.

Josephine laughed. "Mulatto? It's all right. When my mother reached her teens, my grandmother sent her away to New York to work in the home of a relative of the plantation owner. She never told anyone that she wasn't completely white, including the man she married, my father. When I was born with blonde hair and light complexion, my mother saw little reason to reveal her heritage." The woman's eyes became glassy with tears. "Daddy was a Dutch businessman in New York City. He loved her very much. He died of influenza when I was four."

"How did you find out about—"

"About my origins?" She smiled. "When I became a teenager, I had a friend from Georgia. Alexander was apprenticed to our family lawyer. He'd studied at Harvard." She moistened her lips. "He had strong opinions regarding the Negro race and their purpose for being on this earth. After meeting Alexander and hearing his bigotry, my mama decided to tell me about my great-grandfather."

Serenity's eyes widened. "What did you do?"

"I cried. I cried for days, in fact. Then I told Alexander and he broke off our engagement." The woman smiled weakly. "I hated my mother for telling me the truth."

"Oh!"

"It wasn't until she died—I was about twenty-one— that I realized my mistake. That's when I got involved in the slavery movement, and that's how I met and married Mr. Van der Mere."

"And my mother?"

"Yes and met your mother. We were both active in the Capitol Hill Quilting Society. They make and sell quilts to aid the cause to abolish slavery."

"Mama's quilting bee? The one here too?"

"I'm afraid so."

The French doors suddenly swung open. Serenity's father, a wide grin on his face, strode into the sunroom. "He's gone. Did you ladies hornswaggle him! Remind me not to stand on the other side of the state assembly aisle from you two."

Serenity threw herself into her father's arms. "I was so scared I'd say the wrong thing and give those people upstairs away to the sheriff."

He laughed. "Oh, don't worry about them." He gestured with his eyes. "They're long since gone. Caleb rustled them out of here before dawn this morning. Now, Serenity honey, do you have any questions for your dear old father?"

She thought for a moment. "Yes. The day Caleb man-handled me in the stables—"

Samuel laughed. "You were headed for the tackroom where Caleb had hidden fourteen runaways. With all the hubbub that day, we figured they would go unnoticed there. And we were right, except for your unexpected visit."

"I went to free Onyx," she explained.

"I know. But what you don't know is that dog is a vital member of our team. Caleb has trained him to do all sorts of things."

"Like recognize the 'Drinking Gourd' song?"

Her father nodded and laughed. "That's why he charged at you last night. He was trying to round you up and take you to safety."

"And that's why you let him run free some nights."

"Right. Now you know why you've run into poor Caleb so many times. Annie tried to warn us that you'd catch on, but we didn't listen."

"Annie's in on this?"

"Very much so. Sometimes she's a conductor."

"Taking the runaways to the next station," Josephine explained. "I trained your mother and she trained Annie. I started out as a conductor myself."

Serenity staggered to the rocker and sat down. "I can't believe it! All this was going on and I didn't even know it!"

"Honey, we are but one of many stations all the way between Louisiana and Canada," her father explained. "The Quakers, like your mother's family; free-born Negros; and many white people risk their lives regularly to keep the escape route alive."

"I know! I've heard of the underground railroad. It's been in use some twenty years, I'm told. But why us? Why must we be a part of this illegal activity?"

"Your father tried to protect you from knowing." Josephine placed her hand on Serenity's shoulder. The girl shrugged away her touch.

"Now that I know, what happens? I'm not sure I want to be a part of it. I have a serious problem, Papa, knowing you are breaking the law." Serenity's fingers tapped out a rhythm of frustration. Then she heard Eulilia's words coming from her own mouth. "After all, the slave owners have rights too. They paid good money for their slaves."

Samuel looked at Josephine in surprise, then back at his daughter. "But they didn't have the right to buy them in the first place."

"According to our laws, they did."

"But according to God's law—"

"I know, God's law takes precedent over man's. But, does not God's law command us to tell the truth and not steal? You wanted me to lie to Sheriff Broderick today, if necessary, didn't you?"

The man shrugged. "A lie wasn't necessary, was it?"

"That's not the point, Papa."

Josephine squeezed the girl's shoulder. "This is all so new to you, Serenity. You need time to think about all that's happened."

Serenity looked up into the woman's face and gave her a weak smile.

Samuel paced across the room. "What happens from here on out, until you make up your mind?"

Serenity brushed a curl from her face. "I won't give you away, if that's what you mean. But I don't want to know anything about your illegal activities either."

"I think I can live with that." Her father turned to leave, then paused. "Oh, yes, and don't forget our discussion about treating Josephine more respectfully."

Serenity glanced at the woman and smiled a timid smile. "Yes, Papa, I promise to be nicer to everyone from now on." She cast him a coy smile. "At least, I know the 'night sounds' aren't ghosts and goblins anymore. Somehow, though, I almost wish they were."

~22~

Secrets Revealed

 A NEW DAY! SERENITY FLUNG OPEN THE French doors and stepped out onto the balcony, her mother's Bible tucked under her arm. She felt so much better after talking things out with her father. But while she wished he wasn't involved in the underground railroad and wasn't marrying Josephine, at least they'd agreed on a truce. She'd always been "Daddy's girl" and didn't want that to change. *Maybe that's part of my problem,* she thought. *Maybe I'm afraid he'll love her more than me.* Aunt Fay's words entered her mind. "God created us to love and love and love. And each love is different; not more, not less, just different."

Serenity trailed her fingers along the balcony railing. *The woman really isn't that bad a person,* she admitted. *Actually, I can see why Mama enjoyed her company. But Papa, why Papa?* Then her logical mind rejoined. *And why not Papa? He's honest, prosperous, and handsome, I suppose.* She'd never before thought of her father from a woman's perspective. "Yes," she mused, "I can see why Josephine is attracted to him, mustache, beard, and all. And God only knows, the woman's wealthier than the queen of England. She certainly isn't after his money."

Wandering back into her room, she pulled her boudoir rocker over near the French doors and sat down to read her mother's Bible. "Let's see," she mumbled, "Matthew, Mark, Luke . . ." She flipped through the gilt-edged pages. "Hmm, where shall I begin?" She paused at the first chapter of Luke. "Forasmuch as many have taken in hand . . ." She hurried through the first four verses of the book. ". . . There was in the days of Herod, the King of Judea, a certain priest . . ." Quickly, she became engrossed in the story of Zecharias and his wife, Elizabeth. "Imagine," she muttered, "an angel. I wonder what an angel might look like?"

She continued reading. "And in the sixth month the angel Gabriel was sent from God unto a city of Galilee, named Nazareth, to a virgin espoused to a man whose name was Joseph, of the house of David; and the virgin's name was Mary."

"Mary . . ." The name sparked Serenity's imagination. She tried to picture the young woman. *Were you my age? Maybe younger? Did you have black hair like me or was it brown? Blond? No, not blond. The Jewish people I met in Albany were seldom blond.*

She'd heard the story before, every Christmas, in fact. But she'd never thought about it away from the event of the Christ child's birth. *I wonder what Mary was doing when the angel appeared to her?* She thought about all the simple tasks she'd been learning during the last few weeks. Washing and ironing, baking, canning early peas, and making strawberry preserves—it felt good to be useful. She glanced down at her hands. True, they weren't as soft as they'd been when she was at school. *I need some of that French lotion Eulilia uses.*

She rested the open book on her lap and leaned her head against the back of the rocker. She set the rocker to rocking.

Her thoughts returned to the birth of baby Jesus. She imagined Mary seated, much like herself, in a chair holding her baby. After several minutes, she opened her eyes and resumed reading.

"And the angel came in unto her, and said, Hail, thou that art highly favored, the Lord is with thee; blessed art thou among women." A smile spread across Serenity's face. "Highly favored, imagine having the God of the entire universe send a message like that! Highly favored, the Lord is with thee." *What I would give to know for sure that the Lord is with me!* she thought. *Now that Papa has Josephine, I'm alone.* Her eyes misted. *It's like I don't belong anywhere—here, at school—anywhere. And how at home will I be in Josephine's Albany mansion?*

"Dear Father in Heaven, I know I'm not worthy, like Mary, to be considered highly favored by You. I don't ask to be blessed more than other women or singled out for a special mission, but I need to know You're with me. My life seems tilted, out of sorts, ever since Mama died." Her voice caught. "I need something or someone I can count on. Aunt Fay says that You promise to be with Your children. Yet I don't feel Your presence. How can I know for sure You're with me?"

The clop of horses' hooves on the brick roadway in front of the house interrupted her prayer. She rose from the rocker, ran to the far end of the balcony, and peered around the corner of the house. She spied Caleb Cunard's brown suede hat and jacket.

He caught her movement out of the corner of his eye. Turning in her direction, he grinned and tipped his hat. "Good morning to you, Miss Serenity."

Color rushed to Serenity's face. Flustered at being seen

and uncertain why, she ducked back into the shadows. "That was juvenile of me." *Why do I always act like an immature child whenever that man is around?* Disgusted, she returned to her room and placed the Bible on the night-stand. She took the back stairs to the kitchen.

Always before, when she entered the kitchen, Serenity sensed that the staff stopped their conversation. This time they acknowledged her arrival, then continued their discussion about the previous night's events. She was surprised to discover that the servants didn't all agree on the issue of runaway slaves. Pearl and Jasmine, two of the younger and newer servants, were very vocal about their views.

"Why should our lives be placed in jeopardy for these runaways?" Pearl asked. "Every time a group of them passes through here, we are all at risk."

"I agree." Jasmine carried a fresh pot of hot water to the sink and dumped it into the dish pan. "It's not that I don't feel for their plight, I really do. But that doesn't mean I want to risk everything I've got for people I don't even know."

One glance at Gloria, and Serenity knew the older woman was about to blow. "How very nice for the two of you to have fallen into such a comfortable situation here at the Pownells. Not everyone is as lucky as you, you know. You were both born to free Negroes employed by the Pownell family, which was not of your doing, I might remind you." The woman's eyes flashed with fury. "Take Annie, here, and Dory, and half the stable hands, for that matter. If the Pownells hadn't come along, who knows what would have happened to them by now?"

Deciding that the kitchen was not where she wished to be, Serenity headed toward the back door. "And you, missy," Gloria called after her. "You did a mighty brave thing last night. I'm glad to see that your mother's mercy is runnin' through your veins."

Serenity smiled and simpered, "I just did what had to be done. The baby . . ."

"That's right! The baby. Would you two girls have had the bounty hunters snatch that infant from its mother's arms and beat the mother into submission?"

The screen door slammed closed behind Serenity. She broke into a run. She rounded the corner of the house when Onyx caught up with her. "How're ya' doin', boy?" She scratched him behind his ears. "So you're a conductor on the underground railway too? What other tricks do you have in your cache?"

The dog, trying to please, bounded ahead and leaped at a low-flying butterfly. Doing a half twist mid-air, he ran back to her for praise. She patted his head and laughed. "All right, show-off!"

A week passed before she heard the night sounds again. This time when the voices and the scraping on her wall awakened her, Serenity closed her eyes and prayed for the runaways' safety. Lying awake, she listened and wondered. *How many people are hidden in the attic tonight? Are there children? Babies? Girls, maybe my age?* The face of the young mother filled her mind. She thought of the young Mary giving birth to the Son of God, miles from home and family. The frightened face of the runaway replaced the Jewish girl's peaceful one.

Serenity tried to shake her mind free of the images. The words, "And there was no room in the inn," echoed through her thoughts. She rolled over and punched her down-filled pillow with her fist. "Dear God, is it my responsibility to rescue all of the world's oppressed peoples?"

A tear of self-pity trickled down her cheek. *It's not fair, Lord. Look at my friend Eulilia. She has a perfect life, nothing goes wrong in her family. It's just not fair!* She forced herself to close her eyes and repeat a verse she'd discovered and memorized that morning. "Thou wilt keep him in perfect peace whose mind is stayed on Thee." She fell asleep repeating the promise.

Serenity set aside a part of each day to trek down the path through the woods to the Cunard home to read the Bible with her Aunt Fay. In the evening she discussed what she'd learned with either Annie or Josephine, sometimes both. Josephine especially was eager to learn more about God. Once Serenity invited Josephine to go with her to see Aunt Fay, but the woman declined. Secretly, Serenity was glad. She didn't want to share Aunt Fay with anyone.

Some evenings, Serenity and Josephine would meet in the parlor to "knit," after Samuel adjourned to the library to take care of business matters. One evening in particular, as Annie sat by the fire and mended stockings, Serenity asked Josephine a question that had been nagging her for some time. "Why does religion bother my father so?"

The woman pursed her lips. "I think it's not religion so much as the idea of letting go and letting God control his life. Your father is a strong man. Trust doesn't come easily for him."

"Mistress Charity, oops!" Annie's hand flew to her mouth. "Begging your pardon, ma'am. I mean Mistress Josephine . . ."

"That's all right," Josephine assured her. "Mistress Charity was my friend too. Just because I am marrying her husband doesn't change that."

Annie swallowed hard, then continued. "Mistress Charity used to tell Dory that God would need to use an earthquake or fire, like He did for Elijah, to get Master Pownell's attention."

Serenity's needles clicked, causing her to drop a stitch. "That's an awful thought!"

Josephine chuckled aloud. "She was speaking hypothetically, I'm sure. Besides, I believe God finally reached Elijah with a still, small voice."

"Oh, that's good." Serenity sighed with relief. "The last thing this family needs is more tragedy."

They ended their study early that night. Samuel had promised to take Josephine and Serenity to Syracuse for a mid-summer shopping expedition the next day, and while Samuel also had important business in the big city, Josephine needed to check on the *Silver Garnish* and its crew.

Annie followed Serenity up the stairs to her room and helped her unbutton the long row of tiny bone buttons down the back of her dress. "What's it like in Syracuse?" The servant girl asked.

"You've never been to Syracuse?"

The girl shook her head.

"It's nothing much, really, not at all like New York City and Boston. Now, they're cities!" Serenity's eyes sparkled with excitement. "There are dress shops everywhere, and curio shops, and sweet shops with the most luscious candies imaginable, especially marzipan! I love marzipan." She could almost taste the sweet confection on her tongue. As Annie undid the ties on Serenity's corset, Serenity unfastened the pins holding her ebony hair in place. Her heavy mass of curls tumbled down around her shoulders. "And the divinity fudge in New York is heavenly."

Annie giggled. Serenity looked at her quizzically.

"Divinity—heavenly?"

"Oh, that is sort of funny." She piled her hair on top of her head, allowing several of the tendrils to cascade around her face. "How do you think this hairdo might look at my father's wedding?"

"Fine, if you want to resemble one of those loose women King Solomon was always warning young men about."

Serenity huffed, released the bulk of her hair, and straightened her shoulders in disgust. "Loose curls do not imply loose morals!"

"Maybe so, maybe not," Annie replied, grabbing up the hairbrush and drawing it through the tangled mess.

Serenity grimaced to herself. Nothing she might say or do ever swayed Annie from what she believed.

"So, what else will you see in Syracuse?"

"Canals, factories, I don't know, lots of things. Hey, why don't you come with us? I'm sure Papa won't mind."

Annie looked startled. "Really?" Her face fell. "Oh, I don't think Pansy will want me to go. I'm suppose to help her beat the rugs tomorrow."

"Beat them the next day instead. What's the difference? I think it's a jolly idea for you to accompany Josephine and me." She studied her face in the mirror from several angles. "Hmm, do you see any wrinkles around my eyes?"

Annie shook her head.

"Perhaps we will go to one of the little English tearooms on Main Street and eat shortbread cookies." Serenity paused for a moment. "Actually, I don't remember if Syracuse has any English tearooms. Oh, well, whatever they have, I'm sure we'll enjoy the trip immensely."

Annie laughed and tugged the brush through a difficult snarl.

"Ouch! If you keep that up," Serenity snapped, "I'll be searching for a wig shop instead of a candy store."

With her hair braided and a nightcap restricting the long braid, Serenity climbed into bed and pulled the quilts up to her neck. "Oh," Serenity wailed. "I left Mama's Bible in the library. I wanted to read for a while before going to sleep."

"I'll get it for you." Annie turned toward the door.

"No, don't bother. I'm so sleepy, I don't think I could make much sense out of what I was reading. Thanks anyway."

"I'd be glad to—"

"No, really. I am very tired." She yawned and burrowed further under the covers. Annie started for the door.

"I would appreciate it if you opened the balcony doors. It's kind of stuffy in here."

Annie opened the doors a crack, then turned down the flame on the lamp beside the bed. "If there's nothing else, I'll say good night."

As the door closed behind the chambermaid, the room grew dark. Serenity let her mind wander through the day, then turn toward her Unseen Friend. "Dear Father, I have to admit, You are becoming more real to me every day. It's like Mama's Bible is a letter from You. But it's difficult for me to read it without Aunt Fay's help. Is that how Mama felt?" Serenity recalled a passage from her mother's diary. She'd been surprised to read of her mother's deep feelings about not having more children.

"Serenity is such a joy to Samuel and me. I'd love to have five more daughters like her, but God knows best. Of course, Samuel would enjoy having sons to carry forth the Pownell name, what man wouldn't? So far, it hasn't been in Your plans, has it, Lord?"

Serenity stared up at the darkened ceiling. *Mama actually believed that God had a plan for her life, even to the number of children she and Papa had? I wonder what His plan is for me? And how will I know it?*

She closed her eyes, recalling more of her mother's words. "Samuel couldn't love our little curly head more, but it would help dear Seri to have younger brothers and sisters as well. According to Doc Hanson, that's never going to be."

Serenity wondered what it would have been like having a baby brother or sister. According to Eulilia, they were, at the very least, a bother. *Eulilia, dear Eulilia.* Serenity drifted into a twilight type of a sleep, dreaming herself to be back at the finishing school in Boston.

Outside her dormitory room, she could hear the girls in physical education class, shouting and laughing. *What's so funny?* she wondered as she settled down to study her Latin. Suddenly, Eulilia burst into the room and began shaking her.

"Serenity, wake up! Wake up!"

"Go away, I've got to study this stuff! Amo, Amas, Amat . . ."

"Wake up! Serenity, you must awake!"

Serenity opened her eyes to discover Annie's dark, shiny face peering down at her instead of the blond Eulilia's.

"Huh? Oh! What? What's happening?" The light from Annie's lamp blinded her. She shaded her eyes with her arm.

The girl shook Serenity by the shoulders once again. "Miss Serenity, wake up. Something terrible is happening outside. Wake up!"

"Uh, oh, it's you." Then Serenity remembered the promised trip to Syracuse. "Did I oversleep?"

"No, no. Sheriff Broderick and his men are outside with two bounty hunters from Alabama. They're rousting everyone out of the servants' quarters, searching for the runaways. Please! You gotta' help."

"Bounty hunters?" The girl recoiled in terror. "Go get my father, not me."

The oil lamp in Annie's hands trembled. "I tried, but I couldn't waken him."

"What do you mean, you couldn't waken him?"

"I pounded on his door and no one answered."

"Well, there must be someone who can—"

"There isn't. Abe's leg is still mending and I don't know where Mr. Caleb might be at this hour."

"What about Josephine? She knows about this stuff."

Annie widened her eyes. "But she's a . . . a . . . a guest, Miss Serenity."

Serenity groaned, slid her legs over the side of the bed, and shoved her feet into her house slippers. "A guest more in touch with what's happening around here than I. Go waken her while I see about my father."

"Yes, ma'am."

Serenity drew on her robe and whipped out of the room into the hallway. "I'm sure my father's in there, just sleeping soundly. Mama always said he sleeps like a bear during hibernation and is about as friendly as one when disturbed."

She rushed down the dimly lit hallway and pounded on the door of the master suite. "Papa! Papa! Wake up." When no answer came, she pounded again. "Papa! You must waken—" She turned the brass knob and flung open the door. Light from the hallway shone on the massive master bed—it was empty. Serenity froze.

Hopefully he's just gone to see about the disturbance. She tightened the belt of her robe and hurried toward the stairs. At the landing she met Josephine and Annie. Annie had taken the time to light a lamp for Serenity. "Here, take this one." Annie handed a lamp to Josephine. "I'll go get another."

Josephine's pale face told Serenity the woman shared her apprehension.

"Where's my father?" Serenity demanded of the frightened woman.

"I don't know. How would I know?"

"Well, I just . . . I'm sorry. That was uncalled for." Renewed shouting outside spurred the women to action. They rushed down the staircase and out the front door onto the portico. The area in front of Abe and Dory's cabin was ablaze with flaming torches.

"Whatever is happening?" Serenity hissed.

Josephine took a deep breath. "I would assume the sheriff is searching for runaways."

"I don't know what to do. Where's my father?"

Josephine tightened her shawl about her body.

"Caleb! He'll know what to do." Serenity reasoned. "Annie, run next door to Reverend Cunard's place. Tell Caleb what's happening, and try not to let anyone see you."

Annie shot into the darkness. The two women looked at one other, each took a deep breath, then strode toward the torchlights. As she walked, Serenity's lips moved, but no sound came. A promise came to her mind as clearly as printed in her mother's Bible. "He that dwelleth in the secret place of the most High abideth under the shadow of the Almighty."

~23~

Through the
Flame

SHERIFF BRODERICK AND THREE OF HIS deputies stood, torches in hand, at the door of Abe and Dory's cabin. The two bounty hunters Serenity had seen by the lake completed the semicircle of torchlight. Dory stood in the doorway of her home, her feet planted and ready at any moment to swing the weapon in her hand—a kitchen broom. "Just what you doing here anyway?" The woman's ebony skin shone in the torchlight. Her customarily gentle brown eyes flashed with anger.

"Where's that husband of yours, girl?"

"In bed, where all decent husbands belong at this hour."

The sheriff extended his free hand toward the woman. "Look, we don't mean no trouble, here, girl." He clutched a piece of paper in his fist. "See this here paper? It's a writ that gives me permission to search these premises for stolen property." The sheriff waved the paper in the woman's face.

Behind her, the cabin door opened. Her son stepped out. "Mama, Papa says for you to come in. Don't make this your fight."

One by one, the servants from the other cabins silently surrounded the small band of law officers, their faces set, their eyes hard and ready to defend their homes if necessary.

The sheriff glanced about nervously. He recognized that he and his men were outnumbered. "Ain't no fightin' here, sonny," the sheriff explained. "Just step aside and let me do my job. These here men from Alabamy believe you might be harboring runaways. And I'm here to prove them wrong."

"This is not my property, Sheriff." Dory had regained her composure. "I need Mr. Pownell's permission to allow you to search any of the buildings on this estate."

"You may, but I don't." The sheriff waved the paper in the air. "The only permission I need is Judge Hargood's."

"Excuse me, Sheriff Broderick," Serenity's voice boomed loud and strong, much stronger than she felt. The men turned toward the voice. The servants parted to make way for the two women. "I understand you are here to see my father? Really now, did you expect to find him in the servants' quarters at this hour?"

"I did not come to speak with your father, Miss Serenity. I came to search your property, and that's what I intend to do."

Before Serenity could reply, Josephine pushed to the front of the crowd and gently placed her hand in the crook of the sheriff's arm. "But, of course, you did, Sheriff. But a gentleman such as you would always announce himself to the master of the house before he trespasses on his property. I'd very much like to see that writ, if I may." She urged him toward the main house. "Do you know that I have never before seen an official document like this? I would so much like to read it. . . ."

"You read?" The sheriff looked surprised.

"Not as well as you, of course, but I'm trying." She gazed up into his confused face. "I still have trouble sometimes with those big words, but I can manage my little romance novels, from the continent, you know."

She nestled close to the sheriff's arm. "Why don't you have your men search the outbuildings while I try to make sense out of this official document, over a cup of hot chocolate, of course?" She batted her eyelashes up into the sheriff's face. "I make the best hot chocolate west of Belgium."

Serenity stared in amazement as the woman skillfully maneuvered the lawman away from the conflict.

The sheriff stopped to give orders. "All right, men. You heard the lady. Fan out, check the stables, the barns, and the hay lofts for any strays that may be hiding. Don't forget the bunkhouse. And Johnsby, I will put you in charge of searching each of the servants' cabins."

"Please hurry, Mr. Johnsby. Our dear servants have a full day of work tomorrow. They need their sleep," Josephine cooed.

The young deputy named Johnsby tipped his hat toward Josephine and Serenity. "I won't be long."

Serenity nodded curtly. "Thank you, I appreciate that." As Josephine and the sheriff headed toward the main house, Serenity followed after the deputy, watching as he searched each of the servants' premises. His search was halfhearted at best. As they left the last cabin, the deputy apologized, "Sorry, ma'am, for the inconvenience."

Serenity studied his strong young face in the torchlight. "How can you do what you do? Turn helpless people over to those animals." She rolled her eyes in disgust.

Johnsby shrugged. "Bounty hunters are only men, trying to make a living just like me."

"But they're crude brutes dealing in human cargo."

He shrugged again. "Like me, they're just enforcing the law."

"The law? What kind of law terrorizes women and children in the middle of the night?"

Johnsby blushed. "I don't make the laws. I merely enforce them. That's my job. It's men like your father who make the laws in Albany and in Washington."

"Well, I, for one, do not appreciate what you do!" Serenity stopped at the first cabin and knocked on the door. Dory answered it immediately.

"Is Abe all right?" Serenity asked.

"He be fine once these hooligans leave us alone." Dory's eyes held malice in them as she gazed at the lawman, who stepped away from the house and waited to escort Serenity back to the main house.

With the deputy out of earshot, Serenity whispered, "Where's my father?"

The woman shrugged.

"Is there any chance the deputies will find anything tonight?"

"Not down here they won't."

"You mean?"

Dory nodded slowly, glancing toward the house and the darkened gable.

"Oh, dear God . . ."

"That's right, Honey, pray like you've never prayed before."

Suddenly a shout erupted from the stables. "Look! There goes one!" A shadow dashed across the lawn and around the side of the main house. One of the bounty hunters and the deputies broke into a chase toward the house.

"Annie!" Serenity whispered. "That was Annie!"

"Oh, dear Heavenly Father, no!" Dory clutched her hands together in an attitude of prayer.

"Onyx! Onyx! Where is that dog when you need him?" Serenity gathered the skirts of her night clothes and charged after the lawmen. She sensed Deputy Johnsby close behind, but she didn't slow to take a look.

She raced around the corner of the house where the lawmen had disappeared, stopping at the basement's open trap door. *Oh no!* Loud, angry voices were coming from the basement, along with Annie's terrified sobs.

Deputy Johnsby put out his arm to bar Serenity's way. "Ma'am, I wouldn't—"

"Then don't!" She pushed his arm aside and hurried down the stairs. She faltered when she saw the man she'd accosted on the beach. Red welts from her fingernails striped his bristled cheeks.

"Tell me." The man held his torch as close as possible to the lace on Annie's night cap without touching it. "Where'd those runaways go?"

As the man inched closer to the frightened maid, Serenity breathed, "Thou shalt not be afraid of the terror by night . . ."

The grizzled man leered in Annie's terrified face. "Or maybe, just maybe, you're one of 'em. Huh? Is that it? You're a mighty pretty—"

". . . or the arrow which flieth by day." Serenity marched across the basement and pushed the bounty hunter. "Sir, unhand my chambermaid this instant!" The startled man released Annie's arm. Serenity wrapped her arm about the girl. "Must be a boring business you're in, scaring innocent young girls."

The bounty hunter peered into Serenity's face. "I know you. You're the crazy lady from the beach."

"Crazy? Crazy? You think that was crazy! I can become a total lunatic when I lose my patience. And I must confess, I am feeling very close to . . . to—" She closed her eyes and weaved from side to side as if she were having a seizure.

"Miss Serenity!" Annie patted Serenity's cheek. "Are you all right?"

The man's eyes widened. He stepped back. "Keep this crazy lady away from me!" His elbow knocked several jars—including the jar of plums—from the shelf. Serenity caught her breath. The man examined the broken jar, then raised his torch to the spot where the plums had set. "Well, what do we have here?" He grinned toward Serenity, then pulled the leather strap. The latch snapped open. "Hmm, interesting! Get over here Peters, and give me a hand."

Serenity stared in horror as the two men slid the canning shelf to one side. The bounty hunter shined his torch in the hidden stairwell. "My, oh my." A look of triumph spread across the man's face. "Papa's going to eat well tonight!"

"Ma'am . . ." Johnsby grasped Serenity by her upper arms. "Please come upstairs with me. It could get ugly down here."

Serenity whirled about to face him. "Ugly? What do you mean? I won't leave without Annie."

At the mention of the servant girl, the bounty hunter whipped about and grabbed Annie's upper arm. The girl squealed in pain. "This little gal's coming with me. You don't think I'd be stupid enough to go up those stairs first, do you?"

Serenity gasped, "Let her go!"

The bounty hunter peered into Serenity's face and grinned. "You ain't in no position to make demands, missy, not if this hideout is what I think it is."

Bad breath caused by the man's rotting teeth hit Serenity full face. She grimaced and backed away. "What's the matter, missy? Not so brave now, huh? The little kitten's got her nails clipped!" He released Annie from his grip and lifted his hand to slap Serenity across the face, only to have the vice-like grip of Deputy Johnsby grasp his wrist.

"I wouldn't do that if I were you." Johnsby eyed the bounty hunter for several seconds, each man considering his next move.

"Yeah! Well, we've got more important fish frying in Denmark." He shoved Annie toward the passageway. "Move, girl! Get up those stairs!"

"No!" Serenity grabbed Johnsby's arm. "Stop him! Don't let him hurt her."

Johnsby signaled for the man called Peters to follow the bounty hunter up the stairs. "You men, keep him in line. Don't let him hurt that girl."

The two deputies nodded and disappeared up the darkened stairwell behind the bounty hunter.

"And now, Miss Pownell, I think it best we go upstairs to where the sheriff and your house guest are, um . . ." He gestured toward the staircase leading to the kitchen. ". . . sharing hot drinks."

Serenity glanced over her shoulder at the hidden stairwell. Her steps faltered. The deputy took her arm and assisted her up the stairs to the kitchen.

The sheriff looked up from his cup of hot chocolate as Serenity and Deputy Johnsby entered the kitchen. A mustache of creamy milk chocolate rimmed the full mustache of hair above his lip.

"Sir," Johnsby started, "one of the bounty hunters uncovered a hidden staircase in the basement. He took one of Pownell's maids with him. I don't trust that man."

Josephine, who'd been standing in front of the iron cook stove, gasped. The mug she'd been filling slipped from her hand and crashed to the floor, splashing the hot liquid on her robe and feet. She screamed.

Instantly, the sheriff rushed to her aid. Serenity ran to

the pantry for a clean rag to mop up the spilled drink.

"Go!" the sheriff shouted at Johnsby. "Don't leave him alone with any of them blackies or we'll have another crime on our hands."

"I sent Peters and Wilson with him," Johnsby explained.

Suddenly a woman screamed. *Annie!* Chills skittered down Serenity's spine. She lunged toward the kitchen stairs. Johnsby grabbed her arm, then ran past her through the open door. The sheriff bounded down the stairs after him.

"You ladies stay put!"

Serenity and Josephine shot one another a look, then dashed down the stairs after the lawman.

At the foot of the stairs, Johnsby turned and shouted, "I thought I told you—"

"Who are you to tell me what I can and can't do in my own house?" Serenity countered. A second scream came from the attic. Serenity pushed against the lawman's chest. "Let me past!"

The man grabbed her wrists. When the sheriff opened the secret door, a wave of smoke gushed into the basement. "Fire!" he shouted, choking on the smoke. "Fire!"

At the same moment boots thundered down the hidden staircase and two deputies emerged through the doorway, coughing and gasping for air. "Fire! Sheriff, that crazy bounty hunter torched the hay!"

"Oh, no! Oh, please God, no! Annie! Where's Annie?" Serenity darted up the stairwell.

"No! Miss Serenity, no!" the sheriff cried, lunging for the girl's waist. He caught her on the first step.

Serenity kicked, screamed, and flailed her fist at the lawman. He danced about to avoid the blows. When he tried to catch one of her flailing hands to restrain her, she grabbed his hand and sank her teeth into the side of his thumb.

"Yeow!" In the instant he relaxed his hold enough to acknowledge his wound, Serenity broke free and dashed for the stairwell only to come face to face with Deputy Johnsby who had Annie cradled in his arms.

Serenity saw her friend's pain-distorted face and cried. She looked at the girl's burned hands.

"I tried to put out the fire, honest I did," Annie moaned.

Johnsby pushed past Serenity toward the trap door. "Let's get her out of here."

Serenity shot a quick glance about the burning attic. The loose hay had ignited the rafters, flames skittered across the heavy oak floor gobbling everything in their pathways. *What about the cargo? Where are the runaways?*

The sheriff and his two deputies grabbed several gunnysacks and began fighting the fire. "You two women get out of here! Go with Johnsby." The deputy carried Annie from the burning building. The women followed.

They ran to the side lawn where Deputy Johnsby had gently placed Annie on the grass and then had returned to the house. Serenity stood helplessly watching Annie roll on the grass in agony. Josephine knelt beside the girl to comfort her. Behind them, someone rang the fire bell on the stable wall and shadows bearing water buckets raced toward the burning building. Dory appeared. She and Josephine carried Annie to Dory's cabin.

Serenity stood motionless, watching the yellow flames dance against the evening sky. Suddenly she stiffened. "Mama's Bible!" she gasped. "In the library!" She darted for the front portico. As she bounded up the steps, her boot caught the hem of her nightdress and ripped a portion of the skirt from the bodice.

Serenity ducked inside the house. She ignored Deputy

Johnsby's shout. She had only one thing on her mind—her mother's Bible. Covering her mouth with a portion of her torn skirt, she ran through the smoke-filled entry and into the library. She felt her way across the room to the chair where she'd been reading earlier in the day. Blindly, she ran her fingers over the brocade-covered chair.

"No!" she wailed. Someone had moved the book. Tears streamed down her face, "Oh, dear God, how will I ever find Mama's Bible in all this smoke? I've lost so much. Please, I can't lose this last connection with Mama as well. If You'll help me rescue Mama's Bible, I'll give my life to You!"

Serenity slid her hands along the arm of the chair to the lampstand. She followed the curve of the arm until she felt the side table's smooth surface. Her heart leaped when her fingers rested on the nubby texture of leather. The Bible! She grabbed the book and three of her mother's journals that lay beneath it. "Thank You," she gasped and rose to her feet.

Now, how do I get myself out of here? The library door should be right over here. Her free hand slammed into the marble mantle, her boot stubbed against the hearth. Stunned, she shook her head. *This shouldn't be here. I'm completely turned around.* She held onto the mantle for a moment to regain her bearings. "If I am facing the fireplace, the door will be behind me and toward the right. Yes, that's it."

Whirling about, she took a step and ran into the sofa. "No!" she gasped, staggering in confusion. "Where am I?" As she righted herself, she tripped over her torn skirt. Both she and the books fell to the floor. "No," she cried as the books flew from her hands.

Heavy smoke billowed in from the hallway. Her lungs ached with every breath. For the first time since she'd entered the burning building, Serenity considered the possibility that she might not escape alive. "No! Oh, God, please, no!" Frantically, she ran her hands across the Persian carpet. Her left hand brushed against the edge of one of the journals, then another and another. Finally she found the Bible.

Pressing the books to her chest, she scooped up her skirts in her free hand and once again tried to find the door, only to slam into another wall. She dropped her skirts and felt along the chair molding to a picture frame. *A picture frame?* Her mind reeled in confusion. *There are no pictures hung near the doorway!*

The smoke above her head thickened. She coughed, then dropped to her hands and knees where it was easier to breathe. *I'm going to die in here, Lord. I'm going to die!* The idea frightened her. "Oh, God, I said I could do this myself. I admit it! I can't. I need You." The fire above her head roared, yet for Serenity it felt as if she were surrounded by silence, a calming silence. She felt a strange peace flood through her. Curling into a ball beside the baseboard, Serenity closed her eyes and prepared herself for death. *Is this how Mama felt the instant before she perished?* she wondered.

From somewhere in the turmoil, she heard Deputy Johnsby shouting her name. "Miss Serenity? Miss Serenity? Where are you?"

"Here! In the library," she called, rising to her feet. A wave of relief rushed through her. She would live, not die. The library door swung open bringing with it a wave of fresh air.

"Miss Serenity?"

"Deputy Johnsby? I'm right here." She reached out and grabbed the lapel of his jacket.

"Miss Serenity, thank God I found you! The fire's spread throughout this entire end of the house. The ceiling could collapse on us at any moment!"

She fell into his arms.

"What were you doing in here?" the man said, leading Serenity through the doorway.

"Mama's Bible. I came back for Mama's Bible."

"A Bible? Are you crazy?" He clutched Serenity's upper arms, nearly dragging her.

"It's all right. I found it. It's right here." She gasped for air, staggered, then swayed against the deputy's heavy woolen jacket. Deputy Johnsby caught her, scooped her into his arms, and dashed for the front door.

When they emerged from the burning building, a cheer went up. Dory rushed to Serenity, crying and scolding the girl. "That, missy, was a fool thing to do. If I hadn't seen you run in there, no one would have known what happened to you."

The deputy set her on the ground. Dory immediately knelt beside her and gathered her into her abundant arms. "Why in the world did you run into that burning house? Your mama would have been furious with you!"

"I know, but I couldn't lose Mama all over again."

The deputy hovered protectively over Serenity. She looked up into the lawman's smoke-stained face. She reached out her arm. "I'm sorry. I didn't mean to risk your life . . ."

He smiled down at her. "It was an honor, ma'am."

A dark figure lunged out of the shadows. "Are you all right, Miss Serenity?" Caleb Cunard bounded to a stop beside her. "That was one fool thing to do, you know, run into a burning house!"

Serenity bristled. "How in the world did you—" For some reason, she could take censure from the man who saved her life, but not from Caleb Cunard. "I am fine, thanks to Deputy Johnsby. Nice of you to ask."

Caleb shot a quick glance at the deputy, then back at Serenity. "Where's your father?"

"I don't know. We couldn't find him earlier."

Caleb frowned.

Johnsby brushed his hair back off his forehead. "Excuse me, miss. We need a bucket brigade!" He ran to join the neighbors and the servants fighting the fire. By now, Fay and the Reverend had arrived. Shouts and confusion filled the air. Horses whinnied as they were being led from the stables. Caleb waited until the deputy got out of earshot, then asked Serenity, "What about the cargo? Were they found?"

Serenity shook her head. "I don't know. But I didn't see any strangers come down the attic stairs."

"Good. Then that explains where your father must be— delivering the cargo to the next station. He must have gotten word that the sheriff and his posse were coming."

"But who? Who would warn him?"

"The night has eyes and ears. Now if you're sure you're all right, and not going to do anything foolish again, I'll go fight the fire."

Serenity watched him run across the lawn and join the brigade. Soon he joined the silhouette of Deputy Johnsby at the front of the line, tossing pails of water onto the ravenous fire.

Tiny sparks flew into the air, then cascaded down like fireflies on the band of fire fighters as they passed bucket after bucket of water. Serenity's throat was raw; her eyes smarted; her back ached; the muscles in her arms cried for relief, but she kept passing buckets of water. Blisters formed on the palms of her hands. Soot and sweat covered her face, neck, and hands. Her soiled and sweat-soaked robe hung in shreds, revealing large portions of the night dress beneath.

Suddenly a flash of lightning filled the sky. Thunder cracked. A cool drop of water pelted her nose, then a second. A cheer went up from the exhausted firefighters. Rain!

"Rain? Rain! It's raining!" She felt like dancing, but instead flung her hands wildly in celebration. Josephine joined her and helped her to her feet.

No one had noticed the summer storm gathering over the lake, but within a few minutes, the first few droplets of water multiplied into a driving rain.

"Isn't this utterly beautiful?" Serenity's skirts billowed as she tried to whirl across the lawn, but stopped abruptly when she found herself in Deputy Johnsby's startled arms.

"Miss Serenity!"

Stunned, she stepped back from the deputy, her face flushed with color. "I . . . I . . . I'm sorry."

A bemused smile crossed the lawman's face as he steadied her. "That's perfectly all right, Miss Serenity."

"I guess I became a little lightheaded."

He tipped his head toward her. "Glad to be of service."

Flustered, she turned and slammed into another chest, that of Caleb Cunard's. "Huh?" she said, startled.

Caleb glared at the deputy. "My mother sent me to fetch you home to rest. Who's your friend?"

"Friend?" She looked up at Johnsby. "Johnsby? I barely know him." She paused to note Caleb's set jaw. Whether from deviltry or design, Serenity slipped her arm in the crook of the lawman's arm. "Deputy Johnsby saved my life tonight."

"So I've heard," Caleb muttered.

"He was here when I needed him." She cast a saucy smile up at the deputy.

"Well, I'm here now." He reached for Serenity's arm. "I'll take care of Miss Serenity."

The lawman smiled. "I guess that's up to the lady, isn't it?"

Caleb's chin jutted forward. He started to speak, but was stopped when Serenity looked adoringly at the deputy. "That's all right, Mr. Johnsby," she cooed. "I'll go with Mr. Cunard. His mother is a dear friend of mine."

"If you're sure you'll be all right." The deputy looked uncertain.

"I'll be fine."

The lawman frowned. "Perhaps, in a day or two, I can come by to make certain you have recovered?"

She grinned up into his face. "Thanks for coming to my rescue tonight."

"Anytime, ma'am, anytime."

She slipped her arm from the deputy's to Caleb's. Caleb's body stiffened at her touch. He started toward the fence where he'd hitched his horse.

"Wait! My books!" Serenity slipped her arm from his and ran to the lilac bush where she picked up her precious treasure. She paused to bow her head. "Thank you for protecting my books, Heavenly Father. And please, please, be with Papa, wherever he is."

~24~
Into the Night

 "WHAT WAS THAT ALL ABOUT BACK there?" Caleb demanded as he helped Serenity mount his chestnut-brown mare. With one swift move, he leaped behind her onto the saddle.

Her nerves frayed and her patience exhausted, she whipped her head around, her wild windblown hair slapping Caleb across the face. "I beg your pardon?"

He pawed the heavy locks out of his eyes and away from his mouth. "It certainly looked like you and Johnsby were becoming quite friendly."

"Oh? Tell me now? How does one treat the man who saves one's life? I'm afraid I didn't learn the proper protocol for such a situation at Martha Van Horne's Finishing School for Young Ladies." She turned her face away from him, again whipping the tangled tendrils across his face.

"Will you stop doing that?"

She whirled her head around a third time and asked, "Doing what?"

"That!" He swatted the hair away from his face. "Come on, Lulabelle." He urged the horse into a trot.

"I'm sorry I am such an inconvenience to you!" Serenity sniffled and pulled away from his grasp.

He tightened his arm about her waist. "Sit still, woman."

"What else do I do to displease Your Highness?" Tears slipped down her smudged, tear-stained face.

"I'm sorry. Please don't cry." He wiped his hand across his face, trying to dislodge another swat of hair glued to his sweaty cheek.

"Ouch!" She yelped and grabbed for her head. "You're pulling my hair!"

"Sorry . . ."

He reigned in his horse at the edge of the woods.

"Why are we stopping?"

He slid off the horse and extended his hands toward her. "I want to apologize for my behavior back there around Deputy Hornsby. I don't know what came over me."

She allowed him to help her down from the saddle. When her feet rested safely on the ground, she expected him to release her. Instead, he held her for several seconds longer than necessary. She glanced up at him questioningly. He gazed at her. "Miss Serenity, I am sorry, but I have the strangest urge to kiss you."

Her jaw dropped open in surprise.

He released her as he would a hot stove. "I'm sorry."

Recovering from her surprise, Serenity shot him a coy smile. "Do you always apologize to the young ladies you intend to kiss?"

"No, ma'am—I mean I don't go around kissing young ladies, I assure you," he stammered.

"Well, maybe you should." Her eyes twinkled with deviltry.

"Is that an invitation?"

She batted her eyelashes and grinned. "If you have to ask, I guess you'll never know." Serenity giggled, then ran for the Cunard home.

Before her feet hit the porch, Caleb's ten-year-old sister Becca burst from the house. "Are you all right, Miss Serenity? Mama made me stay here and wait for Daddy while she went to fight the fire. Is she with you? She hasn't come home yet."

"Daddy's watching the embers for a few hours and Mama's helping care for Annie," Caleb said, heading for the barn. "The girl's hands were badly burned."

"Aaron went to help with the fire. Did you see him?"

"No, I didn't," Caleb confessed. "Take care of Miss Serenity." He hopped back into the saddle. "I've got some things to do."

Serenity and Becca climbed the steps to the porch. "I drew a hot bath for you, Miss Serenity," Becca said as she took Serenity by the hand. "Come on, Mama told me to add her special Italian bath salts to the water. The whole house smells like lemon-verbena!"

The idea of a hot steaming bath hastened Serenity's steps. As she shed her ruined night dress and robe, she caught a glimpse of herself in the mirror and gasped. Her two gray-blue eyes peered out of a blackened face. She touched her disheveled hair and brushed the back of her hand across her smudged cheek. *Deputy Johnsby saw me looking like this?* She giggled to herself. *Of course, he didn't look much better by the time I left him!*

Serenity stayed in the sweet-smelling water until it became tepid.

"Here's a nightgown of my mother's you can wear," Becca volunteered. The girl held out a voluminous white flannel nightgown, one with lace and tiny rose buds embroidered around the neck and cuffs.

"I remember this." Serenity took the garment into her

hands, lifting it to her nose. "I can almost smell the rose-wood it came in."

"I wondered if you'd remember." Becca smiled. "Mama stores it in the box."

"Of course I remember! My mother and I went shopping in New York City for this. We had a delightful time shopping together. She bought me a doll with long golden curls and a dress of pink satin." A wave of sadness brushed across Serenity's face. She cast a glance in the direction of her home. "It probably burned in the fire."

Rebecca bit her lip. "I'm sorry."

Serenity swallowed hard and nodded. She slipped into the nightgown, then climbed into Becca's rope-spring feather bed. Despite her concern for her father's whereabouts and the loss of her earthly possessions, Serenity fell into a dreamless sleep the moment she closed her eyes. She awakened sometime later to the sound of loud voices in the parlor.

"They're safe. That's the important thing. They're safe."

Papa's voice? Serenity sat up and gazed about the unfamiliar room.

Again her father spoke. "I don't care about the house. Houses can be replaced, people can't. Where's Josephine?"

"Mrs. Van der Mere chose to stay with Dory and care for Annie. My wife's with them."

The Reverend's voice? Nothing made sense to the disorientated Serenity.

"Why? What's the matter with Dory?"

"The bounty hunters caused such a fuss at not finding the runaways, the sheriff dragged Abe off to jail, broken leg and all. His way of pacifying them, I guess."

"Why Abe?

"Said he was the male in charge of an illegal operation."

"Hmmph! Illegal operation. That's presuming on fact not in evidence. Besides, Abe doesn't even live in the main house!"

Serenity's mind began to clear. She recognized her surroundings. Lacking a robe to cover her nightgown, she wrapped the bed quilt around her shoulders and padded barefoot to the bedroom door and opened it.

"Papa?"

"Serenity!" Her father took two long strides and scooped her up in his arms. "You're safe. I would have died if I'd lost you!"

"I'm fine, Papa."

He set her down and gazed at her for several seconds, gently caressing her face with his hand. "Oh, Puddin'-tuck, I am so proud of you. Caleb told me about your bravery. You are truly your mother's girl."

Her eyes filled with tears. "I was so worried about you."

"I know, it couldn't be helped. When I got word that the sheriff and his posse were coming I had to get the cargo out of the house and to the next station immediately. That's where Caleb found me. I came back as soon as I heard."

"Josephine was a big help, you know."

Samuel smiled. "She's quite a woman. Not your mother to be sure, but quite a woman in her own right."

"What happens now? The house is—"

"Don't worry about the house, darling. What I need to do is turn myself in to the sheriff. I can't let Abe suffer in my place."

"Papa! No! What will they do to you?"

"Oh, they'll shout a lot, lecture me on obeying the law, and levy a fine against me for harboring fugitive slaves."

"That's all? Are you sure? Those bounty hunters were really mad."

Her father grunted. "They were mad because they didn't get their payment for catching those runaways. Those men have no jurisdiction around here, or in the South, for that matter."

"Sir?" Caleb stepped out of the shadows. "The sheriff was pretty hot as well. I wouldn't completely trust him."

"Naw . . ." Samuel dismissed the suggestion with his hand. "I've known old Broderick since he went a courtin' Lucy, his wife. He gets fired up, but calms down quick enough." He shook his head, his eyes twinkling. "He's a good man, just don't tell him I said that."

Reverend Cunard laughed. "Sounds kind of like you and me, huh, Sam?"

Serenity's father laughed. "Now, Eli, you know how I feel about your Bible-thumping preaching. And besides, first you win over my wife, now my daughter? You are one dangerous man!"

The preacher snorted. "I'm not what's dangerous, it's this." He held up his well-worn Bible. "I think the power in this book scares you, Sam."

"Nonsense." The assemblyman waved him away. "I haven't time for the esoteric problems of first-century radicals. Got my hands full with modern ruffians."

"Same difference, wouldn't you say?" Eli Cunard strode over to the fireplace. "Maybe you'd find a few answers to your modern-day problems if you attended church once in a while."

Samuel Pownell picked up his hat from the kitchen table and rolled the rim in his hand. "Maybe so, Preacher. But for now, I got a job to do. Abe's been incarcerated too long on my account. I want to speak with Josephine before I turn myself in."

Caleb reached for the doorknob. "I'll accompany you, sir."

"Oh, Papa!" Serenity ran into her father's arms and buried her face in his suede jacket.

"No, son," Samuel said to Caleb as he stroked his daughter's hair. "You might be implicated in this as well. Eli, would you accompany me, as my pastor?"

Eli's bushy eyebrows shot into his hairline. "Your pastor?"

Serenity's father grinned. "But don't go getting your baptismal garb ready yet."

Eli Cunard slapped Samuel on the shoulder. "My robe's always ready. You just give me the word."

Serenity's father eased his daughter from his arms. "Now, I'll be fine. And I'll be out of jail in no time, you'll see." Still holding her hands, he turned to Caleb. "Caleb, I'm placing my most precious possession in your care. Don't let anything happen to her."

Caleb straightened his shoulders and nodded solemnly. "Yes, sir."

Reluctantly, Serenity released her father's hands. She followed him and the preacher as far as the porch. Streaks of pink and orange filled the eastern sky as the two men climbed on their horses and disappeared down the road toward the wafts of smoke still rising from the burned-out mansion.

Serenity turned and slowly reentered the Cunard home. Her eyes appeared gray and lonely. She sensed Caleb watching her.

"Perhaps you should try to get some sleep."

She sighed. "I suppose so."

"Look, if it will make you feel any better, I'll take you to see your father this afternoon, when I'm sure it's safe to do so."

"Really?" She turned and gave him a big smile. "Oh, I'd like that, Caleb. I'd truly like that."

A strange look passed over the young man's face. He was about to say something, but instead he cleared his throat and grabbed his hat from the rack behind the door. "I'll go find Ma and try to get you some clothes to wear." He glanced down at her bare feet. "Your feet must be freezing."

She looked self-consciously down at her bare toes.

"If you'll excuse me, Miss Serenity?" He turned to leave.

"Thank you for everything."

He glanced over his shoulder, nodded, then bounded off the porch. As he did, Onyx came trotting out of the woods. Before mounting his horse, Caleb scratched the dog's head. "Stay with her, boy."

A few hours later, Serenity awoke to find a brown, home-spun broadcloth dress laying across the foot of the bed, along with a pair of black-buttoned leather shoes and a plain, off-white slip and other necessary undergarments. She slipped into the undergarments, then into the heavy cotton stockings.

Examining the dress in the window light, she shook her head. *Even the uniform at school wasn't this ugly,* she thought. The roughness of the starched fabric scratched her skin as she lowered the outer garment over her head. Resigning herself to her fate, she buttoned the bodice. She wriggled a bit at the unaccustomed feel of the fabric on her shoulders and arms.

She glanced down at the Bible laying beside the bed. Picking it up, she opened to Psalm 136 and read, "'O give thanks unto the Lord; for He is good: for His mercy endureth forever.' All right, Father, I give You thanks for this dress, the slip, the shoes . . ." She wriggled her toes, then lifted her skirts. " . . . and these ugly stockings."

Laughing to herself, she opened the bedroom door. Fay stood in front of the fireplace, stirring something in the large iron stew pot hanging over the fire. Becca sat in the rocking chair beside the fire, darning socks. Fay smiled. "Well, you did manage to get some sleep, didn't you? I see you found the clothing Pansy sent over for you to wear?"

"Pansy? That was nice of her. I'll have to thank her later. What time is it?" Serenity glanced toward the mantle clock.

"About seven. I'm fixing a late breakfast for the men when they return from town. I'll bet you're hungry."

Serenity's stomach growled on cue. She crossed to the small window behind an oak reading desk. She brushed the yellow gingham priscilla curtain back with her fingertips. "How is Annie?"

Fay continued stirring the pot. "She was resting when Josephine and I left for home. She'll have to keep her hands bandaged for a few weeks until new skin forms. Probably she'll have scars the rest of her life."

"Oh, poor Annie! She doesn't deserve—"

"Good morning." Josephine stepped out of the master bedroom and stretched. Fay's abundant house robe wrapped around the tiny woman's waist and dragged on the floor behind her as she walked. She stretched and groaned. "I used muscles last night that I didn't know I had!"

"Me too." Fay massaged the middle of Mrs. Van der Mere's back with her free hand. "How are your hands?"

"Pretty sore. I imagine yours are, too, Serenity?"

"Yup. I have blisters."

"Becca, go into my room and get the petroleum jelly, please. It's the best stuff for healing blisters." Fay placed the wooden spoon on the spoon holder and wiped her hands on her red calico Mother Hubbard apron. "It could have been a lot worse last night than it was."

"Thank God, no lives were lost," Josephine said, then

thanked Becca for the jar and began rubbing the jelly on her hands. "Would you like some, Serenity?"

"Yes, please." She scooped a dollop from the jar and gently dotted it on the water-filled blisters. "Did you see Papa?"

"Yes . . ." Josephine cast a wary glance at the young woman.

"He's in jail?"

"I suppose so." The woman sighed. "Abe's oldest boy brought his father home before we left. The man's in a lot of pain with that leg. Riding to town and back didn't do much for it, I suppose." Josephine's stomach growled as she spoke. "Oops, excuse me!"

Fay laughed and waved them to the table. "Fresh baked johnny cake and barley stew should solve that problem. Becca, could you set the table for our guests?"

Josephine chuckled. "Guests? After all we've been through together, we're as good as family. Just where do you keep your flatware?"

"In the breakfront." Fay gestured toward the large oak cupboard. "I can't help but think we've not heard the last of those two bounty hunters. They've picked up the scent, and I doubt they'll let it go."

"You're right. This station is as good as closed," Josephine said. "Your husband and son will continue to be targets, though, along with Samuel and Abe. The bounty hunters won't let up." Josephine placed the appropriate flatware on the table beside each of the bowls and sandwich plates. "Have you thought of leaving the area for awhile?"

A shadow passed across Fay's brow. "Eli and I talked about it before he and Samuel left for town. He's been wanting to go to California ever since hearing the news of the gold find at Sutter's Fort. Obviously, like any sane wife and mother, I'd rather not."

Josephine nodded, but didn't comment. The women and the two girls sat to the table to enjoy the simple fare. They ate in silence for several minutes. The hot corn bread slathered with freshly made peachbutter melted in Serenity's mouth. And for a moment she could almost forget the troubles beyond the cottage walls.

~25~

Out of Control

"I WANT TO GO WITH YOU!" SERENITY stamped her foot at Caleb, who stood with his hand on the doorknob. "If you don't take me, I'll walk to town." She added.

Caleb chuckled. "Twelve miles is a pretty long walk."

"Aunt Fay, tell him! Make Caleb understand how important it is for me to see my father."

"Don't put me in the middle of all this." Fay threw her hands in the air and retreated to the dry sink.

Serenity turned toward Caleb. "Can't you see how important this is to me? He's the only family I have. Please, I beg you!"

Josephine touched the young man's arm. "I think we should take her with us, Mr. Cunard. I'd want to be there if I were in her shoes."

"But the jail is no place for a sensitive young lady," he defended.

"And what am I?" Josephine reminded. Caleb's face reddened.

"Sorry, ma'am. I didn't mean—"

"I know you didn't, young man, but I really do understand Serenity's position here."

"I just want to do what's best for her. Samuel put her in my charge, you know."

Serenity grabbed the calico bonnet Aunt Fay lent her and plopped it on her head. She whipped past Caleb onto the porch. "I'm hardly a child, you know!" Yet her dash to the buckboard—even Serenity had to admit—was hardly that of an adult. She plopped herself in the middle of the seat, determined that the only way Caleb would make her stay behind would be to bodily evict her.

The warm July sun bore down on the driver and two passengers as they crowded together on the wooden seat of the buckboard. Serenity sat with her arms squeezed to her sides like a daisy pressed between the pages of a book. She glanced at Josephine's strong, determined profile—a woman on a mission. The woman caught her eye and smiled.

Serenity returned the smile, then glanced sideways at Caleb. She studied his chiseled profile. *His jaw is too squared to be handsome,* she thought. *But I do like the dimple. And his ears, he has nice ears. But I don't know about the hair.* She'd seldom seen his straw-like brown hair. He always kept it hidden beneath his weather-beaten suede hat. *Eulilia thought he was quite dashing,* Serenity remembered. She narrowed her eyes and studied his bristled face.

"Any questions, Miss Serenity?" A teasing dimple appeared in his cheek. Serenity blushed and dropped her gaze to her hands folded in her lap, trying to ignore the chuckle that followed. She stole a glance toward Josephine and was relieved to find the woman gazing at a field of young corn plants they were passing. If the woman saw the exchange between Serenity and Caleb, she had the courtesy to pretend she didn't.

They arrived in Auburn at suppertime. The streets swarmed with people, most of them hurrying in the same direction. Caleb scowled. "This place should be empty by this time of day." He drew the buckboard alongside a tall, well-dressed businessman crossing the street. "Mr. Porter," he shouted. "What's up?"

The banker looked up at Caleb. "A mob is gathering at the saloon. A couple of rabble-rousers from Georgia are stirring up trouble. Been a good ten years since this town's seen a lynching."

"A lynching?" Serenity shot a frightened glance toward Josephine. Josephine's face remained set. Caleb shook the reigns, hurrying the horses toward the sheriff's office and town jail.

After helping the women from the buckboard, Caleb dashed inside. Serenity and Josephine ran to keep up. He burst through the door. "What's going on around here?" he demanded, pounding his fist on the large oak desk just inside the entry.

The sheriff, leaning back in his chair, ignored Caleb's thunder.

"Good day to you, Mr. Cunard. Surprised you got the guts to show your face around here after all the goings-on. We know you're up to your bootstraps in this mess. We're watching you, you know."

Caleb removed his hat and plunked it on the desk in front of the sheriff. "Banker Porter tells me those trouble-makers from the South are trying to foment a lynching mob." His eyes flashed with fury.

"Tempest in a teapot. I assure you, we have everything under control here." He waved a hand toward the three deputies across the room, cleaning their rifles. "And I got

Deputy Johnsby over at the saloon keeping an eye on the Southerners.

Noticing Josephine and Serenity standing in the doorway, the sheriff leaped to his feet and nodded. "Mrs. Van der Mere, Miss Pownell. I suppose you're here to see the assemblyman. He's just finishing his supper." The sheriff called, "Hey, Shepley, take the ladies back to Pownell's cell."

A lean, wiry man with a salt-and-pepper beard and mustache, stringy brown hair, and one bushy eyebrow straight across his browline, laid aside his rifle and rose to his feet. "Yes, sir! Be mighty proud to escort such purty ladies anywhere." Serenity shuddered when he winked and brushed against her shoulder as he passed.

The iron-barred door squealed in protest, then clanged against the brick wall as the deputy swung it open. "This way, ladies." Deputy Shepley's voice echoed off the brick walls as he led them down a narrow hallway lined with empty cells. He stopped and unlocked the door to her father's cell. Serenity rushed past the deputy and into the darkened cell.

"Oh, Papa, are you all right?" She threw herself into his surprised arms.

"I'm fine, dear, just fine." Seeing Josephine standing behind Serenity, he rubbed his beard. "Sure could use a good bathing, though."

Serenity clung to him. "I've been worried about you. Are you sure you're all right?"

"I'm fine." Gently setting her aside, he gathered Josephine into his arms. In a soft, concerned tone, he asked, "How are you doing?"

She smiled lovingly into his face. "About like you'd suspect. I'm worried about you."

"Porter says those two bounty hunters are stirring up trouble down at the saloon," Caleb said, striding into the cell and placing himself squarely between Serenity and the deputy. "I'm mighty worried this thing is going to get out of hand."

"Naw, they're a lot of hot air, that's all." Samuel linked his arm around Josephine's waist. Besides, the people of this county voted for me, they're not going to listen to a couple of Georgia crackers."

Caleb shook his head. "I hope you're right, but I'd feel a lot better if I could go down there and see for myself."

Samuel frowned. "I don't know if that's such a good idea. Your involvement in this movement is in question too. Your presence might be the trigger to incite a mob."

"Wait a minute." Josephine placed her hand gently on Samuel's chest. "Isn't the saloon two doors down from the telegraph office? What if Serenity and I strolled down that way? I still need to send a couple of messages to Albany, like we talked about earlier."

"You ladies can't enter a saloon!" Caleb looked horrified.

"No, but we can walk by it. It's surprising what one can overhear from the sidewalk. Besides, don't you gentlemen have lots of details to talk about while we're gone?" Josephine shot a wicked grin toward Serenity.

Samuel chuckled. "Sounds like you speak from experience."

She slapped him gently with her fingers. "Mr. Pownell! There are some things a gentleman may think, but not say!" To Caleb, she whispered, "I've been in this fugitive business a long time, successfully, I might add."

She turned to Serenity and smiled. "Are you ready?"

The girl's eyes brightened. "Yes, Ma'am!"

Her father studied her face. "Are you sure? Just yesterday, you didn't want anything to do with this business. And, by the way, where did you get that dress?"

"From Pansy." Serenity sashayed, as if to show off the latest frock from London. "Don't you like it?" She giggled. "It seems all my clothes were lost in the fire. As far as this ugly business is concerned, you have to admit a lot has happened in the last twenty-four hours."

"Everyone has been so wonderful to us," Josephine interjected, "supplying us with clothing, food, and shelter. I feel nothing but gratitude."

Samuel dipped his head. "I am soundly chastised for my insensitivity."

Josephine laughed and gave his arm a squeeze. "Actually these dresses are part of our disguise. No one will look twice at two housewives hurrying along the street at this hour." She gave Samuel a coy grin. "We'd better be going and see what we can sniff out." Josephine took Serenity by the arm and escorted her from the cell.

The ladies pranced through the office and out onto the wooden sidewalk. "Now, let's see . . ." Josephine paused, putting her finger to her lips. " . . . just where is this famous saloon?"

Serenity laughed aloud. "You don't know? I thought you had it all planned."

"I do," Josephine argued, "once you steer me toward the saloon, that is. But first, we need to buy a few things at this general store." She ducked into the store and Serenity followed. "I'd like two five-pound sacks of sugar, please."

Sugar? Serenity scowled. *What is she up to?*

While the storekeeper measured out the sugar, Josephine strolled through the crowded aisle to the back of the store where the dry goods were stored. "I also need two one-yard pieces of flannel."

The storekeeper hobbled over to the dry goods counter. "A yard each? Any particular color? We have pink, blue, yellow, white, and green."

Josephine sighed as if deliberating on color choice. "I'll take one yard of the yellow and a second of the blue. I always did want a son."

"A son?" Serenity whispered.

"Yes, little mommy!" Josephine giggled like a school girl caught playing a prank. She paid for her purchases and walked out onto the street. "Just in case one of the men from last night might think he recognizes us, we'll each be carrying . . ." She wrapped one of the sacks of sugar in the yard of yellow flannel and dumped it into Serenity's surprised arms. " . . . a baby! And what would you like to name your little one?"

Speechless, Serenity stared as Josephine wrapped the second sack of sugar in the blue flannel. Surprisingly, it did look like she held an infant in her arms when she was through. Josephine pulled the flannel back a bit and said, "Here, meet Herbert." With a little adjustment, Serenity's "baby" also took on the shape of a newborn.

"So, what's her name?" Josephine teased.

Serenity stared down at the lump of sugar in her arms. "A girl, I guess—Mergatroid. How do you like that name?"

Josephine laughed aloud. "The poor child!" Clutching the flannel-wrapped bundle to her chest with one hand and gathering her skirts with the other, she stepped her way across the muddy roadway. "You said the saloon is down this way?"

Serenity nodded and followed the woman's example, gingerly watching her step to avoid puddles and piles of horse manure. Josephine paused long enough to adjust the flannel over Serenity's bundle. "Better keep that blanket close to little Mergie's face or she'll catch a death of consumption!" The two women giggled. "I wouldn't hold her quite so tightly, you'll suffocate her."

Serenity glanced down at her "child" and found her smashed against her bodice in a death grip. "Oops! I guess I'm not used to this mothering thing."

"Hmmph! And I am?" Josephine skirted around a hitching post and stepped up onto the boardwalk. The two women strolled up the boardwalk, eyeing the swinging sign suspended over the open door to the Oaken Barrel Saloon. The sound of angry voices poured out onto the street. Above the general din, catchphrases caused Serenity to bristle.

"I wish I could go in there and tell those people a thing or two," Serenity muttered under her breath.

"Sh," Josephine hissed. "We're here to gather information, not take on the male population of Cayuga County." Josephine stretched her neck toward the doorway. "Listen . . ."

" . . .teach him a lesson."

"Even a state assemblyman shouldn't be above the law!"

"Aw, some fancy lawyer will get him off, mark my words!"

"Well I didn't vote for the varmint!"

"Me either."

The two women paused at one side of the doorway. They backed further away when the combined odors of stale pipe smoke, ale, and body odor accosted them. Posing, as if talking about their babies, Serenity and Josephine listened with keen interest to the happenings inside the saloon.

"He'll just pay the fine and go on breaking the law," someone cried.

"Like it or not, the law's the law!" someone else shouted.

A decidedly Southern accent shouted, "We could string

'em up—that'd send a message to other lawbreakers."

"Yeah," another male voice shouted. "Let's string 'em up!"

Other voices joined in the clamor. "String 'em up, teach 'em a lesson!"

Serenity shot a terrified glance at Josephine. Josephine put her finger to her lips. "Wait," she whispered. The woman inched closer to the opening and carefully peered around the edge of the doorjamb. She ducked back when a familiar figure strode from the bar, Deputy Johnsby. The two women pressed themselves against the rough-hewn wall and held their breath. From his determined stride, it was evident that Deputy Johnsby had other things on his mind and had not seen them. They watched him cross the street and disappear in the direction of the sheriff's office.

The women lingered several seconds longer as the most loquacious of the two bounty hunters continued stirring up the crowd's thirst for blood. They decided they'd heard enough when someone yelled, "Jake, go over to the livery and get us a rope!"

"Make it a thick one," someone shouted. The crowd laughed.

Josephine whirled about, scooped up her skirts, and started back across the muddy street. Her "infant" dangled from her left hand as she walked. Serenity's "baby" didn't fare much better as she ran to keep up with Josephine. With every step, the woman sputtered, "Why those wormy little toads aren't worthy to walk on the same sidewalk as your father! How dare they judge him!"

All Serenity could do is nod and hurry in her footsteps. By now, neither woman cared about the bundles they carried, nor did they notice the startled looks of female passersby.

Josephine sputtered all the way to the sheriff's office. She threw open the door; it slammed against the wall behind it. "Sheriff Broderick, we have a major problem on our hands."

The sheriff looked up from where he and Deputy Johnsby were talking. Deputy Johnsby looked startled, first at Josephine, then at Serenity, then at their burdens.

The sheriff drawled, "I am aware of the problem, Mrs. Van der Mere."

She stopped directly in front of the massive oak desk, her hands firmly planted on her hips and the "child" hanging suspended by the piece of flannel. "So, what are you going to do about it?"

"I've been working on it since before you arrived."

"Yes?" She nodded insistently. "Go on!"

Sheriff Broderick took a deep breath, obviously reluctant to share his strategy with this insistent woman. "Now, get a hold on yourself, Mrs. Van der Mere."

"I have a hold on myself. What I want to know is what kind of a hold do you have on those disgusting, unwashed cretins down there at the saloon? They're ready to riot!"

Serenity stepped to her side. "They sent some guy named Jake to the livery for a rope, sir."

The two lawmen looked at one another, then at the other deputies lurking in the gathering shadows of the office. The sheriff raised one conciliatory hand. "Ma'am, I am sure . . ."

"You are sure of nothing. You heard your own deputy's report. Those men are serious! They're out for blood."

"My men and I are ready for them." He gestured toward his deputies.

"Oh yes, I'm sure. Five of you against a mob of thirty or more enraged animals." Josephine paced across the floor, then back again. "Is Caleb Cunard still here?"

The sheriff shook his head. "No, I sent him on an errand."

She whirled about, pounding her pack of sugar on the top of the desk. "An errand? At a time like this?"

"Ma'am, I don't need to defend myself. I'm the sheriff of this county."

"Oh yes, you are the sheriff. And what kind of a reputation will you have if these hoodlums break in here and steal your prisoner, a state assemblyman, at that?" Blond corkscrew curls slipped free of the borrowed calico bonnet. She brushed them back impatiently.

Serenity watched the woman in awe. Where was that sweet-talking diplomat who lured the sheriff into the house for hot chocolate last night? Suddenly, the thought hit Serenity. *She really does love Papa. What a firebrand!*

Her respect for the widow continued to grow with every word Josephine spoke. As she studied the sheriff's beleaguered face and the pugnacious gleam in Josephine's eye, Serenity almost felt sorry for the sheriff. She swallowed the urge to giggle, in spite of the seriousness of the situation.

"Well," Josephine thumped the "baby" on top of the desk and turned toward the cowering deputies. The men stared at the inanimate bundle in horror, unable to erase their first assumption of it being a live infant from their minds. She huffed impatiently. "Where do you keep your extra rifles?"

"Ma'am?" The sheriff leaped to his feet.

"Please, spare me. My dearly departed husband taught me how to shoot, and my aim is a good as any man's in this room."

Deputy Johnsby glanced at the sheriff's ashen face, then at the tiny blond woman, whose face was filled with fury. "My, my, Mrs. Van der Mere, you are a woman of varied talents!"

Josephine closed her eyes and shook her head. "Please, spare me your admiration and give me a gun!" She turned to Serenity and added, "My husband believed it was as important for a woman to know how to handle a rifle as it was for her to handle a washboard." She paused and smiled wryly. "Of course, thanks to his wealth, I never needed to learn the latter."

"Mrs. Van der Mere," the sheriff rounded the desk slowly. "I can't arm a woman."

"Sheriff, if I must, I will go next door to the general store and buy my own rifle and ammunition. Or you can make it simple for all of us by allowing me to use one of those." She pointed toward the rifle rack behind his desk. "What will it be?"

The sheriff retreated behind his desk, admitting defeat. "Let her use the Springfield, Johnsby. Women! Next thing you know, they'll be wanting to go to work in the factories!" He slumped into his chair.

"Hmm . . ." Josephine paused a moment. "Interesting concept."

The sheriff glanced up at Serenity. "I suppose you want a gun as well?"

Horror swept across the girl's face. "Oh, no, sir. Not me! But I'll be glad to reload the rifle if that will help."

"That's a relief! At least all the women in this country haven't gone mad!" He caught the glare from Josephine. "Hey, Barrett, let's get a few lamps lit in here, at least until the mob shows up."

"Yes, sir." One of the deputies rose to his feet to carry out the command.

Suddenly the front door flew open, causing everyone to jump in fear. "I got it, Sheriff!" Caleb slapped a piece of paper on the desk. "Judge Hargood signed the release. He wants the assemblyman out of here before nightfall."

"Right—before nightfall! What does he think it is out there, dawn?" The sheriff held the paper up to the wall lamp. "This is a political hot potato," the judge wrote. "It won't sit well in Albany if a bunch of yahoos accost a state assemblyman, no matter what the man . . ." Color climbed from the sheriff's collar up his face. He finished reading the writ silently.

"He's right, Sheriff," Deputy Johnsby interjected. "This is one hot potato you don't need in an election year."

"Besides, Sheriff," Josephine smiled sweetly at the man. "The judge took you off the hook by signing that paper. No one can blame you for following the judge's orders." She batted her eyelashes several times. Neither Serenity nor the sheriff missed the irony of her behavior.

"Sheriff, we have no time to waste," Johnsby volunteered. "Give those numbskulls another hour swilling corn whiskey and it will be too late."

"The man makes good sense." Josephine arched one delicate eyebrow.

The sheriff leaned his elbows on the desk, his chin in his hands. "I gotta think."

"While you're thinking, can we go back and spend a few minutes with the prisoner?" Caleb suggested.

The sheriff waved them toward the iron-barred door. Johnsby jumped up, grabbed the iron ring of keys, and unlocked it. He gestured toward Serenity. "Come, Miss Serenity, I'll take you to your father."

She cast a quick glance over her shoulder at Caleb, then smiled at the young deputy. "Why, thank you, Mr. Johnsby. You are such a gentleman."

~26~

Terror by Torchlight

"Iron bars do not a prison make," Serenity mumbled as Deputy Johnsby led her past the empty cells.

"Excuse me?" he asked. "Did you say something?"

"Oh, uh, just recalling a little poem my mother once taught me."

"Here we are."

Samuel Pownell rose from the wooden slab of a bed as Deputy Johnsby unlocked the cell door. "Well?" he said. His visitors filed into the cell, their faces drawn and worried. "That bad, is it?"

"I'm afraid so." Caleb, hat in hand, worried the brim with his fingers. "Those two Georgia crackers are stirring up a ruckus down at the saloon. And you know the kind of ruffians who hang out there."

"Not the elite of Cayuga County, to be sure." Samuel laughed and slid his arm around Josephine's waist.

"This is not funny, Samuel," she scolded. "These men are serious. They're talking—" She paused unable to speak the words.

The man's face sobered. "A lynching? And what does my friend, the sheriff, have to say to all of this?"

"Judge Hargrove recommended he release you." Serenity's eyes glistened with hope.

"Well, regardless of the outcome, we have plans to make." He took both of Josephine's hands in his. "You, my dear, must do as we talked about—go to Albany and defend my case. Take Annie with you. I'm sure the doctors in Albany can help her more than old Doc Adams. Also, I'll need you to liquidate my assets, sell the townhouse, the stables, my carriage."

"Isn't that a little drastic?" Caleb interjected.

Samuel shook his head. "I don't think so. If the sheriff tries to fight off a mob in the mood for a hanging, chances are he'll lose. If he chooses to let me go, I am sure one of his stipulations will be that I leave the state, pronto." Samuel tightened his lips. "Either way, Josephine will be of more help in Albany than here."

"Whatever you think is best, Samuel." Josephine caressed the top of his hand.

"It's best, my love. The sooner you all get out of here, the better I'll feel." Samuel stared into the woman's tear-filled eyes.

He released Josephine's hands and gathered Serenity into his arms. "Caleb, I want you to get Serenity away from here as fast as possible." He took a deep breath, squeezing her tighter than she ever remembered him doing. "I don't know where I'll be. But I want you to vow before your God that you will care for my daughter, be her guardian, until either she marries or I return."

Serenity looked up in surprise. "Papa—"

"I would ask your father but his hands are full caring for your mother and the other children," Serenity's father continued, ignoring his daughter.

"But you asked Uncle Joel to be my guardian," Serenity protested.

"I've had second thoughts. My brother has had a streak of greed coursing through his veins ever since he was a young boy." Samuel shook his head. "I trust him with your life, but I don't trust him controlling your inheritance. So, Caleb, what'll it be? Can I trust you with my prized possession?"

Caleb straightened. His face hardened with determination. "Absolutely, sir. By God's grace, I will protect her or die trying."

Samuel reached out and took the young man's hand. "That's all I ask, son. I've asked Josephine to have the legal documents drawn."

"Pownell . . ." Sheriff Broderick strode into the cell. "We have a situation brewing here. After discussing it with the judge, we agree that the best thing for everyone concerned is get you out of here." He laughed nervously. "You've become a political liability, I'm afraid."

Samuel laughed. "You're speaking my language, friend!"

"The other deputies don't know it, but Johnsby has gone for a horse. You'll have to ride fast and hard while we try to hold off the mob. Get out of the state as fast as you can." His face sobered. "I'm sorry—I must put out a warrant for your arrest.

Serenity gasped. "No!"

"Thank you, Broderick." Samuel shook the lawman's hand. "I won't forget this."

The sheriff chuckled. "Actually, I wish you would. I can't believe I'm doing this." He glanced around the solemn gathering, then strode off.

"Oh, Papa, what are we going to do?"

Tilting Serenity's chin upwards until their eyes met, her father spoke in whispered tones. "Plenty. I have a very important task for you. There is a wooden cask hidden in the cave. You know the area by the 'prophet'?

"The prophet, sir?" Caleb asked.

"Yes, Serenity knows where it is." He glanced at Caleb, then returned his attention to Serenity. "Consider it your dowry, darling, at least until I can get more funds to you." Caleb will help you retrieve it. It might be wise to go to Uncle Joel's place in Buffalo. We don't know how far those bounty hunters will go if they're thwarted from stretching my neck; your uncle can protect all of you."

"Yes, sir." Caleb nodded.

"But Papa—"

"Don't make this more difficult than it is, Puddin'-tuck. And don't worry." He took one of Josephine's hands in his. You either, Darling. I'll see you in Albany, I promise."

Johnsby stepped into the cell. "The horse is ready. There's a cache of food in the saddle bags and a flask of water."

Samuel smiled at the young lawman. "Thank you, Mr. Johnsby. You've been nothing but kind to me. And I'll always owe you for rescuing my daughter from the fire."

"Mr. Pownell, I'm just sorry we're on opposite sides of this conflict. Maybe someday . . ."

They shook hands.

"Now, my lovely daughter and my precious Josephine, I'd better hightail it out of here."

Serenity felt Caleb's strong hands on her upper arms, drawing her from her father's grasp. She watched as Josephine and her father said good-bye. For an awkward moment everyone stood and stared at each other. Johnsby glanced anxiously toward the sheriff's office, then back at Samuel.

"I know," the assemblyman said.

Serenity's eyes misted as she watched her father place a tender kiss on Josephine's quivering lips.

"Go, Samuel, go!" Josephine pushed herself free from his arms. Her outstretched arm lingered in the air. "Go with God!"

Samuel Pownell swallowed hard, kissed his daughter once more on the forehead, and waved. "Pray for me, my loves."

A hysterical laugh erupted from a tearful Josephine. "Just every minute of every day!"

Without another word, the politician bolted through the open cell door and down the hall toward the rear exit. Johnsby followed hard on his heels.

"Well . . ." Josephine reached for a handkerchief in her pocket and blew her nose. "Do you think the stage office is still open tonight? I need to get a ticket for Syracuse."

"Yes, ma'am." Caleb withdrew a silver watch from his pocket. "In fact, the last stage leaves town in fifteen minutes."

"Don't worry, Serenity. God is in control of this, I am sure." Josephine kissed Serenity on the cheek. "Tell Dory that I'll send for Annie in a day or two." The life force that seemed drained from the woman a moment ago returned with incredible power. Her eyes sparkled with determination. "I must go, dear. See you in Buffalo, or who knows where?" She whirled about and marched from the cell.

"I guess we'd better get out of here before the mob arrives." Caleb's low, steady voice comforted the young woman's nerves.

Sheriff Broderick gazed at the two young people for a moment. "I suggest the two of you stay awhile. If you leave too soon, someone might get wise to your father's absence."

Caleb's hold on his charge's shoulders tightened. "I need to get Miss Pownell away from any potential danger."

"Every minute we can keep those animals from knowing of your father's escape . . ." The sheriff arched his brow and gazed at Serenity. " . . . the more likely he'll be able to successfully evade them."

"Then we'll stay, I suppose."

Serenity glanced at Caleb, then the sheriff. "Can we do anything to help?"

Sheriff Broderick stroked the day-old growth on his chin. "I don't rightly know, Miss Pownell. I've never dealt with a mob bent on lynching a man. I guess we'll have to play it by ear." He gestured toward the cell door. "Why don't we head out to the office and discuss the possibilities?"

Tension filled the office. The three deputies stood poised at the windows, guns in hand. "Sheriff, they're comin'," one of the men growled. "Should we start shooting?"

Sheriff Broderick shot a glance out the closest window. "They sure enough are, Lenny."

The flames from the torches danced in the night, revealing the men's angry faces. Crude shouts filled the air.

"Don't get trigger happy. We don't want a blood bath, especially not ours." He chuckled nervously. "You men back me up while I go out and see what these yahoos want."

"You know what they want, Sheriff."

"Yes, I know, Lenny, and so do you. But they don't know you and I know, do they?"

The man lowered his eyes. "No, sir, I guess not."

"Mr. Cunard, go find Johnsby. He knows what to do. Miss Serenity, please stay in one of the jail cells."

"But Sheriff, I can load the rifles!"

"Do as I say!" The sheriff snapped impatiently. "Or do I have to lock you in one of the cells?"

Caleb looked down at Serenity's jutting chin. "You do what the sheriff tells you to do."

"Yes, sir," Serenity replied sullenly.

"Good." As Caleb bolted from the room, Serenity turned to see Sheriff Broderick stride toward the front door.

"Everyone in position?"

"They're crossing the street," Lenny announced. "The bounty hunters are leading the way." He paused. "They're about to step onto the boardwalk."

The sheriff held up one hand, then swung the door open in the mob leader's startled face. "Was there something I could help you with?" the sheriff asked, filling the doorway with his imposing frame.

The surprised bounty hunter stumbled backwards as the sheriff, rifle in hand, pressed forward, the business end of his rifle inches from the man's nose. The crowd dropped back as well, until they stood in the muddy street looking up at the venerable sheriff.

The second bounty hunter shouted from the protection of the crowd. "We're here for Assemblyman Pownell, Sheriff."

"Yeah," another voice in the crowd shouted. "No one will get hurt, except for the politician, har—har!" The mob echoed his laughter.

"String 'em up!" someone shouted, waving a heavy hemp rope above the crowd's heads.

The mob cheered, whistled, and shouted. Serenity shuddered at the vehemence and hatred she heard in their voices. Whatever had her father done to deserve such bitterness? With the deputies' attention focused on their leader, Serenity slipped across the room to get a better view of the action.

The half-open door allowed her a clear view. The man called Lenny snarled for her to get back in the jail, but she ignored him.

Outside, buoyed by the crowd's support, the first bounty hunter whipped his coattail behind the holster strapped to his hip and rested his hand on his side arm.

"I wouldn't draw that, mister, unless you intend to use it," the sheriff growled, leveling his rifle at the man's forehead.

The second man from Georgia swaggered to the front of the crowd. "We're gonna' have a little necktie party, Sheriff, like it or not. If you're smart, you'll take a walk, get yourself some supper."

"Yeah," the first bounty hunter sneered. "You don't 'spect to hold all of us off with that there rifle, now, do you?"

The sheriff emitted a low chuckle. He raised the rifle in the air and pulled the trigger. The explosion rattled the windows of the office and nearby shops. Instantly, the three deputies burst from the office, their rifles leveled at the leaders of the pack. The mob retreated two steps. The startled look on their faces caused Serenity to giggle, despite the gravity of the situation.

The sheriff recocked his rifle and drawled, "Probably not," then leveled it at the most outspoken of the two bounty hunters. "But, between me and these gentlemen, and those behind you . . ." The crowd turned to find Deputy Johnsby and Caleb Cunard aiming their rifles at the rear of the mob. " . . . and those on the roof of the bank and the general store . . ." Again the mob swiveled their necks to look in the direction of the sheriff's gaze. The men stationed on the roofs of the buildings waved at the sheriff. " . . . we'll get off quite a few rounds before you can get even one of us, I should imagine."

A low rumble of doubt swept through the mob. "Now, gentleman . . ." Sheriff Broderick broadened his stance. " . . . isn't it about time you reconsider your plan?" Sensing their uncertainty, the sheriff continued. "Considering the light out here, I can't tell one face from another. But if we're still here when the moon rises, I'll be able to see all of you just fine." Seeing a few in the mob back away, he uncocked his rifle. Behind him, however, his men remained poised for a fight. "The best thing to do is, like these Georgia crackers said, go home, get some supper, and get a good night's sleep. Things will look different tomorrow."

The crowd looked nervously at one another. Several more of those standing on the fringes disappeared into the shadows of the night. Others appeared ready to bolt outright. Noting the shift in mood, the head bounty hunter shouted, "That's what you think, Sheriff! You'd better watch your back. You can't protect Pownell twenty-four hours a day, you know!"

The sheriff touched the brim of the bounty hunter's felt hat with the barrel of his rifle. The hat tumbled to the ground. The man bent to retrieve it. He shoved it back on his head and glared at the sheriff. "You are one—"

The sheriff interrupted. "You and your buddy are no longer welcome in these parts, mister. I want you out of my town and out of my county before midnight. Now that's gonna' take some tall riding, son. I'd suggest you get to it." He cocked his rifle a second time. "Immediately!"

At that the rest of the mob discretely slipped away into the night. The sheriff waved to one of the deputies behind him. "Lenny, you and the boys escort our visitors to the nearest state border."

Lenny and the other two deputies surrounded the two

bounty hunters. "Yes, Sir. Right away! Come on, you two, let's get movin'. We got a long ride ahead of us."

"You can't do that!" the more outspoken of the two men snarled. "The law says we can hunt runaways anywhere we please."

The sheriff's eyes narrowed. "You broke the law and lost that privilege when you fomented my people into a lynching mob. That doesn't set well with me, and it won't set well with Judge Hargrove either."

"I'm not afraid of—"

"Then you are more stupid than you look, son. Northern prisons aren't any less grim than those in the South, I assure you." The sheriff rested his rifle on his hip. "I have a standing warrant for your arrest laying on my desk. It goes into effect at 12:01 A.M. Do I make myself clear?"

Lenny stepped toward the men, who took a defensive stance against the deputy. One of the men went for his gun, but Lenny's vice-like grip stopped his arm mid-swing. "Take your hands off me!" the man cried.

"Aha," the sheriff snorted. "Resisting an officer? I tried to warn you. Lenny, lock 'em up!"

The deputies wrestled the men up the stairs. Serenity pressed herself behind the open door as they passed. Then the sheriff, Johnsby, and Caleb strode into the office before she could escape. The sheriff spied her cowering behind the door and gave her an exasperated look.

A yell erupted from one of the jail cells. "Hey, where's Pownell? He ain't even in here!"

Sheriff Broderick grunted with pleasure. "Hmm, 'magine that."

~27~

The Eve of
Yesterday

 A WAXING JULY MOON LIT THE COUNTRYSIDE as the buckboard bounced over potholes and ruts on the way back to the Cunard home. For Serenity, one question triggered another. "What will become of the house?" she asked. "And the servants?"

"As I understand it, Abe and his family will stay on the place until it's sold. Then they'll join your father, wherever he happens to be. The others will be placed with worthy employers."

"That's good. I'm especially glad Annie will get the medical care she needs." A cool breeze caught Serenity's bonnet and whipped it from her head to her shoulders. She placed it back on her head and tightened the ribbons about her neck.

Caleb looked over at her. "Are you cold?"

"A little."

"Here." He struggled out of his suede jacket and wrapped it around her shoulders. She started to protest. "Don't be foolish. That flimsy little cotton dress can't keep you warm." They rode for several minutes in amicable silence.

"O call back yesterday, bid time return . . ." Serenity said dreamily, just barely above a whisper.

"Excuse me?" Caleb glanced her way. "Did you say something?"

"Nothing really, just a line from Shakespeare's *Twelfth Night*."

"I'm not familiar with Mr. Shakespeare and his writing."

She smiled wanely. "You should be. He was a wise old crow."

Caleb laughed, then returned his attention to his driving.

"Mr., er, Cunard?"

"Call me Caleb."

"All right, Caleb. What's going to become of me?" Her voice sounded weak and lost. "Will I ever see my father again?"

He looked down at her. "Of course, you'll see him again, God willing." He returned his attention to the empty road. "As to your first question, who's to know the future? God never intended man to know what tomorrow might bring. He just wants us to trust it to Him."

"Yes, I guess so." She sighed a deep sigh. "Trusting is so hard sometimes." Her voice caught as she fought back a wave of tears.

Caleb pulled on the reins; the buckboard rolled to a stop. "What's wrong? Are you crying?"

"No," she gulped and sniffed, "Of course not."

He took her face in his hands. "Yes, you are, but you needn't." He wiped a tear from her cheek. "Everything will be just fine."

"All right, you want to know why I'm crying?" The tone of her voice raised several keys. "I'm penniless. I'm wearing borrowed clothing. My home is destroyed. I lost two parents in the last few months. And my future has been placed in the hands of a virtual stranger!" she choked.

Caleb's face filled with remorse. "Oh, forgive me."

She hiccuped, trying to swallow her sobs. "You can't imagine what it's like . . ." Tears slid down her cheeks unbidden.

"You're right, I can't. But please, don't cry."

Her face wrinkled. "I . . . I . . . I can't stop," she wailed. "I want to but I can't!"

"Oh, sweetheart." He drew her into his arms. "I'm so sorry."

Serenity sniffed several times. "I need a handkerchief, please."

Caleb searched his pockets until he found a handkerchief. As she looked trustingly into his eyes, he wiped the tears from her face. A flood of gratitude rushed through her. Her face mere inches from his, she placed her hand on the back of his neck. She drew him to her until she could feel his warm breath against her lips. Serenity had never been kissed by anyone other than family members. She'd heard her friend, Eulilia, tell about the thrill of kissing, but she'd never braved it herself. Her breath caught in her throat. This was her moment. She closed her eyes in anticipation.

"No!" Caleb jerked free from her hold.

"Huh? What happened?"

"I'm sorry, Miss Serenity, but I won't betray your father's trust in me. He's placed you in my care. I can't allow myself to take advantage of your dependence on me."

"What?" Her face flooded with embarrassment.

The man licked his lips and cleared his throat. "I hope you don't go around to other men, offering your, er, lips like that. They just might not be so honorable!"

"I don't understand. I thought you wanted to kiss me?"

"Well . . . not anymore. You'll understand when you grow up a bit more." He flicked the reins. The horses responded to his command.

"Grow up?" She folded her arms across her chest. "Of course I don't go around—" She couldn't finish her sentence in her disgust.

"I'm certainly glad for that. It'll make my job a whole lot easier."

"Your job?"

"My job to protect you until either you marry or your father returns."

She tightened her arms about her chest and huffed. "Don't worry, Mr. Cunard," she said, emphasizing the "mister." "If and when I choose to offer a man a kiss, you'll be the last to know."

He looked at her sharply, then flicked the reigns again. "Giddyap!"

The twelve miles from town to the homestead seemed interminable to the young woman. The gentle clop-clop of the horses' hooves on the hardened road lulled her into a stupor despite her irritation and embarrassment. Even her concern for her father lessened as she drifted in and out of sleep. Her shoulders slumped; her eyes drooped; her head lolled from side to side, coming to rest on the nearest support: Caleb's shoulder. She failed to hear him mumble. "What have I gotten into, Lord? Do you think I'm made of iron?"

Serenity didn't remember being carried into the Cunard home. Nor did she remember Fay's tender ministrations as she readied the girl for bed.

She awoke the next morning to the aroma of hotcakes frying on the griddle.

"Good morning," a voice next to her said. It was Becca.

Serenity jumped. She'd never slept in the same bed with another person. "Oh, I didn't know where I was for a moment."

"I imagine not. You were dead to the world when my brother brought you in last night."

"Your brother?" She looked down at the lacy nightgown she wore.

Becca giggled. "Mama did that, silly, not Caleb!"

"Oh."

The little girl leaped from the bed, tossing the covers as she went. "We have a lot to do today. Oh, you haven't heard, have you?"

"Heard?"

"Judge Hargrove warned Daddy and Caleb that they'd best leave the county before they got themselves arrested too. So, we're heading West! Isn't that exciting?" She whirled in circles in the center of the room. Her summer nightgown billowed about her slender body. "To California, or maybe Oregon! Mama and Daddy were still discussing it when they sent me to bed." Then she leaped back onto the foot of the bed. "They were arguing . . . imagine! I've never heard them argue before. It was scary. Mama wants to go to Oregon and Daddy wants to head for the gold fields of California. I want to see California!"

Serenity sat up in bed. "What do you know about California?"

"I know that it's sunshiny and you can get rich real fast! I will have a trunk full of frilly dresses of real lace, from places like Belgium and Ireland!" The girl's eyes danced with excitement. "Caleb said you almost saw a shoot-out yesterday. What was it like?"

Serenity laughed. "Now, that was scary!"

"Really? Wow! Caleb says you're gonna' be my sister for a while."

"Well, I don't know about—"

The child bounced up and down on the bed several times. "I always wanted a big sister. Did you ever want sisters or brothers? Brothers are pains, of course, but sisters? Did you ever wish you had a sister?" Only the growl in Serenity's stomach stopped further questioning.

"Sorry, I didn't eat supper last night," she explained. Becca bounced off the bed and slipped into her clothing. It took Serenity several minutes longer to wash her face and hands, dress, then comb the snarls from her hair. Once braided and piled atop her head, she checked herself in the small, cracked mirror hanging on the wall behind the oak dresser, then opened the bedroom door.

The family was gathered around the table and Preacher Cunard was reading from the Bible. "And we know that all things work together for good to them that love God, to them who are called according to His purpose. Romans 8:28." Serenity slipped into the open chair between Caleb and Fay. Preacher Cunard closed the Book. "It is our custom, Miss Serenity, to join hands for prayer, forming a circle around the table." He took Aaron's and Becca's hands. "Let us pray." Fay smiled as she took Serenity's hand in hers. Timidly, without glancing toward one another, Serenity and Caleb joined hands as well. When their fingers touched, Serenity felt a wave of heat flow through her body and a flutter in her stomach, which she attributed to hunger.

Shaking her head, she closed her eyes to concentrate on Preacher Cunard's prayer. After the amen, she wasn't sure if it was her imagination or not that Caleb held her hand a while longer than necessary.

During the meal, Caleb reported the activities of the previous night.

"Weren't you scared?" Becca whispered across the stack of hotcakes to Serenity.

"A little," she admitted. She licked the maple syrup from her lips. "A lot, actually."

Everyone laughed.

"This morning, Aaron and I need to go treasure hunting," Caleb announced. "Mr. Pownell told us where to find a keg he hid, for Miss Serenity's welfare, of course."

"You and Aaron? Excuse me? No one's going to uncover any treasure without me. I know exactly where it is."

"Wait just a minute. I need one of you boys to go to Auburn with me to buy a wagon for our trip." Preacher Cunard placed his napkin beside his plate and rose to his feet.

Fay glanced from one face to the next. "We're heading for California," she finally said, her lips tightening into a thin line.

"Hooray!" Becca squealed.

"California?" Aaron dropped his fork in surprise. "I'll go with you, Father. Wow! California!"

Caleb scowled and looked toward his mother. Serenity followed his gaze.

"Oh, well, I suppose I should check to see how Abe and Dory are doing," Fay said. Caleb, maybe Becca could accompany you and Serenity on your treasure hunt?"

"Yippee!" Becca bounced up and down in her chair. "A treasure hunt!"

Serenity caught the smile that passed between her Aunt Fay and Caleb. *She knows*, Serenity thought, *she knows about last night*. Her face suffused with color. She glanced about to be sure no one noticed, then concentrated on finishing her stack of hotcakes.

"Serenity, a couple of the ladies in the community dropped off a few garments for you. They're laying at the foot of Becca's bed."

Serenity looked up in surprise. "Oh, thank you." She looked down at the dress she'd been wearing since the fire. "This one got a little soiled yesterday, I'm afraid."

"Actually," Caleb interrupted, "you might want to keep that one on. You're bound to get more than a little soiled climbing around inside that cave."

Fay stood and began stacking the empty plates. "He's probably right, dear." She glanced down at her elder son. "Take care of your sister, you hear?"

"Yes, ma'am."

"I know I can trust you." Serenity blushed from the obvious double meaning in Fay's tone. No one else at the table seemed to notice. Serenity excused herself and started collecting the used silverware.

"You go on." Fay took the dinnerware from Serenity's hands. "I'll take care of the dirty dishes. I need a little time alone this morning. Hot dish water does wonders for one's spirits!" Serenity couldn't miss the sadness in the woman's eyes.

"It will be all right. That's what you taught me, remember?"

The woman smiled sadly and nodded. "I know. And you're right. Everything will be all right, eventually." She bit her lip and blinked back her tears.

"How long will it take you two to get ready to go treasure hunting?" Caleb asked.

"I'm ready now!" Becca hopped up from the table and dashed into her room for her bonnet.

Serenity kissed Fay's cheek.

Unable to speak without crying, Fay nodded. "You'd better go now. Caleb isn't the most patient of men, you know."

"Mother, I heard you! How can you tell Miss Serenity a thing like that?" Caleb removed his hat from the rack behind the door. "I'll get a torch from the barn and meet you two outside."

"Just a warning, darling! Just a warning." Fay looked toward Serenity, not her son.

Why? Serenity didn't have time to search for the meaning to Fay's cryptic message. She'd barely stepped onto the porch when a black blur bounded out of the woods and up the steps.

"Onyx! Where have you been?" Serenity knelt beside the excited animal and scratched him behind the ears. "You poor puppy. You must have thought everyone abandoned you!"

Caleb laughed. "Are you kidding? This con artist takes care of himself just fine. Come on, Onyx, help us find that treasure!"

The dog barked and leaped off the porch after Caleb.

"Boy! You'd think he's your dog instead of mine."

"He knows who's master."

"Master?" Serenity choked on the word. "How arrogant!" Caleb laughed and headed down the road, the dog tagging at his heels. Serenity rose to her feet and descended the steps.

"Wait! Wait for me!" Becca shouted, bursting from the house. The ribbons to her bonnet fluttered in the breeze behind her as she ran.

"So, come on," Caleb shouted and waved, "the day's a-wasting!"

"Gotcha' last!" Becca tapped Caleb's shoulder and ducked out of his reach. For a moment, Serenity paused to watch Caleb and his sister playfully tag one another. *Having a brother and sister would have been fun.* She smiled to herself, glancing up toward the morning clouds hovering over the lake. "Like it or not, Father, it looks like that's what I got for a while, huh?"

When she once again looked for Caleb and his sister, they were nowhere to be found. Even Onyx was missing. "Hey, you two," she called, "wait for me." She gathered her skirts in her hands and dashed down the road. As she rounded the bend near the footpath that lead to the beach, she heard a shout. Three bodies leaped from the woods. Serenity screamed and turned to run back to the Cunard place. Behind her she heard Caleb and Becca laughing. Becca ran to Serenity's side. "Did we scare you? Really scare you? Huh?"

"You scared me, all right!" Serenity admitted, tugging at one of the girl's braids. "But you'd better watch it, cause I'll get you back, sooner or later!"

"Ha-ha, you can try!" the girl teased.

~28~
Simple
Treasures

BY THE TIME SERENITY AND BECCA started down the pathway to the beach, Caleb and Onyx had already disappeared into the brush. Serenity led the way, holding the branches so they wouldn't hit Becca as she followed. They quickly broke into the sandy clearing. Serenity stole a glance at the ten-year-old as she passed. *It will be fun having a little sister,* she thought.

Becca caught her eye. "This is exciting, isn't it, Miss Serenity?"

"Please call me Serenity, or Seri. And yes, it is exciting, looking for hidden treasure."

"Seri? Ooh, I like that. My real name is Rebecca, you know."

Serenity smiled and nodded. Becca chatted as they trudged across the sand. They followed Onyx and Caleb's footprints in the sand. By the time they arrived at the cave, Caleb had the torch lit and was exploring the area just inside the entrance.

"Ooh," Becca exclaimed, "I never knew this cave was here. Look how well the rocks hide it. Did you know it was here, Serenity?"

"Yes, I did. When I was your age, I used to come down here and hide from my parents when I was angry at them. And as I got a little older, I came down here to be alone and to write in my diary. I even hid it in here for a while."

"Really?" Becca shook with excitement. "Let's go inside!"

"Wait a minute." Caleb appeared in the cave opening. "We gotta' stick together. There are several pathways branching off in different directions. I don't want someone wandering off alone." Onyx pushed ahead of Caleb and disappeared into the darkness.

Serenity clicked her tongue and brushed past the young man as well. "I know this cave like I know my own name," she assured him. "I've explored every branch at one time or another."

Caleb narrowed his gaze, reluctantly following her into the darkness. They passed the keyhole entrance and advanced into what Serenity thought of as the "reception hall." She'd spent many hours playing house with her dolls in this part of the cave; it was in this area that she'd hidden her wooden toy chest.

They'd walked less than fifty feet when, behind them, they heard a plaintiff call. "Hey, you two. I don't feel so good. I'm going back outside and wait for you, all right?"

Caleb turned and hurried to his sister. "Are you all right? You don't sound too good." The child gazed about the cave. "I . . . I don't like it in here. I keep thinking the ceiling is going to fall in on me or the walls are going to crush me."

"Those walls and that ceiling have been there for hundreds of years. They aren't going anywhere," he assured her.

"Still, I want to wait outside."

Serenity watched as Caleb brushed a few stray locks of

hair from Becca's sweaty forehead. "Do you want me to walk out with you?"

She shook her head. "I'll be all right as soon as I get out of here."

"Fine. I'll stay right here until you reach the outside. Then shout and I'll know you're safe."

She nodded, knitting her brow and frowning. He patted her head and waited until he heard her call.

"It's down this way." Serenity pointed toward a pathway branching to the left. "I've seen the rock Papa described."

"I thought he said to take the path to the right."

"No, it has to be the one to the left. The pathway to the right deadends into an underground waterfall." Serenity felt her way along the rough rock walls. "The identifying rock should be right here."

Caleb shined the torch along the walls. Water from a growing stalactite dripped on the flame and evaporated with a sizzle. "I can't see anything. Can you?"

"No! I was so sure this was the spot. See that tall stalagmite up ahead? Didn't he say it was on the lake side of the prophet? That's the prophet."

"Prophet?"

"Yes. See his hood and robe, and the staff in his hands? I always called him Jeremiah the prophet. Papa's secret cache must be around here somewhere."

They scoured every inch of rock between them and the prophet. Finally admitting defeat, Serenity sat down on a recently fallen rock. "I don't know where else to look," she admitted. "We could spend weeks searching this place and still not find one small rock with the initials SWP carved in it."

Caleb braced the torch between two rocks and sat down beside her. "We can't give up. It's your future we're trying to secure here. Without it, you'll be penniless until your father finds you."

She heaved a great sigh.

"Your father told me to help find the treasure." He stood and extended his hands to help her to her feet. "And I intend to carry out my promise!"

"Wait!" she squealed. Leaping to her feet without Caleb's assist, she yanked the torch from its holdings and thrust it into Caleb's hands. "Look! Shine the torch over here." Pawing at the fallen rocks, she held up a piece. Carved in the chip of the rock was the letter P. "It's here!" She stood up and guided Caleb's hand that held the torch. "Up there!"

High above their heads, a deep hole yawned in the side of the cave. "Can you reach it?"

"I can..." Caleb rose to his tiptoes. "...but I think I'd rather look before I thrust my hand in there. I don't fancy having bats in my belfry."

"Let me hold the torch while you take a look," she suggested.

Caleb thrust the torch into her hands and climbed on the fallen rocks to get a better look. "Over this way, shine it over this way. I think I see something."

She obeyed. "What?"

"Something shiny. Possibly a metal latch or handle?" He stretched. "I can't quite reach it."

"Maybe I can reach it," she suggested.

"Hmmph! You're shorter than I."

"But if you held me up . . ."

"Hey, you're pretty smart for a—"

"For a what? A girl?"

"No, for a nitwit."

"Of all the—" She ran her fingers along his side. "Ticklish?"

"Stop it!" he shouted, writhing out of her reach. "We'll never find your father's treasure this way."

"So?" She cast him a devilish grin. "Think of all the fun we'll have trying."

"Give me that." He took the torch from her hands. "Didn't your parents ever teach you not to play with fire?"

She giggled and ducked out of his reach. He braced the torch between two rocks on the far side of the treasure site. "Give me your foot."

He cupped his hands, allowing her to use them as a step. "I see it!" Serenity leaned her body against the uneven ledge outside the twelve-inch hole in the wall. "I need more light."

"I can't give you any more light," Caleb groaned. "I have my hands full, remember?"

She laughed. "Oh, yeah. Umph, wait a minute." She stretched her hand further into the hole. Her fingers brushed against the brass handle. "I can't quite reach it." She dug the toe of her free boot into a crevice of the rock. "Maybe . . . just a little further . . . Oh, oh, no!" The tiny rock ledge beneath her foot shifted. She flailed her arms, knocking Caleb's hat from his head.

"Hey, watch it!" he shouted.

The ledge crumbled and her foot slipped, sending Serenity to the ground atop a startled Caleb.

"Oof!" he grunted.

"Ouch!" she whimpered, rolling off Caleb's back. "I almost had it!"

"Well, I've certainly had it!" He sat up, nursing a bruised elbow. "Woman, you pack a wallop of a punch. Are you all right?"

"No, I'm not all right!" Her lower lip protruded. She spotted a grin teasing the corners of his mouth. "Don't you dare laugh."

"I wouldn't think of it."

"Yes, you would, and you are!" She pushed against his chest and laughed as well.

"If you could see yourself!" He brushed a smudge from her nose and chin. "You would laugh too."

"And you look so great, Mr. Cunard?" She leaped to her knees and tousled his disheveled hair.

"Why you—" He returned the favor. Her curls flew in every direction. She tried to roll away, but he trapped her shoulders and drew her to him. Her breath came in short gasps as she stared into his deep brown eyes. Confusion flooded his face. Slowly, he lowered his lips toward hers, all the while studying her lips. She leaned forward and closed her eyes.

As his lips brushed against hers, he froze. "No, I can't do this."

Her eyes flew open. "What's wrong?"

"No. What I said last night still stands. I can't betray your father's trust in me." Caleb took her hands in his. "Your father appointed me to protect you, like a parent. If I should take advantage of you, in any way, I couldn't live with myself."

"My father's opinion is very important to you, isn't it?"

"Yes, but even more important is my Heavenly Father's opinion of me. When I vowed to protect you, it was before God as well. And nothing is more important to me than that."

"Does this mean that you and I could never . . ." She reddened at the implication of her question.

"Exactly, at least not until either you reach your majority or your father returns for you and I can request the privilege to court you properly."

Serenity gave him a coy smile. Her insides quivered like freshly made blackberry jam. "Is that a promise, Mr. Cunard?"

He raised her fingers to his lips and kissed them, then placed the kissed fingertips on her lips. "Until your father returns . . ."

She ran her fingers along her lower lip. "What happens until then?"

"Until then, we avoid isolated places like this! Come on, let's get that cask and get out of here." He took a deep breath and leaped to his feet. He poised his hands for her once again. She nodded and hopped to her feet. This time, as she placed her foot in his hands and her hands on his shoulder, she did so carefully, avoiding any unnecessary contact.

After much grunting and tugging, the wooden cask slid out of its rock cradle. Serenity pulled it forward enough to allow Caleb to grasp it. He slid the cask to the edge of the rock and lowered it to the rock-strewn floor. "Whew! That's mighty heavy. What does your father have in there—lead?"

She shrugged, examining the small oak cask girdled with two brass strips. On each end was a brass handle. "Let me help. Should we open it here?"

"Let's take it outside where we can see. Grab the torch." Caleb rotated the muscles in his shoulders, then squatted and heaved the cask onto his shoulder. "Lead the way, my dear."

"Aye, aye, captain." She giggled. "All you need is a patch over one eye and a peg leg."

"Aye, me lass. Just call me Blue Beard."

"Or, perhaps, Captain Bligh."

"And who may ye be, me first mate?"

Serenity giggled and charged ahead toward the opening of the cave. "We made it!" she shouted as she emerged from the cave. "We found the cask!"

Becca and Onyx stood ankle deep in the lake. "You found it? The treasure?" She and the dog charged across the beach to the rocks. "A real treasure?"

"Looks that way." Serenity whirled about and gestured toward Caleb as he stepped from the cave. Running to the water, Serenity doused the torch in the water.

She returned in time to see Caleb pry open one end of the cask with the hunting knife he wore in his belt. He gasped. "Oh, my."

"What? What is it?" Serenity rushed to his side.

He turned the open cask toward her. "You are one wealthy woman, Miss Serenity." She looked toward the cask and gasped, "Oh, dear God, it's gold—gold bars."

"Gold!" Becca exclaimed. "I'm gonna go tell Mama." She leaped to her feet and charged up the beach. Onyx followed.

"No wonder the cask was so heavy," Caleb mumbled, his face dark and unreadable.

"I . . . I don't know what to say. How much do you think is here?"

"Enough to keep you in lace and satin for a mighty long time." He avoided her eyes. His tone hardened. "I guess we'd better get this stuff to the house." He squatted and lifted the cask to his shoulder. "Come on!"

She glanced at him, surprised at his abrasive tone. "What is wrong, Caleb?"

"Wrong? What could possibly be wrong?"

"I don't know. Inside you're fighting not to kiss me, out here, you're as testy as a polecat."

He stopped and cast an angry glare toward the cask. "This changes everything. Every man who courts you will be suspect of doing so for your money."

Serenity grinned at him. "Only if he knows it exists."

"That's just the point. It is more important now than ever that we maintain a, a . . ." He sought for the right word. "An emotion-free relationship."

"That's going to be tricky since you and I have never had such a relationship." She laughed and skipped ahead of him, scampering up the trail to the road.

~29~

The Promise of Tomorrow

TOMORROW AND TOMORROW AND tomorrow. Every word, every action, and every thought in Serenity's mind was of tomorrow. "We'll pick up the wagon tomorrow. We'll purchase the foodstuff tomorrow. Tomorrow we'll finish the last dress for my new wardrobe, a new wardrobe without a whisp of silk in it!" While she was only going as far as Buffalo with the Cunard family, the trip would be hard, too hard for dresses of fine linen and French lace. *There'll be time, once I reach Uncle Joel's place, to shop for the daintier things of life,* she decided.

She and Becca had spent several days over at the burned-out Pownell mansion, sifting through the ashes rescuing family treasures. Serenity had cried when she found her mother's favorite porcelain tea set undamaged. The servants had located several pieces of pewter kitchenware and a large silver Revere pitcher as well. But the item she treasured the most was her father's gold pocket watch. Not only was the watch still running, but a second compartment held a silhouette of her mother and a lock of her mother's hair.

Serenity gave the kitchenware and the Revere pitcher to Dory. The watch and the porcelain tea set she carefully wrapped in soft cotton batting and placed in a travel trunk that would hold her entire world until she reached her uncle's home.

Preparations for the journey to Buffalo filled Serenity's days. She had no time to fret about her future beyond tomorrow. While she'd not heard from her father since he fled the jail, Josephine had sent a telegram assuring her that "all was well." Serenity had taken the cryptic message to include her father's safety.

A subflooring was added to the family wagon to safely house Serenity's gold bars. The evening before they were to leave, the Cunard family, along with Serenity, gathered for supper around the oak trestle table. Onyx lay snoozing beside the hearth.

"Have you taken care of that dog?" Preacher Cunard asked Caleb.

"Dog?" Serenity looked up from the string beans and mashed potatoes on her plate. She glanced at Caleb. He avoided her eyes. "What about Onyx?"

"You haven't told her yet?" Preacher Cunard frowned at his elder son.

"Told me what?" Serenity demanded.

The older man shot a pleading look at his wife. She smiled sweetly, but remained silent. He cleared his throat. "Serenity, we've decided—"

"We?" his wife coached.

"Er, I've decided that there's no place for the dog on this trip West. Onyx will do much better if he stays here with Abe and Dory. They've agreed to care for him until your father sends for them."

"And then?" Serenity asked, her fork and knife poised in her hands like medieval weapons of war.

"And then . . ." He cleared his throat a second time. "And then, they'll see he gets a good home."

She glanced at Fay, then at Caleb. They both stared straight ahead.

"Why have you waited until now to tell me?"

The man smiled weakly. "We didn't want to upset you."

"Then you failed. I'm upset!" She inhaled sharply to hold back her tears. "You might as well unpack my trunk. I'm not going anywhere without Onyx." At the mention of his name the dog grunted. "He's the only family I have left. I won't leave him."

"I really think this is the best—"

Serenity straightened her shoulders. She trembled inside, for she knew that Preacher Cunard was not accustomed to being crossed. "Excuse me, sir, but I don't. He's my dog. I promise that I'll care for him. I'll pay for his food. He won't be a problem."

The preacher cleared his throat again, sending a pleading look toward his wife. Fay gazed up at the rafters. "Caleb, tell her," he said.

Caleb looked at his father. "Tell her what?"

"Tell her how impractical it would be to travel on a barge with a big dog like that! The trip is all by canal, you know." The man shot glances at his two younger children, who also avoided his gaze. Preacher Cunard took a swig from his water glass, then broke off a piece of bread and stuffed it in his mouth. No more was said about Onyx during the meal. After the dishes were cleared and packed in the proper barrel, Fay handed Serenity a stack of linen fancy work she'd decided not to take with her. "Here, honey, would you take these dresser scarves and doilies over to Dory? I'll ask Caleb to walk with you."

Serenity sniffed back a fresh bout of tears that had kept spilling out ever since her encounter with Preacher Cunard. "Yes, ma'am."

"Caleb." Fay called at the base of the ladder that led to the loft where the two boys slept. "Just go get your shawl and bonnet, Seri. He'll be down in a minute. Caleb!"

Serenity ran for her shawl and bonnet as told. The last place she wanted to spend the evening was in the stilted atmosphere of the Cunard home that evening. She grabbed the package of fancy work from the table as she hurried past. "I'll wait for him outside on the porch."

The door slammed behind her. She ambled over to the steps and sat down. Onyx's large soft body pressed against her side and licked her cheek. Wrapping her arms around him, she buried her face in the dog's side. Tears trickled down her cheeks and onto his soft ebony fur. Before she realized it, her tears had grown into deep sobs. The dam of strength she'd constructed since her father left broke. The dog, recognizing her pain but not understanding the cause, anxiously licked her face and neck.

Since the preacher's announcement, Serenity had been trying to decide what she'd do if they insisted she leave the dog. Legally she had no recourse but to go with them, at least with Caleb. Would he make her go without the dog? She didn't know. If she stayed, where could she go? What could she do? It wasn't as if a woman of her age and station could travel alone. Even Josephine needed a retinue of servants to protect her good name and honor.

She ran her hands over the dog's neck and chest. Her breath came in ragged gasps. No, if Caleb insisted she leave the dog, Serenity realized she had no other recourse but to do so. A fresh wave of sobs overcame her.

A gentle hand rested on her shoulder. Thinking it was Fay, Serenity sobbed, "Why must everything be so difficult?"

The hand slid around her shoulders, drawing her near. "I wish I knew." Instantly she knew it was Caleb beside her. She knew she should move away, but his arm was so strong, so reassuring, she couldn't force herself to do so. "Let's walk over to Dory's. It will make you feel better."

"Saying good-bye to my home will make me feel better?"

He helped her to her feet and took the package from her arms. She shook her head, kicking at a stone in the road. Onyx bounded after it.

Tucking the bundle under his arm, Caleb took her hand in his. "I'm sorry."

They walked companionably along the moonlit road. A breeze off the lake whistled through the tops of the pine trees. "When I was at the academy, I would hear a similar sound and try to imagine myself here."

"I know what you mean. There've been many nights I've listened to the wind while I waited for fresh cargo to arrive."

She glanced up at his profile, illuminated by the moon. When they reached the edge of her father's land, they cut across the lawn to the house. The ghostly silhouette of the burned-out structure sent shivers up and down her spine. Even though she'd seen the place several times since the fire, she'd never viewed it at night.

Caleb squeezed her hand. "It looks worse than it is."

"I know."

They hurried on to Abe and Dory's place. While Serenity had said her good-byes to everyone that afternoon, she was grateful for a chance to give Dory a special good-bye. A tear fell from Serenity's eye as she hugged the woman's abundant body.

"Now, none of that, missy. You hear?" Dory wiped the tear away with a corner of her apron. "Once Abe's leg heals, we'll be on our way to Albany and your father. And before you know it, we'll all be together again."

Serenity nodded and sniffed. "I can't help it."

"Aw, honey." The woman crushed Serenity to her.

"Did you come by to leave Onyx with us?" Abe asked.

Serenity gulped, casting a pleading glance toward Caleb. Onyx laid on the floor beside his feet. Caleb cleared his throat. "Yes, I suppose so."

Serenity knelt beside the dog and patted his head. "You be a good doggy, you hear?" She sniffed, then rose to her feet. "I'm ready to leave." She hugged Dory and Abe once more, then turned and walked out into the night. As she walked away, she heard Onyx barking to be let out of the cabin.

"No turning back," she whispered, refusing to look toward her burned-out home. No turning back. She managed to control her heartache until Caleb placed his arm around her shoulder, then the tears flowed.

Instead of continuing home when they reached the lake road, he guided her down to the beach. "Here," he suggested, "why don't you sit down on this log until you feel better."

She nodded and settled herself on the weathered piece of driftwood. Caleb stepped back while Serenity buried her face in her arms. After several minutes, she lifted her head and gazed at the silvery path of moonlight across the lake.

"It's so beautiful here." Her voice caught as she realized she may never see this spot again.

"Yes, it is."

"What's going to happen to me?"

He straddled the log and sat down. "The future isn't ours to know."

"What do you mean?"

"God never promised to reveal our futures. He just promised to be with us, always."

She bit her lip. "I have promised, I will never leave thee, nor forsake thee . . ."

"Hebrews 13:5." He smiled. "That's what's really important, knowing God is with us whether we're here in Cayuga County, or in Buffalo, or Sutter's Fort, California. That's what makes every yesterday precious, every today livable, and every tomorrow an adventure."

"An adventure?" She glanced over at him.

"An adventure. Even the Word holds excitement and promise when we know it's safe in God's hands." His eyes glistened with anticipation.

"Aren't you afraid of what tomorrow may bring?"

"Not when I know Who holds my tomorrows. Then I can chase them with confidence."

"Chase tomorrow? That's a strange way of putting it. I kind of like it. It implies not being afraid, but embracing my future." She stood and extended her hands heavenward. *Lord, I think I'm ready now, to chase tomorrow.* She took a deep breath and turned toward Caleb. "Race you back to the road."

"Not in the dark."

"Aw, come on. Where's your adventurous spirit?" She turned and charged up the pathway.

After several bouts of tag and hide-and-go-seek, they arrived back at the Cunard home to find everyone retired for the night. Serenity tiptoed into Becca's room, undressed, and slipped into the big double bed.

The girl stirred. "Is it tomorrow yet?" she mumbled.

"No," Serenity adjusted the bedding around her neck. "Not yet."

Tomorrow arrived with a flourish of sunshine and activity. Before Becca and Serenity emerged from the bedroom, the men were loading the last of the family's belongings aboard the wagon, and Fay was stirring the last pot of porridge over the fire in the giant stone fireplace.

The women of the family had barely finished washing the breakfast dishes when the first of the well-wishers arrived. Within a few minutes it looked like the entire county had shown up to wish them a safe journey.

Joy and excitement filled their good-byes. Serenity could see envy in many of the familiar faces as they bade farewell to their pastor and his family. Finally, the time came to leave. Since the wagon bulged with household goods, all but the driver would walk most of the distance. The first stretch of the journey would be over the farm roads between Lake Cayuga to the canal. Once at the canal, they'd roll the wagons onto a barge and float west to Buffalo, a much easier trip than staying with the land route.

Aaron, Caleb's younger brother, drew the lot that made him driver for the first stretch. After Preacher Cunard assembled his flock for a farewell prayer, he gave Aaron the signal. The boy climbed into the driver's seat and flicked the whip above the horses' heads. The animals took a step. The wagon lurched forward. They were on their way.

Above the din, Serenity heard a familiar bark. So did Preacher Cunard and Fay. The dog pushed his way through the crowd of people and ran to Serenity, barking joyously. Serenity fell to the ground, wrapping her arms around the dog. "Shame on you, Onyx! You ran away from Dory." Tears swelled in her eyes. "You have to go back. You can't come with us."

When she felt a gentle hand on her shoulder, she looked up into Preacher Cunard's stern face. She waved a hand toward him. "I know. I know." She started to stand.

"No, child, we, uh, discussed it last night after you and Caleb left and, er, decided the dog can come with us."

"What?" She leaped to her feet.

"Onyx can come with us, but he must earn his keep."

"Oh, thank you!" Tears tumbled down her cheeks. She glanced toward a surprised Caleb and a smiling Fay. "Thank you, Preacher Cunard!"

"Wait a minute, young lady. Let's get one thing straight."

She stopped and stared. "Yes, sir?"

"We aren't moving one step forward until you stop calling me Preacher Cunard and begin calling me Uncle Eli. Do you understand?"

Startled, she nodded. "Yes, Uncle Eli."

A smile spread across the man's face. "That's better. Now maybe we can get on with being a family." Onyx barked in agreement. "You too, you big old mutt."

He raised his hand. The wagon began rolling once more. "Westward, ho!" He turned toward Serenity, and in a low voice said, "I've been waiting a long time to say that."

She laughed and started after the wagon. "Come on, Onyx, let's go chase tomorrow!"